The Vampire's Fake Fiancée
Nocturne Falls, Book Five

Kristen Painter

THE VAMPIRE'S FAKE FIANCÉE:
Nocturne Falls, Book Five

Copyright © 2016 Kristen Painter

This book is a work of fiction. The characters, events, and places portrayed in this book are products of the author's imagination and are either fictitious or are used fictitiously. Any similarity to real person, living or dead, is purely coincidental and not intended by the author.

ISBN: 978-1-941695-15-9

Published in the United States of America.

Welcome to Nocturne Falls, the town that celebrates Halloween 365 days a year. The tourists think it's all a show: the vampires, the werewolves, the witches, the occasional gargoyle flying through the sky. But the supernaturals populating the town know better.

Living in Nocturne Falls means being yourself. Fangs, fur, and all.

Sebastian Ellingham isn't known for being a happy vampire. And when his long estranged wife comes to town expecting to pick up where they left off, things take a sharp turn toward cranky. Sure he's been protecting her for centuries, but her assumption that he's still available (he is) rankles.

His answer is to hire a woman to play his fiancée. The lucky victim is Tessa Blythe, sister of one of the town's deputies, librarian in need of a job and, oh yes, reluctant Valkyrie. Playing along with Sebastian is all about the end game for her, the position of Dean of Library Studies at the local private academy.

When unexpected sparks fly between them, they agree to mutually deny the attraction. Fate, however, has other plans...

For all those readers who asked
when Sebastian was getting his book.

"A hundred thousand dollars to upgrade the video system to high-definition? I think not." Sebastian snorted as he crossed off yet another line item.

The proposed operational budget for the new wedding chapel was ridiculous. Sebastian shook his head as he looked at the bottom line for a third time. There was no way he was approving a second budget of more than half a million dollars so the lovesick could marry in a Halloween theme of their choice. Especially not after he'd already approved the first budget to get the place up and running.

Julian would have to understand that this new project of his would have to operate on a more reasonable sum.

That was if his playboy brother stayed in town long enough to actually have a conversation. He seemed to spend more time in Las Vegas than he did in Nocturne Falls these days. And if Julian thought he was going to get his usual salary when he wasn't putting in his usual hours, well, that was another thing they'd need to discuss. Sebastian was not about to pick up his brother's slack playing the Vampire On Duty for the tourists.

Thankfully, one of the other vampires in town, Greyson Garrett, had been happy to fill in. Like most vampires, he was well off enough that he didn't need to work. Unlike most vampires, he had his own sort of magic that allowed him to daywalk like all of the Ellinghams, meaning he could fill in whatever shifts necessary. Sebastian suspected the secret was an old Roma spell from Greyson's past. The Romani were a people with their own magic, Sebastian knew that much. He also knew Greyson Garrett wasn't the man's real name, but many vampires changed their names as time went on for various reasons. None of which Sebastian cared about. The man was a hard worker and readily available. Unlike Julian.

Sebastian ran his tongue over his fangs and went back to the budget, picking out another of the line items. Nearly forty thousand alone for décor in a fourth themed room. What kind of theme was Newly Wed and Nearly Dead anyway?

Julian had clearly been swayed by Delaney and Corette on this, but Sebastian wasn't about to let his youngest brother spend like a drunken sailor because of the women in their family and their cockamamie ideas about this new venture.

"Hmph." He crossed out the onsite photographer. There were plenty in town. If people wanted pictures of this nonsense, they could hire one of those. No need to keep one on staff.

The door to his study flew open. "Sir—"

Sebastian held up a hand. "Greaves, I asked not to be disturbed."

"I know, sir, but this is important."

With some concern, Sebastian set his pencil down and gave his rook his full attention. The man wasn't prone to hyperbole, so if Greaves said it was important, it must be. "What is it?"

The man paled and swallowed. "I was in town getting groceries and I stopped by the pub for a pint—"

"You know I don't care about that. How you spend your time is your business."

"I know that, but while I was in the pub, I...ran into someone."

"And?" Sebastian frowned. He wanted this budget finished today. And he was not one for dramatics. "Get on with it, man."

The rook's lip curled and his eyes took on the muddy haze of disgust. He cleared his throat. "Evangeline is in town."

Her name was enough to throw a switch inside Sebastian. Everything in him went numb, iced down by a chill that went soul-deep. The wound inside him, the one he liked to pretend had healed, throbbed anew, and then the promise he'd made—the promise that had bound him to the woman like a ball and chain—rang in his ears. He blinked and found his voice. "You must be mistaken."

"I spoke to her myself. It *was* her."

Sebastian sat there, letting the information soak in. "It's been nearly two hundred years since I've seen her." And over three hundred since they'd meant anything to each other. Or rather, since he'd meant anything to her. Over three hundred years since she'd walked out and left him with the wrenching conclusion that he was not enough for her.

He'd tried to keep tabs on her, but there had been long stretches, years at a time on occasion, when he'd had no idea where she was or if she was all right. Every once in a while, she contacted him. Mostly when she needed money.

Blast it, *only* when she needed money. But these days, providing for her was the only real means he had of keeping the promise he'd made.

"She looks a little different. Changed her hair."

Sebastian nodded vaguely. Her face filled his memories, causing his heart to sting with emotions. "Still beautiful, I assume."

"Yes."

He gave the pain a moment before pushing it

aside. Of course she'd still be beautiful. She was a vampire the same as he was, their looks almost entirely frozen in time. And she'd always been breathtakingly lovely, even as a human. At least on the outside. "What did she want? Money? I'm sure she's down to her last penny again. And most likely she wants cash. It'll be morning before I can access the kind of funds she—"

"No, sir. At least not that she mentioned. All she said was that she wanted to speak to you."

Sebastian stiffened and looked past Greaves into the hall behind him. "Did you bring her back here?"

"No, of course not." Greaves adjusted his collar. "I told her to stay put and I'd be back with an answer shortly."

Sebastian eyed his rook. In their nearly four hundred years together, the man had been a stalwart companion. Trustworthy. Willing to sacrifice. Never duplicitous. A keeper of secrets. All the qualities Sebastian himself possessed. "What answer?"

"When you'd be willing to meet with her. If you're willing, that is."

Sebastian stared at the man. To be face to face with Evangeline again after all this time...a thousand possibilities filled his head, followed by only a few outcomes. "Even if she didn't bring up money, I'm sure that's what this is about. Just find out how much she needs this time and I'll take care of it. I don't need to see her face to face to fill her accounts."

"I really don't think that's what this is about. She wouldn't need to see you in person if she was just running low."

Greaves had a point. Was it possible something in Evangeline had changed in these last centuries? "Then what *do* you think she wants? As best as you can tell."

Greaves pondered the question. "My guess is she wants to apologize."

"Evangeline? Apologize? How much did you have to drink, old man?"

"I know, it doesn't seem like her, but she was different. Almost…contrite. I think you should at least see what she wants."

"Damn it." Sebastian shook his head. "Fine. I'll meet with her. But on my terms."

"Of course."

He hated the hold she had over him and yet felt powerless to do anything but respond exactly as she'd probably guessed he would. No matter the responsibility he still felt toward her, he could not let her have the upper hand. Not this time.

If he did, he would be completely destroyed. "Go back to the pub. Get a number for her. Or find out where she's staying. Tell her I'll contact her when I'm ready to talk and we'll meet where I want to meet. If she wants to see me, it's going to happen how I want it to."

Greaves seemed to puff up a bit. "Very good, sir." He left to deliver Sebastian's message.

Sebastian put a hand to his chest as he leaned back into his chair. If his heart could beat, he felt sure it would be pounding. He closed the file before him. The project budget could wait.

He had a lot to think about. A lot of feelings to sort. Scenarios to play out. A course of action to decide upon. A promise to keep.

After all, it wasn't every day your estranged wife came back to town and wanted to talk.

Tessa Blythe reluctantly put her new kitten, Duncan, down on the floor so she could grab the ringing phone. He scampered off, undoubtedly in search of another roll of toilet paper to shred or catnip toy to disembowel. The little monster was a terror. Cute enough to melt butter, but horribly behaved. She was utterly and completely in love with tiny tabby kitten. "Hello?"

"Hey, it's your sister."

"Hi, Jenna. What's new?" Jenna was a sheriff's deputy in a silly little town that celebrated Halloween three hundred and sixty-five days a year. Sounded like a recipe for disaster to Tessa.

"You're not calling to tell me you got stabbed by a criminal, are you? Or bitten by a zombie or whatever unfortunate element roams the streets there? Oh, please tell me you didn't have to kill someone in self-defense."

A sigh answered her. "Tessa, this is Nocturne Falls, not the dark streets of some crime-ridden city. It's like Tim Burton's version of Disney. I can't even tell you the last time I took my gun out of its holster. I swear, you'd love it here. It's very friendly to supernaturals. And really, considering who we are, you need to get over your fear of living a genuine life."

"I am living a genuine life. And can we please not go into that again?"

Duncan was now climbing the side of the couch, claws digging deep in the ancient plaid fabric that covered the ugly thing. (The apartment had come furnished, but ugly was ugly.) Tessa put her hand over the receiver. "No. Bad cat. Bad." She was never getting her security deposit back.

"Who are you yelling at? Did you say cat? Did you get a cat, Tessa? Holy Loki, please tell me you did not get a cat. You're turning into a cliché."

"Just because I'm a librarian, *possibly* with a cat, doesn't mean I'm a cliché."

"No, but when you also wear glasses you don't need and generally seem to have your hair in a bun, the scales do lean in that direction."

"I wear magnifying lenses because it helps me with my job."

"You wear glasses as way to disguise your looks."

"Are you saying I don't look good in my glasses? That's very cruel."

"Had any dates lately? Or does that birth control bun effectively keep the men at bay?"

Tessa reached up and pulled the elastic out of her hair. "For your information, my hair is down right now. Besides, you wear your hair up all the time."

"I have to, it's a job requirement. You don't have that excuse, but hey, if you want to hide yourself from the world by becoming a cliché, that's your business. I love you, frumpy bun and all, you know that. I wouldn't be trying to get you to move to Nocturne Falls to be near me if I didn't love you. Right?"

"Right." Tessa wouldn't mind moving, even if the town was a tourist trap. She'd moved to Dayton, Ohio, only because it was where she'd gotten her first librarian job. And she'd love to be near her sister, but there was the matter of getting a new job. And quitting her current one. Not that her current one had turned out to be anything that fabulous.

"So listen, that's why I'm calling. I just heard through the grapevine that the private school here is hiring a dean of library studies. And the money will be good. I don't know how good, but Harmswood Academy doesn't cut corners."

"I have a job."

"Are you the dean of anything?"

Now it was Tessa's turn to sigh. "No. But I *could* get promoted."

"The only way you're going to get promoted is if that old battle ax that's in charge dies."

"Jenna, that's unkind."

"It's true, though, isn't it?"

Tessa frowned. "Yes."

"And didn't you call me last week and say that if you could find another librarian job, you'd take it in a heartbeat?"

Tessa took a breath. "Yes. But that was in the heat of the moment."

"It still happened. Now you have a chance. So take a week off, come down here and submit your resume. What have you got to lose?"

"I'd have to bring Duncan."

Jenna gasped. "Do you have a boyfriend?"

Tessa pressed her hand to her forehead, the headache of confession surely on its way. "Duncan is my cat." Who was now chewing off the end of the curtain pull.

"I *knew* you adopted a cat."

"I didn't adopt him, exactly. Someone dropped him in the book return slot, and Mrs. Unger was

THE VAMPIRE'S FAKE FIANCÉE

going to take him to the pound. Can you imagine? The poor thing. He's just this tiny little ball of brown and black striped fur. Some dog would probably think he was a chew toy. Or a snack."

"Told you she was a battle ax."

"She *is* an enormous grump. Constantly nitpicking my work. And between us, she smells oddly like Lipton onion soup mix. All the time."

Jenna laughed. "See? You don't want to work there. You want to be in charge of your own library. The library dean. Doesn't that have a nice ring to it?"

"It does." Tessa closed her eyes. The library at a well-funded private academy could be a magnificent thing. "Do you have any idea what the library at this school looks like?"

"I've only been up to the academy once. They have their own security force. But the campus is gorgeous. I'm sure the library is great."

Tessa bit her lip. A library like that could be really something. And to be in charge of it? That was a little dizzying. "I'll have to put in for time off."

Jenna muttered disgustedly, "What if Battle Ax says no?"

"I don't think she'd do that. I have two vacation days coming. I just have to fill out the form and get them approved. Shouldn't take more than ten days. Two weeks, tops."

"Wait that long and the job could be gone by the

time you get here. Just quit and come here. Bring Dumpling. Bring everything. Move."

"Duncan."

"Yes, him too. C'mon, Tessa. You can live with me until, you get on your feet. I make enough money for both of us to live on. We're not going to be taking a singles cruise anytime soon, but we'll be okay until you start the dean position."

"If I just quit my job, I'm not going to be able to use them for a reference."

"You really think Unger is going to give you a decent reference? Doesn't she blame you for the county deciding the library needed a Facebook page?"

"Yes." That had been an ugly few weeks. Even with the four hundred likes they'd garnered. "But what if I don't get the job? What if something happens and the interview doesn't go well?"

"What's the point of being a valkyrie if you don't use what you've got? If you get a vibe that the interview isn't going well, you can change tactics. Tell them what you think they want to hear. Or you could always become a deputy like me."

"You know how I feel about violence and fighting and all that." And about anything that might cause her to get upset, but seeing as how Jenna knew that already, Tessa didn't see the point in bringing it up again. She stared at the pale scar that transected the last three knuckles of her right hand.

"For crying out loud, do I need to mention *again* that we're valkyries? Warrior goddesses. Protectors of the worthy. Fierceness is in our DNA."

"Maybe for you, but that's not the life I've chosen to lead." Not after the incident. Not after she'd figured out what she was really capable of.

"I know." Jenna exhaled in the sort of long-suffering way she did whenever they had this conversation. "You probably don't even remember how to swing your sword, do you?"

"I do." Probably. "I chose not to." Or ever again, actually. At the thought of her sword, a small trill of energy zipped down her spine. She ignored it. Like she always did.

"When's the last time you had it out?"

"I'm a librarian. The opportunities to wield a sword are few and far between." Which made this job perfect for her. "Now, back to what I'm going to do for work if this job doesn't pan out."

"Something will turn up. There's plenty of other stuff you could do in this town."

"But I want to be a librarian. It's what I went to school for. It's what I'm good at. It's where my heart is." She loved books. In a book you could escape and be anything you wanted, no risk involved. No chance of hurting anyone else.

"You'll get the job, Tessa. How could you not?"

"Because someone with more experience could come along."

"Yes, but you have to also be a supernatural to get this job. And you don't get much more supernatural than being a descendant of one of Odin's shield maidens."

Tessa tapped a finger against her lip. Duncan leaped off the couch and headed for the kitchen. By the quiver of his tail, she could tell he was up to no good. So the usual. "True."

"And I know this is a risk, and you don't take risks. But just this once, please take a chance. Mom and Dad are going to be touring Europe for the rest of their lives. We'll be lucky to see them at our weddings, if we ever get married. Wouldn't it be nice for us to be close enough to hang out whenever we wanted? We could spend Christmas together if you lived here. We could go shopping and do spa days and all that kind of stuff together."

Tessa's librarian's salary didn't allow for much shopping or any spa days, but she got what her sister was saying. "It would be nice to be closer."

Jenna went on. "Also, isn't Ohio like completely covered in snow and ice? Winter in Georgia isn't nearly as bad."

"I don't mind the snow, but it would be nice not to have to scrape my windshield every morning." She looked around at her cramped apartment that her job barely paid for and thought about her sister's house in Nocturne Falls. She'd seen pictures. Not only was it pretty and on a street with big trees, it had a backyard, which meant Duncan could go out and run around. Fresh air. Sunshine. A chance to wear himself out.

And the chance for her to be near her sister.

"Come on, throw that cat into a carrier and start driving. I'll talk to one of the Ellinghams and see about getting you a tour of the school before your interview so you can see for yourself exactly how amazing it is."

"I can't just leave like that. There's a ton of things I'd have to take care of first."

"Like what?"

"I still have to give the library my notice that I'm quitting and turn off my water and electric and let the landlord know I'm breaking the lease and—"

"Find your inner warrior and make it happen. Besides, I already submitted your name. They're expecting you."

"What? Why did you do that?"

"Because you never would have done it."

"I might have."

"Tessa. This is the kind of change you need. The kind of job you *deserve*."

Tessa squeezed her eyes shut. She and her inner warrior hadn't really communicated in a long time, but she knew Jenna was right. She needed a change, and being near her sister would be great. "I can be there in four days."

"You can be here in one."

"Impossible. Two is the absolute minimum."

Jenna whooped into the phone. "Yes! I knew I could talk you into it. See you in two days, sis!"

"Wait—" But Jenna had already hung up. Like she knew she'd just talked Tessa into something she'd only change her mind about.

Tessa blew out a breath. She was already having doubts. What had she just gotten herself into? She shook herself. No, this was a good thing. She really wasn't happy at her current job. And this apartment was dreadful. A change would be good. Being near her sister would be great. Jenna was so brave and daring and didn't let a thing stand in her way. Tessa wanted to be more like that. In theory.

She walked over and pulled Duncan out of the trash can, then hugged him against her chest for a second before holding him up to look him in the eyes. "I realize you're just getting the lay of the land, but don't get too comfortable. Change is afoot."

He meowed at her, a loud, squeaky sound that made her grin. "I know! This is a big step for both of us, but Jenna will be there and she's got a yard you can play in. Plus, I promise you can take all of your new toys, too."

He tried to eat a piece of her hair.

She pulled it out of his mouth and shook her head. What on earth had she just agreed to?

Sebastian would be lying to himself if he tried to deny the slightly righteous pleasure that he'd taken from keeping Evangeline waiting. It had been only three days. And after all, she'd kept him waiting nearly three hundred years. Seventy-two hours seemed a drop in the bucket in comparison.

It had been a calculated move. Not just to keep her waiting, but to time things so that his meeting with her happened the morning of interviews at Harmswood. He'd be dressed sharply and have a place to go afterward, giving him a reason not to linger.

He also wanted her to know he was a busy man. Occupied with many things. None of which were her. He sighed. If only that were true. She did occupy some of his time, which irritated him to no end, but it was a responsibility with which he'd learned to live. A duty.

A chore.

And then of course, there was the matter of the time they were meeting.

Eight in the morning. A time that, despite the blazing sun high in the January sky, did nothing to deter his ability to be outside. Unlike most vampires. He had the bespelled amulet that he and all the members of his family wore to thank for that miracle. Unless Evangeline had found similar magic on her own, she had no such amulet. She'd left him before Elenora Ellingham, his grandmother and the woman who'd turned him, had saved the life of a very powerful witch.

In thanks, the witch had created the amulets for them.

Being able to daywalk gave Sebastian an edge over Evangeline. Something, quite frankly, to hold over her. Had she stayed, she'd have an amulet too. Not that he was about to reveal that. The amulets were a closely guarded family secret.

And so, because he'd chosen to meet her at such an early morning hour, they were meeting at the bed-and-breakfast in which Evangeline had ensconced herself. When Sebastian chose to leave, she'd be unable to follow.

That's what he wanted. The complete advantage. After all she'd put him through, it was only fair. On some level, he continued to feel *something* for her. He must, he supposed. Not even the vampire council would consider them still married, but they were bonded and always would be. He'd turned her. The council took the role of sire very seriously. For that reason, and another that had been decided before they'd married, he was responsible for her. So yes, he was always going to take care of her. But *she'd* left *him*.

He needed her to suffer a bit before he took her back.

He froze. What was he thinking? Before he took her back? At best, it was *if* he took her back. He reminded himself that was the attitude he had to adopt if he was going to come out ahead with Evangeline. She was far too cunning for him to assume things would go off without some sort of hitch. He would be aware of everything she did, keenly appraising her moves and words and gestures for some deeper motive.

He would not be made a fool of twice.

He pulled his Aston Martin into the small parking lot of the Black Rose. The establishment was a known D&B, or dead-and-breakfast—a small inn that catered to vampire clientele and other supernaturals. There were three in town, but it was no surprise Evangeline had chosen the Black Rose. It was the most luxurious of the trio.

He locked his vehicle and went inside.

He could hear Mrs. Turnbuckle, the D&B's owner, in the dining room talking to some of the other guests. She was elf or hobbit or some such creature, and known for her hospitality and small talk. The latter being a loathsome practice he considered a waste of air. And since he had neither the time nor the desire to engage in such a purposeless activity, he headed straight for the stairs and Evangeline's room.

"Mr. Ellingham?"

He'd almost reached the landing too. He steeled himself and turned, keeping his tone civil but free from encouragement. "Mrs. Turnbuckle."

She was a spry thing in her seventies, with piercing brown eyes behind wire-rimmed glasses and pointed ears that peeked through her wiry blue-gray curls. "Visiting a guest?"

Why else would he be in this miserable establishment? "Yes. Good day." He attempted to take his leave.

"Wouldn't be the pretty one in the Thorn Suite, would it?"

He sighed. "Yes. And she's expecting me."

"Eva Wynn?"

Was that the name she was using these days? At least she hadn't used Ellingham. "That's the one." He forced a smile and what he imagined would pass for a jovial nod and a polite dismissal. "Good day."

He escaped the innkeeper and knocked on Evangeline's door as quickly as possible.

Evangeline let him stand there until he was just about to knock again. His hand was raised when the door opened.

She smiled like she'd just seen him yesterday. She wore a slinky, floor-length black negligee with a matching robe and feathered mules. Her hair was shorter, a darker brown and streaked with deep red, but otherwise, she looked the same. She sucked in a breath and put her hand to her chest. "Sebastian. It's so good to see you. Thank you for coming. I wasn't sure I was going to see my husband at all after you made me wait all week."

"It was three days." Seeing her combined with the flood of her perfume and the sound of her voice hit him like a punch to the gut. The edges of his vision seemed to dim and blur, and his mouth went dry. He wanted to kiss her and shake her and run from the room all at the same time. *Get ahold of yourself, man.* He pulled himself together and frowned. "And I hardly think you have the right to call me husband after all this time."

Her smile widened and she backed up, opening the door to let him in. "Oh, Sebby, come now. Sure, it's been a few years, but that doesn't change the fact that we're married."

A few years? Is that how it felt to her? The woman had never been good with sums, but she was certainly aware of how much time had passed. He walked into her room with a great deal more composure than he felt. "It's been more than a few *years* and our marriage exists in memory only. There isn't a court of law in this world that would uphold that bond after the length of time we've been separated."

She closed the door. "Yes, I'm sure you're right. And I'm terribly sorry about that, I am. Mistakes were made, but I was hoping we could move past that. After all, you are still my sire." She sidled past him to take a seat in one of two chairs by the windows, bathing him in a cloud of her scent.

He filled his lungs with it, then immediately wished he hadn't. With every passing moment, he was growing more intoxicated with the need for her. Damn his weakness for her. Damn his sense of responsibility to her.

Maybe that's all it was. His sense of duty kicking in. Or maybe it was the fact that he'd not had the companionship of a woman since Evangeline had left him.

Oh, he'd thought about other women. Desired them. But he'd never done anything about it. Another wretched side effect of loyalty and duty and bloody responsibility. And perhaps his desire not to have to explain the mess of his life to anyone else.

He distracted himself by studying the suite. The windows behind the alcove where she sat were covered with room-darkening shades on the inside and UV film on the outside. That was standard in every D&B.

She poked at the other chair with the tip of her shoe. Her toenails were painted blood red. His fingers itched to touch her skin. He liked to imagine he still remembered what it felt like to hold a woman in his arms. To feel the press of a woman's soft curves against his own unyielding angles.

She fluttered her lashes. "Please sit. I can't bear to have you standing there, judging me."

"I'm not judging you." He should be, but he wasn't. Instead, he was judging himself. Taking the measure of his weaknesses. He took the seat.

A sharp laugh burst out of her. "Now we both know that's not true. But I'm okay with it. I've been a very bad girl. Just awful to you, my darling. I deserve your judgment."

"I suppose you do." She had been awful to him, especially when she'd made him realize all those years ago that he wasn't enough. Not for her. Maybe not for any woman. So why was she waltzing back into his life now?

She lowered her eyes and pursed her lips as a dramatic shudder went through her. "Do you hate me, Sebby?"

He sighed. The answer to that question was not a simple one. And whatever game she was playing, he wanted to know what she hoped to accomplish and fast. Before he made a foolish decision based on another foolish decision made centuries ago. "Why are you here, Evangeline?"

"That's the Sebastian I know. Right to the point." Her expression saddened and she folded her hands in her lap. "I did you a terrible wrong, Sebastian. I acknowledge that and I ask your forgiveness."

He'd heard this before. Well, not heard exactly, but over the years he'd read versions of it in letters, telegrams, and emails.

"How much money do you need?" He was fully prepared to advance her some funds, just as he'd done in the past. Just as he always had. Just as he'd promised to do.

She put a hand to her heart. Assuming she had one. "I'm not here asking for money. I have enough of my own, thank you. And if that's all I needed, I wouldn't have come here in person."

"Then what?"

She stared at him, truly stared into his eyes, as hers went soft and liquid. "I miss you, Sebby. I was stupid and foolish and I know enough about life now to realize that you were the best thing that ever happened to me."

He narrowed his gaze, mostly unmoved by her outpouring of emotion. He'd seen similar displays from her too many times to be fully drawn in. And focusing on the pain she'd caused him helped temper any soft feelings that arose. "You told me becoming a vampire was the best thing that ever happened to you."

She nodded. "And it was. For a long time. But life without you just isn't...life. And I'll be honest, because you deserve that from me. The men I've met, well, none of them has compared to you. You and I? We were meant to be together. I know that now. After all, what's eternity without your soulmate?"

She'd never called him that before. He tried very hard not to react. He'd dreamed about her coming to him like this. Begging for his forgiveness. Telling him she would be faithful and true and how he was the only man who'd ever meant anything to her. "What are you saying, Evangeline?"

She reached out and took his hand. "I'm ready for you to be my husband again."

His lips parted but he was momentarily speechless. *She* was ready for him to be her husband again? What about what he was ready for? What about what he wanted? Her assumptions were numerous and staggering. And where was the groveling and the promises of fidelity? She'd just admitted there had been other men. Was he just supposed to forgive the many affairs she'd undoubtedly had while she'd been cavorting her way around the world? Where was her apology? Her sense of contrition? Her profession of love? "Just like that."

She grinned. "Just like that. We can go right back to being husband and wife. Just like old times. I can move in tomorrow. Or tonight!" She fluttered her lashes at him. "We could get *reacquainted*."

A curious anger built in him. He'd once thought this was what he'd wanted, to have Evangeline back in his life. But now that the opportunity faced him, he realized that she was taking his love for her for granted. *Like she always had.* Everything inside him shifted. What he thought he'd wanted and what he actually wanted were two different things.

He might not have been enough man to keep her at his side all those years ago, but time away from her had taught him that he could do just fine without her. Perhaps not as happy or as content as he would have liked. Maybe even a little bit lonely, but he'd managed.

Time had also taught him he didn't need to be at her side to keep the promise he'd made. Not so long as he defined taking care of her by financial standards, which is all she'd allowed these past centuries.

He shook his head, flush with the power of his new realization. "You're assuming I haven't moved on."

She laughed and waved a hand at him. "Come now, Sebby. You still carry a torch for me. You know it. I know it. Let's stop playing games and get on with our life."

His anger breached the boundaries of common sense. He stood and glared down at her. "For your information, I have not only gotten over you, but I am involved with someone else."

Her smile disappeared. "You're not serious."

"I bloody well am."

Her mouth tightened into a little knot of disbelief. "If you're trying to get me to fawn all over you and tell you how much I missed you, fine, but let's not pretend that—"

"Are you calling me a liar?" He *was* lying, of course, but falsehoods were not something to which he'd ever been disposed so she had no reason to doubt him.

She crossed her arms and the twinkle of a challenge danced in her eyes. "You expect me to believe you've found another woman who is as equally enthralled with you as you are with her? A woman who can bear your moods? Who doesn't weep with boredom when you go off on your academic tangents? Sebby, I grew to love you despite those things. Our match, arranged as it was, worked because you are a good man, as loyal as a hunting dog and as predictable as the chimes for dinner, *not* because you kept me entertained. But I've always been a resourceful woman and capable of doing that for myself. Why do you think we hosted so many balls and dinners and house parties?"

And there was the side of Evangeline he'd come to despise. The cutting, cruel woman who could tear him down faster than she could look at him. That side of her had been evident even in their early years of marriage, but he'd chalked it up to her youth and unhappiness at the arranged marriage.

His time away from her had helped him see some truths, but it had done little to thicken his skin. Her words hurt, even after all these years. Perhaps in some part because he knew they were true. The pain pushed his lie to new heights. "My fiancée thinks none of those things. She adores me."

She blinked. "You're engaged?"

Bloody hell. He'd said fiancée. There was no retreating now. He lifted his chin. "Yes. Happily."

She snorted in disbelief.

Red edged his vision and logical thought gave way to spontaneous reaction. "Come to dinner at my house and see for yourself. Tomorrow at seven. That's safely after sundown."

"Seven it is, then."

Something dark sparked in her eyes but he ignored it. "I'll send Greaves with the details."

He stormed out before she could say another word. He was fuming. He'd expected her to be petulant and egotistical. That's who Evangeline was. A spoiled, willful child of a woman. But for her to carry on like she was his last hope for companionship—and that he should be *grateful* for her willingness to return to his life? Her nerve was astonishing, even for Evangeline.

She had no appreciation for what he'd been doing for her all these years. The way he'd watched over her to the best of his abilities and taken care of her financial needs without question, to say nothing about turning a blind eye to her disloyal ways. He could have sent someone to gather proof of her affairs and used it to dissolve their relationship in the eyes of the council, but he hadn't. He'd clung to the promise he'd made and his old-fashioned sense of responsibility.

He stopped at the driver's door to his car, seething with rage. His heart was irreparably broken. He'd acknowledged that years ago. He'd learned to live with the pain of her abandonment and betrayal. But this assumption that he was waiting with open arms to take her back, no apology needed, *this* was galling.

He got in and slammed the door shut. She'd see how wrong she was. How he truly didn't need her anymore. How very over her he was. Tomorrow night's dinner would be the absolute end of his emotional relationship with Evangeline.

Or perhaps... Perhaps it would be the start of a new relationship with her. One in which he held the upper hand and she finally saw him as more than just a...loyal dog. Tomorrow night's dinner would change everything one way or another.

He could always tell her about the promise. But that wasn't part of the deal he'd made and he was a man of his word. That promise would remain his secret. He'd kept it these many years, he could keep it awhile longer.

He shut his eyes and swallowed as the fine points of the impending dinner came back to him. There was one small detail he'd have to work on. Quickly.

He did not actually *have* a fiancée.

Tessa had thought being the dean of library studies at a private academy sounded intriguing, but after Jenna had given her a tour of the campus and allowed her to linger in the utterly gorgeous library that she'd be in charge of (three floors, stained glass windows, dark wood paneling, antique tapestries, and the most up-to-date touch-screen catalog system she'd ever seen), Tessa thought she might weep if she didn't get the job.

She couldn't stop smiling. If this actually happened, moving to Nocturne Falls might be the smartest thing she'd ever done. She nudged her sister. "The rare-book room has medieval manuscripts."

Jenna nodded. "Cool, right?"

"Cool? Don't be such a Philistine. They're priceless works of art that give us a glimpse into another age. They're the ability to time travel on a page. And I would be in charge of them."

"Like I said, cool." Jenna pointed ahead. "That's reception. I'll just tell her we're here for the interview, then I'll introduce you to the Ellinghams and you're on your own."

"Thank you." Tessa sighed. She couldn't expect her sister to understand. Jenna was a cop. The things that excited her were guns, catching criminals and cold beer. And those things were great, if you were a cop. But Tessa's mind needed art and literature and beauty. Those were the things that kept her sane and reminded her of all the good life had to offer. Those things and her pursuit of them helped balance the parts of her she wasn't so fond of.

Jenna nudged her. "You ready?"

"Yes."

"Then let's go. They're waiting. The receptionist will take us back."

The woman smiled at them. "Right this way, ladies."

Nerves seized Tessa, but she reminded herself that she was smart and capable and she knew her library sciences. Not only could she do this job but she could do it well.

She and Jenna followed the receptionist to a door near the end of a long hallway decorated with oil paintings of past deans. Not one of them looked fully human. The woman knocked on one of two doors in an alcove.

A voice called for them to enter. The receptionist smiled, opened the door and stood out of the way.

Jenna went in first. In her uniform, she was an ever greater presence than she usually was. But then, Jenna had embraced being tall and beautiful and a valkyrie.

Jenna nodded at the imperious man on the other side of the table. "Hugh."

"Deputy Blythe."

"I know we're early, but I thought it would be you and Sebastian."

Hugh smiled tightly. "It will be. He's running a little late. This is your sister?"

"Yes, this is Tessa Blythe. Librarian extraordinaire." Jenna smiled at her. "Tessa, this is Hugh Ellingham, one of the founders of the town and this academy."

Tessa nodded and shook his hand. "Thank you for the interview."

"Your resume is exceptional. Perhaps a little light on years of experience, but otherwise very impressive. I apologize for my brother's tardiness. If you'll just have a seat, I'll text him and see how much longer he's going to be."

Tessa nodded as Hugh picked up his phone.

Jenna leaned in and whispered, "I'm gonna go. Knock 'em dead."

"Thank you. I'll see you later."

The door burst open before Jenna had taken two steps toward it. A tall, handsome, and very agitated man strode into the room with all the dark, stormy presence of Mr. Darcy. He looked like a slightly older, sterner version of the man she'd just met. "Apologies for being late, Hugh, but bloody hell, you will not believe the morning I've had. Evangeline is in town."

Hugh's mouth gaped. "Are you serious?"

"Yes, very." He shoved a hand through his hair. "I won't go into it all now, but I need a woman. Who do you know that might be willing to pretend to be my betrothed for an evening?"

Jenna snorted. "That's gonna be a short list."

Both men turned and the man who'd just come in eyed Jenna and Tessa like they were interlopers. He looked back at Hugh. "You could have mentioned the interview was here."

"You didn't give me a chance." Hugh gestured toward Tessa. "This is Tessa Blythe, Deputy Blythe's sister. Tessa, this is my late brother, Sebastian."

Tessa lifted her fingers in a small wave, hoping the man's less than cheerful disposition didn't affect her interview.

Jenna laughed. "I see what you did there. *Late*

brother. Funny." She nudged Tessa. "Because he's both a vampire and not on time."

"I get it," Tessa whispered. Her sister's fearlessness around these men was astonishing. Sure, they were vampires and they looked appropriately intimidating, but they were also in charge of the hiring. That was a far more daunting bit of information where Tessa was concerned.

Sebastian gave them a curt nod before turning back to his brother. "I can't do this interview right now. I need to sort out this problem. Evangeline's coming to dinner tomorrow night and expects to meet my fiancée."

Hugh shook his head. "Why on earth would she expect that?"

Sebastian frowned. "Because I told her she would."

"And why did you tell her that?"

Sebastian's frown hardened into something more serious. "Pride."

Hugh glanced at Jenna. "How about the deputy here?"

Jenna crossed her arms. "Yeah, that's not happening."

Sebastian's brows knit together, his unhappy expression unchanged. "Why not? I'll compensate you for your time."

"I appreciate that, but, and I say this with the utmost respect, no one would buy it. As best I can tell, we have nothing in common. You rarely leave your house, and when you do, you're dressed like you're off to a business meeting. Which you probably are because you're the CFO of this town. And that's all great, but my idea of fun is four-wheeling through the mud or getting a little range time in with my service weapon."

"Or wrestling a perp to the ground," Tessa added.

Jenna nodded. "Exactly. See? My sister gets me. Hey!" She looked at Tessa with a bright smile. "You could do it."

Tessa swallowed as a surge of anxiety attempted to close her throat. "What?"

Sebastian expelled a gruff sound of disbelief. "This mouse? No offense, but Evangeline would eat her for breakfast."

Tessa's eyes rounded.

His hand shot up. "Not literally. I just meant—"

Jenna cut him off. "I know what you meant. You think because my sister looks like a librarian and *is* a librarian that she's too timid and quiet for anyone to buy that she'd be your fiancée. Well, I'll have you know that she might look harmless but she's a valkyrie, same as I am, and one of the fiercest women I know."

Tessa almost groaned at Jenna's lie. Fierce? She might as well have said Tessa could leap tall buildings in a single bound.

Sebastian's brows lifted as his gaze swept Tessa

from head to toe. "She doesn't look like a valkyrie."

"Well, I am," Tessa said. Did Jenna really see her as fierce? "I have to be, don't I? I mean, my sister is one. It's not a thing that skips generations or only affects one child."

Jenna jabbed a finger at him, clearly not done. "What she looks like and what she's capable of are two different things. You want help with this situation? Tessa can do it. But you'd better promise her this job when this charade is all said and done. Otherwise, no deal."

Tessa poked a warning finger into her sister's back, but the Kevlar vest beneath her uniform shirt didn't allow for much pressure. There was no way she could do this. Pretend to be a vampire's betrothed? And this vampire, who was clearly a difficult man to get along with? No. Way.

"I'll promise her the job, but I must warn you both. Pretending to be my fiancée could be a little dangerous."

Dangerous? Tessa bit her lip. How could pretending be dangerous?

Jenna laughed. "Don't worry about Tessa. She can take care of herself."

Sebastian's brows knit. "Are you sure? She doesn't look like she could defend herself from a kitten."

Jenna leaned in. "You have no idea what she's capable of."

Tessa wanted to disappear. She knew exactly what Jenna meant by that even if Sebastian didn't. *Please don't let her explain further.*

But Jenna's words seemed to have Sebastian considering the deal. "And when she can't pull it off? Then what? No, I think you should do it, Deputy. It's only for a night."

"I'm on duty. And also, I already said no. If Tessa can't pull it off, then you don't have to hire her. But she will. You'll see. And then she'll be the new library dean."

"Dean of library studies," Tessa corrected. Was this really happening?

Sebastian's gaze narrowed in calculation and his jaw twitched in a very unhappy way, which matched the deep sense of skepticism coming off him. "You'll need to be at my house first thing in the morning. You'll have to be familiar with my house and me. We'll need the whole day together if this is going to work."

Tessa felt very much like she was on a roller coaster climbing toward the peak of a very sharp drop. But how hard could it be to pretend for an evening? Especially when it meant guaranteeing herself the amazing position of dean of library studies. "I can be there as early as you need me."

He snorted. "Wonderful, but the early start is hardly the difficult bit. Fooling Evangeline is where things get tricky. She's a master of deception and manipulation, and a vampire as old as I am. Pulling one over on her will be a Herculean task."

Tessa nodded. Her valkyrie senses told her he wasn't lying. A new wave of nervousness rattled her. Moving to Nocturne Falls was starting to feel like a very questionable decision.

Sebastian stared into his backyard, seeing nothing of the gardens or the purple sky brought on by twilight. All he could think about was that he'd made a stupid, rash decision. Evangeline's presence had that kind of effect on men. And his bold claim of being engaged was proof that she most definitely still had that effect on him.

There was no way the meek little sister of Deputy Blythe was going to convince Evangeline that she was his fiancée. Valkyrie or not, the woman was so bland as to be almost unnoticeable, and if her personality matched her looks, he was doomed. She wasn't ugly by any stretch, but she was just so plain that she would be impossible to pick out in a crowd. He doubted Evangeline would ever believe he was attracted to Tessa.

The poor woman couldn't help who she was, though. And he was indebted to her for coming to his rescue, fully aware that it was a tremendously kind act on her behalf. Of course, she stood to gain the dean of library studies job, which she was infinitely qualified for anyway, but he was appreciative regardless. Job or not, he owed her. She barely knew him.

He couldn't remember the last time anyone had put themselves out for him in such a manner. A tiny spot of warmth bloomed in his heart for Tessa Blythe. The first he'd really felt for anyone outside of his family, which naturally included Greaves. He stayed on that thought for a moment. No matter the outcome, Tessa had proven herself a good person.

Sebastian rubbed his chin. Perhaps Tessa being Evangeline's exact opposite was a good thing. Maybe Tessa's mousiness would startle Evangeline into thinking this setup was the truth. That he must really love the woman to be keeping company with her. He couldn't say.

But no matter how he played the outcomes in his head, he couldn't shake the feeling this whole mess had the very serious potential to blow up in his face. Tessa should have the job either way. She should not suffer if this plan didn't work. Because if it didn't, Evangeline would surely make her suffer.

Sebastian vowed he would protect Tessa from Evangeline, no matter the cost to himself or

Evangeline. Tessa didn't deserve to be hurt because of his problems. Or Evangeline's unpredictability.

Yes, he'd see to it that Tessa had the job, but he wouldn't tell her that. He needed her to be motivated, after all. This was not going to be an easy task.

If only they had more time to prepare. But then, they *did* to some extent. Not much more time, but he could go see Tessa tonight. In fact, he almost had to. A day would never be enough to get their stories memorized and become familiar enough with one another so as not to appear like strangers. He sighed loudly.

"Everything all right, sir?"

Sebastian turned. He'd told Greaves everything the minute he'd gotten home. "I need to go see Tessa. There are too many details. We'll never get them right if we don't start now."

"You could just tell Evangeline the truth."

"And look like a fool in her eyes once again? No. I can't have her thinking I've been waiting for her return all these years. That I've just been pining away."

"Except that you have been." He held his hands up. "Respectfully."

Sebastian frowned. "I know what a pathetic fool I am, old man. No need to remind me." He pinched the bridge of his nose. "She looked at me with utter disbelief. As if the thought that another woman was willing to have me was completely preposterous. That I could not possibly be interesting enough to hold the attention of another woman. It may be my downfall, but my pride will not let that lie."

"No, sir."

He looked at Greaves. "Am I that difficult of a man just because I am firm in my beliefs and have little tolerance for imperfection in others? Is that enough to make me…hard to love, do you think?"

Greaves pursed his mouth. "I can't speak for the female population, but you are not Julian, that's for sure."

Sebastian snorted derisively at the mention of his youngest brother. "And I never will be if treacly charm and loose morals are what make a man attractive."

Greaves grunted in agreement.

A hard thought struck Sebastian. He let a few seconds pass before speaking again. "Am I boring, then, Greaves?"

Greaves tipped his head slightly. "I suppose that depends on what a woman finds stimulating. Evangeline's interests lay beyond the realm of the cerebral, so you two were never going to be a good match. You're a brilliant man with a mind that seeks higher pleasures. You need a woman with a similar mind."

"Thank you for that." Sebastian rolled his shoulders to relieve the stress of the day. It failed to help. "I'm going out to see Miss Blythe. We have work to do. I'll see you in the morning."

"Very good, sir."

Deputy Blythe lived in one of the residential neighborhoods the Ellinghams had set aside specifically for town employees. The houses weren't enormous but they weren't shoe boxes either and the yards all showed pride of ownership, something that pleased Sebastian. Order was a thing of beauty and these streets had it in spades.

He parked in her driveway next to her patrol car and went to the front door to knock. Deputy Blythe answered a few moments later and he knew immediately by her expression that he was not who she'd expected.

"Sebastian."

"Deputy Blythe. I realize I should have phoned that I was coming. My apologies for interrupting your evening. I was hoping to speak with Tessa."

"Did you decide to call the whole thing off?"

"No. But that is why I'm here. Is she available?"

"Sure, come in. She's in her room. I'll get her." Jenna pointed at the couch in the living room. "Have a seat."

He remained standing. The house was as neat inside as it was out and not overly accessorized. He liked it.

A few minutes later, Tessa walked into the

room. She pushed her glasses back and blinked at him. "H-hello."

A more tentative greeting he could not imagine. He did his best to be casual. "Hi. I'm sorry to drop by unannounced, but I was thinking we should start the process of getting to know each other now instead of trying to cram it all into the hours before dinner tomorrow."

She nodded, looking relieved. "That's a good idea. I have to confess, the whole thing is making me nervous. I don't like being unprepared."

"No, neither do I. Would you like to go out? Get some coffee perhaps?" He hadn't actually intended that, but it seemed like he'd become quite impulsive lately.

She tucked a loose strand of dirty-blonde hair behind one ear. It was the only piece that had escaped the chignon at the nape of her neck. "Um, sure. I guess if we're supposed to be engaged, being seen in public together makes sense, doesn't it?"

"Yes. Although now it's my turn to confess that I hadn't even thought of that."

She raised her hand, palm to her chest, and wiggled her fingers. "Something else you might not have thought about. Do you have a ring for me to wear?"

"A ring?"

"An engagement ring. Won't this other woman expect to see one on my hand?"

He closed his eyes and sighed. There was so much he hadn't considered. This was why he was rarely impulsive. Actions spawned by emotion were prone to failure. "Yes, she absolutely will. And no, I don't have one. We'll remedy that this evening as well. Why don't you get ready and I'll make a call and see what I can do about that."

She glanced down at her nondescript pants and blouse. "I...am ready."

"Oh." Plain did not begin to describe the poor woman.

Her mouth thinned to a perturbed line. "No, never mind. I'll go change. I'll be quick."

"Take as long as you like. I'm happy to wait."

She headed back down the hall and he heard her calling for her sister. He shook his head. He had only himself to blame when Evangeline saw through this. He pulled out his phone and dialed Willa Iscove, the jeweler in town. He needed a ring and he could think of no one else who could provide him with one on such short notice.

There would be no half-measures, either, because in all of this mess, he knew one thing. If he was going down in flames, it was going to be the largest bonfire Nocturne Falls had ever witnessed.

Tessa slipped into her sister's room and shut the door, leaning against it. "You have to help me."

Jenna looked up from where she was sitting on her bed playing with Duncan who was chasing a feather on a string, but mostly falling over his own feet in the process. "What do you need? Whatever it is, I'll do it. It's my valkyrie duty to protect the worthy and you certainly fit that description, even if you are another valkyrie. Wait, you're not going to ask me to take your place as Grumpy's fiancée are you? Because I love you but my answer to that is still no."

"No, it's not that and don't call him Grumpy. That's my future boss you're talking about. *If* this works out. He wants to go out for coffee and by the way he looked at my clothes, I could tell he didn't think much of this outfit. If I'm supposed to be his fiancée, I need to look like a woman he'd actually be seen with. Which I'm guessing I don't now."

"And that's what you want my help with?"

Tessa nodded. "Yes. Please."

Jenna hopped off the bed and squealed with delight. "I've been trying to give you a makeover for years."

"Hold up. This is not a makeover. I just need help picking out something else to wear. Something more like what a vampire's fiancée would wear." Tessa shook her head at the ridiculousness of that statement. "Whatever that is."

Jenna went over and opened her closet.

Tessa's brows knit. "My clothes are in the guest room."

"Which is why I'm looking in here." She stared into her closet. "Do you have any skinny jeans?"

"Do I look like a hipster?"

Jenna shot her a look. "Regular jeans will have to do."

"I don't have any of those either."

Jenna looked at her sister. "You're kidding, right?"

"No. I don't wear jeans. They're not work appropriate."

Jenna tipped her head to the side. "You have a life outside of work."

Not really, but Tessa kept that comment to herself.

Jenna pulled a stack of jeans off a shelf and plopped them on the bed. "The skinnies are on top. Lucky for you, we're the same size."

"You're an inch taller." Why would one person own so many pairs of jeans? Weren't they all essentially the same? Blue and denim.

"Half an inch and that won't make a difference." Jenna waved her hands at Tessa like she was trying to shoo flies away. "Let's go, strip, get into the jeans. And lose that old lady blouse."

"It's not an old lady blouse. This is Ann Taylor, I'll have you know."

47

"Forgive me. Lose that middle-aged lady blouse."

Tessa huffed out a breath but took off her navy chinos and silk shirt and climbed into the pair of jeans Jenna indicated. They were *snug*. "Are these jeans or leggings?"

Jenna rolled her eyes. "Jeans."

"Are they supposed to be this tight? I think I'm losing circulation in my thighs."

"Yes, and no, you're not." Jenna pulled out a couple of tops on hangers before turning around. "Holy Loki, you actually have a body. And boobs!"

Tessa wrapped her arms around her bare stomach. "Of course I have a body. And a chest."

"Yeah, but who knew the whole package was this hot? Although, Tessa, seriously? That bra is a real snooze. White cotton? Do you have to special order those from Amish-R-Us?" Jenna curled her lip. "We might be sisters but we are not related by fashion."

"It's practical. And I can bleach it." And they matched her underwear, but Tessa was sure her sister wouldn't think that was a plus.

Jenna lifted her brows. "What are you doing in your bras that they need to be bleached?" She held up a hand. "On second thought, don't answer that." She thrust out the handful of shirts. "Try these on."

Tessa took the hangers but stared at the shirts. "All together?"

"Oh my word, no. One at a time." Jenna shook her head and went back to digging in her closet. "You still wear a size eight shoe like me, right?"

"Yes." Tessa pulled the first top on. It was plum-colored and sort of twisted at the neck but then the fabric fell away in a draped cowl. It was pretty. Lower cut than the tops she normally wore, but not uncomfortably so. Not a color she would have typically picked either, but this was about looking different, so mission accomplished.

Jenna turned around with a pair of tall, brown leather boots and a long, chunky brown cardigan. "That top is perfect. Forget the rest of them. Here, boots and a sweater. Do *not* button it."

"What if I get cold? It's January, you know."

"Yes, but it's a warm January. And we're valkyries. Suck it up, you'll be fine. Besides, beauty isn't always easy or convenient."

"Says the woman who normally wears a uniform. That's about as easy and convenient as it gets."

"Yes, but when I go out, I let my light shine. Unlike you, who has yet to actually turn your light on. At least I know now there's a bulb in there. Okay, hair and makeup time."

"Jenna, settle down. My hair is fine and I don't need makeup."

"Your hair belongs in the same store as that old lady blouse. The bun is not happening. We have gorgeous dirty-blonde hair with all kinds of natural highlights that human women pay big bucks for and you're hiding them in a knot. The hair is coming down. And look, no one *needs* makeup, but trust me, a little mascara and lip gloss are not going to kill you and they'll work wonders to show off your blue eyes. Which are the same phenomenal blue as mine. You'll see when I'm done. You, only better."

Ten minutes later and Tessa's hair was down and brushed and mascara and lip gloss had been applied. Tessa had even allowed Jenna to tweeze her eyebrows a little. Jenna was impossible to say no to. But as Tessa looked in the mirror, she knew that she looked nice.

"Well?" Jenna asked. "What do you think?"

"I look less whore-y than I thought I would."

Jenna put her hands on her hips. "That's a fine compliment for all my hard work. You look beautiful. Well, you always were, but now it's apparent. Just think what I could do with a few more minutes."

"This is plenty, thanks."

"Yeah, I get it. All right, go. Have fun and figure out all this fake fiancée stuff."

Tessa doubted fun would be part of the evening. She hesitated. "You'll watch Duncan?"

They both glanced at the bed. The kitten was passed out on his back, his fat stripey belly exposed. Jenna laughed softly. "I don't think he needs much watching right now."

"No, I guess not. But half of the pizza is mine when it gets here. I'm going to want it when I get home."

Jenna crossed her arms. "I'll do my best but Salvatore's is one of my downfalls. If there's less than half left, I can't be held responsible. Now quit stalling and go."

Tessa sighed. "Fine."

"Seriously, have fun. Or at least try to."

"Sure." Tessa left her sister and walked out to the living room.

Sebastian was facing the fireplace, one hand on the mantel, as he finished up a phone call. "Yes, that'll be fine. Thank you."

He hung up and turned around. His eyes widened. Then narrowed again. "Tessa?"

"Do I look that different?"

"I...yes, a bit, with your hair down." He smiled and she had a moment of surprise herself.

He was shockingly handsome when he wasn't frowning. She took an extra breath to get rid of the weird fluttery feeling in her stomach. Something she'd had for lunch must not have agreed with her. "Thanks. I guess."

He nodded. "You look lovely."

"My sister did it." The fluttery thing wasn't going away and she realized it had nothing to do with the burger she'd had at Mummy's. Great. It was one thing pretending to be his fiancée, but to actually find him attractive? That was not going to help. "So, coffee?"

"Yes. But first we have a stop to make. I hope you don't mind."

"No, that's fine."

The stop turned out to be downtown Nocturne Falls. Tessa hadn't spent much time in town yet as she'd only just arrived the day before. Lunch at the diner had been her only foray and it had been brief since Jenna had to get back to the station after her break. The town was pretty at night with the shops all lit up and twinkle lights in the trees. From the Halloween colors to the cobwebs on the lamp posts and the occasionally crooked-on-purpose building, it was like visiting a theme park.

She watched out the window as he parked in a spot reserved for town employees. "Does it always look like this or is this just left over from an event?"

"No, it's always like this. Keeps the atmosphere festive, I suppose. It's more my brother Julian's department. He's in charge of theming and characters. And occasionally new businesses."

She looked at him. "What do you do? I should know that."

He nodded as he turned the engine off. "I'm the CFO of Nocturne Falls."

She'd already assumed he had money. Knowing

he was also in charge of the town's money made sense. He seemed like the type to run a tight ship and an even tighter purse. "You must be good with numbers."

His eyebrows lifted in response. "Better with them than with people."

"Why's that?"

He went silent a moment. "I'm a bit of a loner, I guess. People can be so..."

"Exhausting?"

His mouth bent in a half-smile. "Amongst other things, yes." The remnants of the smile faded and his gaze shifted to the street. "Let's go see about this ring, shall we?"

"Is that what the stop is about?"

He nodded. "The jeweler is very accommodating."

Tessa imagined most business owners would feel that way toward the CFO of the town, although Sebastian didn't seem like the type to throw his weight around. Especially if what Jenna had said about him never leaving his house was true.

They got out of the car (she realized too late that he was coming around to open her door) and she walked with him to a pretty little shop called Illusions. This time, he reached the door ahead of her and opened it. She went in. There were a few people in the store and two women behind the counters waiting on them.

One of them, a stunningly beautiful fae woman,

greeted Sebastian, then Tessa, with a smile. "Hello there."

Sebastian answered with a nod. "Evening, Willa."

She excused herself from the customers she was waiting on. "I'm all set up for you in the back. Come around the counter and into my office."

She went ahead of Sebastian and Tessa, slipping into the back room but standing at the door until they were in. A large orange cat lounged on the desk.

"Hi there, kitty cat." Tessa smiled and gave him a little scratch. Without opening his eyes, he stretched and put his paw on her arm.

"Now you've done it," Willa said as she shut the office door. "You're his new best friend."

"He's very sweet. What's his name?"

"Jasper. Feel free to put him on the floor, too. We're going to need that desk."

Tessa couldn't bring herself to move the sleepy beast. "But he's so comfortable."

Sebastian cleared his throat. He wasn't interested in cat talk apparently. "Thank you for seeing us on such short notice. And for understanding."

Willa gave a little nod. "I know all about how your past can sneak up and bite you." She opened a safe and pulled out a large, covered velvet tray, then carried it over and gave Jasper a little shove off the desk. "Sorry, baby, but I need the space."

He jumped down and skulked off, finding a new place to lounge on top of a low filing cabinet.

Willa put the tray down and lifted the top.

Tessa sucked in a breath. There had to be twenty diamond rings on display, all of them enormous and sparkling like the sun and completely over the top. She hated to think of such assuredly expensive baubles gaudy, but to her that's what they were. Not that she would say that to either Willa or Sebastian. "Wow."

Willa laughed softly. "I feel that way too. All the time. Which one do you like?"

She looked at Willa, then Sebastian, then back at Willa. Clearly they both expected her to swoon over them. "They're all lovely."

Sebastian came closer and motioned to the tray. "Pick one."

She looked at the rings again and finally shook her head, unable to make a decision. "None of these are really me."

He sighed. "This isn't about which one best suits your personal taste, it's about fooling Evangeline."

She frowned at him. "I understand that, but it seems to me that picking a ring that's unlike something I'd actually wear goes against the whole idea here. You want it to be convincing, don't you?"

His expression took an exasperated turn.

"Choose a ring. You only have to wear it tonight and tomorrow night."

Willa put her hand on Tessa's arm. "Just a moment. I have something else."

She took the tray back to the safe and returned with one half the size. She put it on the desk and opened it. The rings inside held diamonds just as large but all in much simpler settings, some without any accompanying side stones. "Better?"

"Yes," Tessa answered.

Sebastian shook his head. "These are too plain."

"These are more me," Tessa shot back. If that meant she was plain, so be it. "But they're all still so large."

"I'm not compromising on that. I'd never buy the woman I love anything less than…that one." He pointed to a ring that held the second-largest center stone with two long tapered diamonds on the sides.

Willa smiled. "A classic round solitaire with two tapered baguettes set in platinum. An enduring style for sure." She looked at Tessa. "A good choice, don't you think?"

The center stone was the size of a fat, spring pea and Tessa was already having palpitations at the thought of how much such a ring cost and what would happen if she somehow lost it, but Sebastian was right. To a point. It was a prop, not a symbol of his *anything*. Unless his desire to fool his ex-wife counted. "It's beautiful." And it was.

Just so unlike anything she'd ever thought would end up on her finger.

Willa pulled the ring free of the insert that held it in place and offered it to Sebastian. "Why don't you see if it fits your bride-to-be?"

He made a gruff little noise of complaint but took the ring anyway.

Tessa offered her hand. And realized he was about to touch her. She went very still, unable to focus on anything but the ring in his fingers and the subtle trembling of her own. No man had ever put a ring on her before and she suspected no man might ever again.

To have the whole thing be a sham made her unexpectedly sad.

He wrapped his fingers loosely around her wrist while he guided the ring on.

His fingers were long and perfect and slightly callused, which surprised her. She'd thought a man who worked with numbers would have smooth skin. She couldn't help but think that he had the kind of hands that looked like they'd be nice to hold. Large enough to envelope hers. And his touch was surprisingly gentle and warmer than she'd expected. Of course, she'd never touched—or been touched by—a vampire before.

She stared at the ring shining like a spotlight on her finger. It sparkled and glittered, demanding attention.

"It fits perfectly," Willa said.

Tessa just nodded, a little blinded by the diamond's brilliance.

Sebastian grunted, which apparently was a big part of his vocal repertoire. "I'll have it back day after tomorrow."

"No rush." Willa's voice held a smile. "I know where you live."

"Indeed. Shall we?"

It took Tessa a moment to realize he was speaking to her. "Oh, yes. Of course. Thank you so much, Willa. Nice to meet you."

The fae smiled back. "You too. Good luck with everything."

Tessa left with Sebastian. It was impossible to ignore the ring. First of all, it was heavier than she'd imagined an engagement ring would be. Secondly, she felt like everyone was staring at it. Or maybe it was just her. She couldn't help but glance down at it. It glittered like a disco ball and was about as out of place on her hand.

"Don't fall in love with it. Keeping it isn't part of the deal."

She jerked her head up. "I know that. Trust me, I have no designs on you or your money. All I want is the job."

He snorted softly like he didn't totally buy that.

The noise and the sense of disbelief radiating off him raised her valkyrie ire, a rare occurrence. Mostly because she did everything to avoid it. Alarms started going off inside her. She clenched her right hand until the scar on her knuckles stood out white. She needed to fix this and now.

She stopped cold, forcing him to do the same, then backtrack to her. "What's the matter?"

She kept her voice low but her tone clear. "This was your idea. If you're going to disparage my character or imply that I am somehow *out to get something* beyond the job that was promised to me, then perhaps you should find yourself another fool."

Her ire still rising, she pulled the ring off, shoved it into his hand and spun to walk away from him. Cooling off and calming down was paramount.

She'd seen his mouth come open, but had no idea if he was following after her or not. It was bad enough that he thought she wasn't up to the task of convincing his ex that she was worthy of his affections, but for him to even slightly imply that she was somehow in this for financial gain was ludicrous.

Just like this insane scheme.

She wanted the job desperately. Actually, she

needed it desperately. But if it meant spending time with a man who was going to rile her up and test her temper, she was done.

Nothing was worth risking another life over.

Sebastian stared after Tessa, mouth open, head full of disbelief, the ring still warm in his hand. The little mouse had roared and it was oddly stimulating. He found himself again and took off after her, nearly needing to jog to catch her. "Tessa. *Tessa.*"

She refused to slow. "I don't want to do this anymore. Find someone else."

"I apologize."

She stopped, but the unhappy curve of her pretty mouth said she wasn't going to be still long. Pedestrians streamed past them. She wrapped her left hand over her right, her thumb rubbing at her knuckles. At a scar there. "You're not a nice man. And I say that knowing full well this could cost me the job of dean, but this is a mutually beneficial situation. You're getting as much out of this as I am. Maybe more. So you making me feel like I'm trying to...to...*grift* you is—"

"You're absolutely right. I'm sorry. My people skills are not what they should be. Which is no excuse for my behavior." He held out the ring. "Please. Give me another chance. I need you." That was something he hadn't said—or needed to say— to anyone in many, many years. To be saying those words to this particular woman was a rather surreal experience.

The passersby slowed and from the smiles and glances at the ring, it was obvious they thought they were witnessing a proposal.

He took her elbow and led her out of the path of traffic and prying eyes. "What do you say? Another chance? I have been told I am a difficult man. Most recently by Evangeline. Perhaps I am, but I have no desire to change, especially not for her. The most I can do is attempt to temper my natural tendencies. Which I will. But you must accept that dealing with who I am is part of this arrangement."

She made a face. "Well, when you put it that way, how can a girl resist?" Resignation filled her gaze. "I said I would help and I'm a woman of my word."

"Thank you. I appreciate that."

She stuck her hand out, palm up. "The ring?"

He gave it to her, letting her put it on herself this time since that seemed to be her desire. It was fine with him. He knew very well the softness of her skin. He didn't need the temptation of it again.

This was a business arrangement, nothing more. "Coffee, then?"

"I suppose."

"You don't seem very enthused by the idea. We do still need to get to know each other."

She let out a soft breath. "I think I'm getting to know you just fine." She narrowed her eyes slightly. "Coffee is good, but I might need something stronger."

He raised his brows. "Alcohol?" He hadn't pictured her as the drinking type.

"Chocolate."

"I can manage that." He took off walking, a new destination in mind.

From behind him, he heard the sound of throat clearing. He glanced over his shoulder. She was still standing there, a look of expectation on her face. He returned to her side. "Did I forget something?"

"We're supposed to be engaged. Not only didn't you wait for me, but couples in love hold hands."

He blinked. "You want to hold my hand?"

She glared at him. "Not particularly, no. But you could at least offer me your arm."

"You're right. I'm not thinking like an engaged man." He stuck his elbow out.

She looped her arm through it. "If you want this to work, you'd better try."

"Again, you're right. Shall we?"

She nodded and he started toward the coffee shop again. A few locals glanced at him with curious expressions. He wasn't sure if it was because he was out in public or because he was with a woman. Either way, it would cause the town gossips to wag their tongues. Good. Let them talk.

Maybe Evangeline would get wind of it. He hoped. That was sort of the point.

He walked Tessa straight to Delaney's. She'd be closing up soon, but they still had a few minutes. He held the door for Tessa, then went in after her.

"It smells like heaven in here." Her eyes closed and she took a deep inhale. A look of sheer pleasure washed over her face, highlighting its symmetry.

He watched her intently. Not only had he been wrong about her being plain, but he was starting to realize she was rather pretty.

"Sebastian, is that you?" Delaney walked out from the back, carrying a stack of flattened boxes. "Is the world coming to an end? What are you doing in here?"

He straightened and approached his sister-in-law while Tessa was still marveling at one of Delaney's show cakes in the front window. "I trust Hugh filled you in on my recent circumstances?"

"He did." Her gaze shifted to Tessa. "That must be the selfless saint who's agreed to martyr herself for your cause."

He frowned. "I hardly think it's that dire a situation."

"She's got to spend time with you, doesn't she?"

He felt a growl building in his throat. "Now see here—"

Tessa walked up before he could say anything more and smiled at Delaney. "Is this your shop?"

Delaney tucked the boxes under the counter. "It sure is. I bet you could use one of everything."

Tessa laughed and Sebastian blinked at the sound. He hadn't heard it from her before and it was lovely. Light and sweet and musical. Not at all what he'd expected.

Delaney pulled one of the boxes off the stack and folded it together, then lined it with wax paper. "What do you like?"

Tessa suddenly grew more serious. "Oh, maybe just a cookie."

Sebastian had a feeling he knew what had dampened her mood. "Give my...*fiancée* whatever she'd like and put it on my account."

Delaney snorted. "Like I wasn't already going to."

Sebastian sighed and turned to Tessa. "Tessa, this is Delaney, my brother Hugh's wife."

Delaney stuck her hand out. "Which makes me your pretend sister-in-law-to-be. How are you holding up?"

Tessa shook her hand and suddenly seemed to relax. "I'm...all right."

"Sebastian's bark is much worse than his bite." Delaney made a face. "Or maybe that doesn't really apply to vampires, but you know what I mean. I hear you're Deputy Jenna's sister."

Tessa nodded.

"That is so cool. You're a valkyrie too, right?"

"Yes."

The more Delaney engaged Tessa, the more the woman seemed to come alive. That gave Sebastian an idea. "Delaney, you and Hugh must come to dinner tomorrow night. The two of you can help steer the conversation in case Evangeline gets too inquisitive."

Delaney's eyes rounded. "Done. And that will save me the trouble of getting Hugh to wrangle us an invite. I can't wait to meet this woman you've been tormenting yourself over."

He scowled. "I have not been tormenting myself over her."

"Sure, sure." She waved him off and looked at Tessa again. "Okay, seriously, what's your poison? What's your favorite flavor combo?"

Tessa swept her gaze across the cases again. "I love chocolate and orange together."

"I have just the thing." Delaney moved a few steps down the display. "Dark chocolate blood orange truffles dusted with fennel pollen." She reached in with a sheet of waxed paper and plucked one out, then handed it to Tessa.

She took it and nibbled a little bite. Her eyes closed and a moan of pleasure rumbled out of her. And straight through Sebastian. The sound was even better than her laugh. He straightened as she swallowed and opened her eyes. "Wow. You made that?"

"I sure did." Delaney preened. "How about you let me make up a box of goodies for you?"

Tessa's mouth was full of chocolate, so she just nodded and murmured, "Mm-hmm."

She walked back to Sebastian, licking her lips.

It was highly distracting for reasons he didn't care to think about. "Enjoying yourself?"

"Yes." She licked the tip of one finger. "Aren't you getting anything?"

"I don't eat sweets."

"You're a vampire, not a robot. Who doesn't eat sweets?"

"I don't." They were an indulgence and indulgences led to weaknesses. "You can add that to the list of things you've learned about me."

She nodded, but there was a little sadness in her eyes. "You're kind of a mess, aren't you? I'm sure most people see your proper uprightness as part of who you are, but to me it seems like a defense mechanism. Valkyries once judged the souls of men on the battlefield, you know. Who deserved to live, who deserved to die and who deserved Valhalla. We're still exceptional judges of character.

It's why my sister is such an outstanding deputy. She can tell when someone's really innocent. Or truly guilty."

His skin itched at her assessment. "Your job is to pretend to be my betrothed. That is all. I do not need your analysis or sympathy or judgment. Understood?"

She stared at him for a long second. "More than you know."

For the first time since this whole charade had started, Tessa saw Sebastian in a very different light. He was broken by betrayal. It practically radiated out of him. It also explained why he was gruff and defensive and not particularly open to new things. On some level, she understood that reaction.

This Evangeline had done a number on him. Tessa couldn't help but feel for the man. To her, it was clear he was damaged and yet, she doubted that anyone outside of his family really grasped that.

Then she reminded herself that it wasn't her job to fix him. Just pretend to be his fiancée. If he wanted his ex-wife back, then maybe she could help him with that. If that's what he wanted.

Delaney returned with a small paper shopping

bag and held it out. "Let me know what you think of them." She winked. "I can always send more if your new boyfriend wears you down."

Tessa made herself smile. "I'm sure we'll be fine. Thank you so much. I guess I'll see you at dinner."

"I wouldn't miss it."

Sebastian nodded. "Thank you, Delaney. You'll let Hugh know about tomorrow night, then?"

"Yes, but you should still call him."

"I suppose I should," Sebastian said. "Very well. We're off for coffee."

"The Hallowed Bean?" Delaney asked.

"Yes."

"Good choice." She looked at Tessa. "If you're still in the mood for something sweet, try the drinking chocolate. It's phenomenal."

"Thanks, I will." Tessa lifted the bag. "And thanks again for the treats."

She and Sebastian went across the street to the coffee shop. A good number of customers filled the spot, leading her to believe the cute little shop had to be a local favorite. She stood with him at the counter and ordered the drinking chocolate Delaney had suggested, along with a slice of vanilla pound cake.

Sebastian got black coffee. "Why don't you find us a seat? I'll bring everything over."

"Okay." She chose a table near the window. If they were going to be seen, that was a prime location. She put the bag of sweets from Delaney on the seat next to her.

Sebastian joined her a few minutes later, tray in hand. He put her drink and her cake in front of her, then sat. He took his coffee off the tray, then handed the tray to a passing worker. He sipped the dark brew, then nodded at her selections. "I suppose you have a rather high metabolism, given your true nature. Or you do something else to stay fit."

That almost sounded like a compliment on her figure. She cut a bit of cake with her fork. "High metabolism like most of...us." She wasn't sure if using the word *supernatural* in public was okay. "And I suppose your first choice of sustenance isn't cake."

He gave a little laugh. "No, not quite. But that's not to say I don't partake on occasion. Although those occasions are rare. I prefer moderation in all things."

"That doesn't surprise me."

"Why? Because I seem like someone who doesn't know how to enjoy himself?"

She sipped her chocolate, watching him. "You said that, not me. I was going to say because you seem like a person who favors control above all else. I respect that."

His brows lifted slightly. "You do?"

She nodded. "Did you think I was going to give you grief about it?"

A moment passed before he answered. "Yes. My brothers both do. Delaney does. Even my grandmother now and then." He sighed and looked out the window. "I sometimes feel as though I spend more time defending the way I've chosen to live my life than actually living it."

She snorted softly. "I understand that more than you know."

"And how is that?"

She cut another bite of cake, but didn't eat it. "I'm a valkyrie who's become a librarian. Most of my kind take very different career paths."

"Like your sister."

"Exactly like Jenna." Tessa ate the cake. It was good. Not as good as the drinking chocolate, which was extraordinary, but nice enough. She swallowed. "What is it about your life that your family doesn't agree with?"

He shrugged and twisted his ceramic mug until the handle was at a right angle to his spoon. "I tend to avoid gatherings and social events as often as I can. I prefer to stay at home. With my books and my work and the pursuits that I enjoy. I live a simple life and that's the way I like it. But I have often been told that I am boring."

"I've heard that a few times myself."

He lifted his mug. "Here's to boring, then. Perhaps Evangeline will believe we are a couple after all."

71

She clinked her cup of chocolate to his. "Maybe she will."

He sipped his coffee. "Let's hope."

"What's your goal for this dinner with her? I know you want her to see that another woman finds you desirable, but what else? You must want something more than that."

He stared into his mug, going silent.

She stabbed another little square of cake she'd cut with her fork. "You don't have to tell me, but it would be helpful if I had some idea of what the end game is."

"I want..." He sighed. "You will think me ridiculous."

"You don't know that. And why do you care what I think anyway?"

He lifted his head. "Because I'm going to be your boss."

"That hasn't happened yet. And if you don't tell me, I won't know how to help you."

His mouth bent with frustration. "I guess I want her back. As much as I wish that weren't true, it would be the simplest solution to everything."

Tessa narrowed her eyes. "You really want your ex back? Just being honest here, but I don't understand how that would be the simplest solution to anything unless you're trying to drive yourself crazy."

He smiled briefly. "It's complicated."

"She is your ex, isn't she?"

"Not technically, no. There was never any formal divorce. She just...left."

"How many years ago?"

He frowned. "Nearly three hundred."

She failed to hide her surprise. Talk about carrying a torch. "There has to be a statute of limitations on that sort of thing."

"I'm sure there is. But the marriage isn't really the issue. I am Evangeline's sire, something the vampire council takes very seriously. When you cause another to become immortal, things change. A sire must protect those they turn to the best of their ability. And so, I am responsible for her. And I will be until the day one of us ceases to exist. Unless she signs dissolution papers. Which I doubt she will ever do."

"Do you still feel married?"

"I feel..." He paused. "More like a parent with a prodigal child. Hmm. That's the first time I've put that thought into words, but it's true. It also sums up why it would be easier to have her back. So I can protect her. That is, more easily than I do now."

She understood the desire to protect and assist those who needed it. That was another trait of being valkyrie. Although for a valkyrie, it was more about those who were worthy of protection, not a sense of responsibility. That was probably a big part of why she'd agreed to help him. It was in her makeup. Finding the right book for a person was the same thing, just on a much smaller scale. "And if she doesn't want you back? Not saying that's going to be the case, just curious what you'll do then."

He leaned forward, resting his forearms on the table. "I don't know. I've spent my years waiting for her to return. I always knew she would. I never wanted to think about if she didn't. But she has, and she claims to want us to be together again. All I need from dinner is for her to realize she's going to have to make me want that too."

Tessa nodded. "You want her to work for it. To make up for all the time you've spent waiting." She smiled. "You want to make her pay a little too, don't you?"

A glimmer of something lit his eyes. "Does that make me an awful person?"

"I think it makes you shockingly normal."

He smiled and laughed a little, giving her a glimpse of his fangs. "I can't say I've been called that very often in my life. Thank you for doing this. I confess I judged you harshly at first but I see now that you are an intelligent woman and very capable of carrying out this charade. You'll make an excellent addition to Harmswood."

"Thank you. I certainly hope I get the job."

"Unless this thing goes horribly wrong, I rather think you've earned the job just by being a part of this. You're certainly qualified. And I think we'll work very well together."

"Well, that's good to know. And appreciated. I hope this all works out for you the way you'd like." She drained the last of her chocolate. The sugar rush was almost instantaneous, but so were the images of her and Sebastian working well together. Images she was sure he hadn't intended to create. Images that had nothing to do with work.

She cleared her throat, desperate for a new topic. "With that in mind, we'd better dig a little deeper."

Sebastian nodded, slightly distracted by the flush of color in Tessa's cheeks. "We should dig deeper, I agree, but are you feeling all right?"

"Yes, why?"

"You look flushed."

She laughed nervously. "Probably just the sugar rush. It tends to do that to me."

"I see. Well, looks good on you." A new thought hit him. "Say, would you like to get a drink?"

"I just had one."

"I mean an actual drink. An adult beverage." The desire for a glass of whiskey had hit him hard and with a kind of rare pull he almost never gave into. Perhaps he was changing as a person after all, because this new impulsive side of him was certainly not something he'd experienced before.

"Oh. All right, I suppose I could have one."

"Not much of a drinker?"

She bobbed her head back and forth. "I prefer to remain in control of my faculties."

Which confirmed his earlier thought about her. "I can understand that, but one won't hurt, will it?"

She made a face that was a cross between a smile and a grimace. "I haven't had dinner yet."

"And yet, you just had cake." He smirked. "Isn't having dessert before your meal breaking some sort of rule?"

"Yes, but, well, I was hungry and there wasn't much else to choose from but sweets."

He put a hand to his chest. "Barely engaged an hour and already I've failed you. How about some dinner, then? To go with our drinks."

"Okay. That would be great. You have a place in mind?"

"I do."

And ten minutes later, they were walking into the Poisoned Apple, the local pub. Or the nearest thing to one. It wasn't a place he frequented often, but neither was any other place in town. He'd heard Delaney mention it and her taste was decent enough.

He slipped the hostess some cash to get them a good table quickly. Unlike his brothers, he wasn't as well known and couldn't trade on his name as easily to curry favor, but he was fine with that. Privacy was more important to him.

They were seated at a booth in the back corner.

It was quiet, unlike the bar, and secluded enough to feel like a safe space to carry on a personal conversation. He looked at Tessa as the server greeted them. "What would you like to drink? A nice red?"

Her mouth curved up on one side. "Beer." She glanced up at the server. "Whatever lager you have on tap will do."

The waitress nodded. "And for you, sir?"

"The best whiskey you have. Neat."

"I'll be right back with your drinks."

As the girl left, he leaned toward Tessa. "I hadn't expected you to drink beer."

"What did you think I'd order?"

"White wine? Or maybe a wine spritzer. But definitely not beer."

She laughed. "It's a valkyrie thing. We have fairly simple, rustic tastes."

"Simple and rustic now seem the least two likely adjectives I'd use to describe you."

She smiled and went a little shy at the compliment, which was oddly endearing. Then he realized she probably didn't get many compliments. The thought that she was being underappreciated by those around her bothered him.

She smoothed the edge of her placemat. "We should work on our stories."

"Our stories?"

She nodded. "How we met, how you proposed, those stories. They seem like things your ex will ask about."

"Ah, yes, very good. I'm sure she will. We ought to figure out what we want to eat first. I'm having the steak, I know that much."

"The sirloin?"

He scoffed. "Not hardly. The aged porterhouse. It's the only choice if you like steak, which most vampires do. It's one of their specialties." At least that's what he'd heard from Hugh.

Her gaze slid down the menu until she found it. No doubt she was looking at the price. It was the most expensive choice. "That's a lot of meat."

"You can take the leftovers home to your sister. Proof that I fed you, in case she asks."

Tessa smiled. "Okay. Oh, that reminds me. I should text her that I'm eating out." She closed her menu, pulled out her phone and sent the message. After she tucked her phone away, she gazed at him, her line of sight going right through him. "Where on earth would we have met? You said you don't like to leave the house."

"Easy. We'll say we met at one of my grandmother's social functions. She hosts them all the time. Balls for all sorts of things. Charity events. Whatever the town needs. I think it's one of her best ways of gleaning gossip. We'll say you were there as a guest of your sister."

Tessa nodded. "That works, but we should be specific. Which event?"

"How about the Black and Orange Ball? While it's not actually a charity event, it is one of the most popular things that happens around here. It's the Halloween party my grandmother's been throwing for years. It's a huge deal. People come from all over to attend. It's a perfectly legitimate way for us to have met as I am forced into attending every year."

"Okay. Where is it held?"

"My grandmother's estate."

"Any chance I could see that tomorrow? Just to have a sense of what it looks like?"

He hesitated. "That would mean bringing my grandmother into this and I'd prefer not to do that. I have pictures from past events I can show you though. As for Elenora, well, she has an intense dislike for Evangeline—"

"I'd be surprised if you said otherwise. Most grandmothers are pretty protective."

"Mine is no exception." He grimaced, thinking about what Elenora would do if given the opportunity to confront Evangeline in person. "What else do we need to work out?"

Tessa bit her lip. "Well, we've only been seeing each other since the end of October and we're already engaged? You don't seem like you'd act that quickly."

"I wouldn't." Although he wasn't entirely sure. His and Evangeline's marriage had been arranged, so no proposal necessary. "We'll say we met at the ball the year before. Good enough?"

"Yes. Now, how and where did you propose?"

He smiled. "At this year's ball, since that's where we met."

"I like that. It's romantic."

"Evangeline won't buy me being romantic."

Tessa made a face. "Then she doesn't know you very well. I think anyone can be romantic under the right set of circumstances."

He smiled. He very much liked the way she thought.

The server returned with their drinks and took their order. When she'd left, Sebastian raised his glass. "To success."

Tessa lifted her beer. "To success."

They clinked glasses and drank.

He swallowed and tipped his head to one side. "What if she Googles you?"

Tessa shrugged. "What if she does?"

"Is she going to find anything about you online that says you live elsewhere? I apologize, I don't recall where you moved from."

"Ohio, and no, I doubt she'll find anything. I used to run the Northeast Ohio Library's Facebook page, but my name wasn't on it, just the head librarian's."

"You're not listed on the library's main website, then?"

"Hah. Like Mrs. Unger would approve that." Tessa rolled her eyes. "Nope, not listed on the website either."

"Very good. I take it Mrs. Unger is your former boss?"

"Yes." She wrinkled her nose.

"And not someone you're fond of."

"No." Tessa sipped her beer. "I think she felt challenged by me. She'd been the head librarian for years and then I get hired right out of school with all these new ideas and..." Tessa's brows lifted. "You know how it is."

"Hmm. I guess I do, but I believe I might be Mrs. Unger in that scenario."

Tessa grinned. "Why? Do you hate change?"

He nodded, reluctantly. "It's not my favorite thing, no."

"Why's that?"

He leaned back, slowly turning his glass of whiskey. "If things are working the way they are, why change them?"

"What if there's a better way to do something?"

"I don't know if I believe that's enough reason. And better by whose definition?"

"So if it's not broke, don't fix it."

"Exactly."

She stared at him over the rim of her glass. "Is

that why you've never gotten officially divorced from Evangeline? That seems like a broken situation that would have been fixed by changing it, don't you think? Plus, you're not a bad-looking guy. You could have found someone else to be with."

He took a small amount of pleasure in her compliment, but didn't dwell on it. Vanity was a weakness. "*No*." The word came out sharper than he'd intended, but bloody hell, she was asking questions she had no right to.

Her brows went higher. "Forget I asked."

He sighed. And lowered his voice. "I never pursued any sort of official separation from her because I couldn't." For several reasons, not the least of which was the promise he'd made. He'd always hoped she'd come back. It would have made his life easier, that was for certain.

"Why couldn't you?"

"For a sire to divorce the spouse they've turned, it requires either the signature of the spouse, something Evangeline wouldn't have given me, or proof of infidelity."

"That sounds like something you could have managed."

He stared at the table. "Yes, I can. I choose not to."

"Because?"

The tablecloth blurred in front of his eyes.

"Because I am an old-fashioned fool. I don't want to ruin her. Or be the one to end things so distinctly."

She peered at him. "So you ended up paying the price for her sins. I can't imagine in all those years of being alone you never once thought about being with someone else."

He kept his gaze on the table. "What I thought about and what I wanted were two different things. Evangeline was always foremost on my mind." Then he picked his head up. "Some might think my loyalty a respectable quality. Especially in this day and age."

"I'm not judging you. Just curious. You must have had some kind of amazing marriage to hold out like that. To still be holding out."

Except that wasn't really how he was feeling these days. He frowned. "Our marriage was arranged. Most marriages back then were, especially for those of wealth and position."

"Then I get the loyalty, which is definitely admirable, but letting her go at this point would be completely understandable. No one expects you to keep the vows you made three hundred years ago."

"Almost four, actually."

"Maybe you could talk to this council. Explain things. They might make an exception."

He thought about it. No one had ever really questioned him about this before. His brothers had tried, but he'd always shut them down as soon as they started. Eventually they knew the topic of Evangeline was off-limits and stopped bringing her up. "And yes, maybe they would make an exception, but that's not who I am. I am a man of my word. And I value the bond we had."

Tessa swallowed a mouthful of beer. "Does she? I'm guessing not if she left you like that."

"She was young and impetus. Becoming..." He lowered his voice. "Becoming a vampire was an enormous change. She had wild oats to sow. And she did. Now she's done. Ready to be my wife again."

Or so she claimed. Was he reading too much into Evangeline's return? Perhaps. But he knew her better than anyone. She had been a good wife. Adept at the social aspects anyway. She had never been particularly warm or affectionate toward him, but he'd always chalked that up to them getting to know each other as husband and wife.

Tessa looked unconvinced. "I just don't get it. What on earth is holding you to her?"

The truth was on the tip of his tongue, but before he could speak, a body shoved into the seat beside him.

Julian threw his arm around Sebastian's shoulders. "Well, look at you, out on the town. I must remember to put a big red circle around today's date on the calendar when I get home. This has to be some kind of lunar eclipse or unknown holiday, or did some alien force invade your body and take control of your faculties?"

"Julian, this is not the time—"

"Nope, you definitely sound like Sebastian." Julian unhooked his arm and leaned forward, planting his elbows on the table and propping his chin on his hands as he grinned at Tessa. "And you must be my dear brother's *fiancée.* How wonderful."

"I..." She looked at Sebastian as if unsure how to answer.

Julian plowed on. "Nice ring. I hope you get to keep that in the deal. You're certainly going to earn it."

"No, she does not get to keep the ring." Sebastian glared at Julian. "I thought you were in Las Vegas. Again."

"I was. And now I'm home. Miss me?"

"Not particularly. We're trying to have dinner."

"Please tell me you got the porterhouse." Julian looked at Tessa. "It's the best thing you'll ever put in your mouth." He wiggled his brows and laughed. "Well..."

"*Julian.* Enough." Sebastian had never hit his brother, but the idea suddenly had merit. "Did you have a reason for interrupting us or was it merely for sport?"

With an enormous sigh and a huge eye roll,

Julian slouched in the seat. "I wanted to see where you were on the wedding chapel budget."

"Nowhere. It's ludicrous. The entire thing will have to be reworked."

Tessa perked up a little. "What's this about?"

Julian let out another sigh. "I've just opened a wedding chapel in town."

"Like the ones in Las Vegas?" Tessa asked.

"Exactly. That's where I got the idea. It's all kinds of fun, something Sebastian hates, but the tourists will go nuts for it. We already had several weddings a month going on in town so adding this chapel seemed like a no-brainer. There are themed rooms and packages and all kinds of great stuff." He glared at Sebastian. "I just need the working budget approved so I can do my grand opening."

Sebastian scowled. "You asked for half a million dollars. It's not happening."

Tessa almost choked on her beer. "Wow, is that what it takes to run a wedding chapel?"

"No," Sebastian said at the same time that Julian said, "Yes."

Sebastian shook his head. "Nothing's happening until this dinner with Evangeline is over with."

Julian sat up. "Dinner? What dinner? When? Where? Are we going black tie or business casual? Hmm, what does one wear to a meal with one's brother's estranged wife?"

Sebastian snorted. "*You* are not invited."

Tessa's mouth curved into a little half-smile. "Why not? He would be great at distracting Evangeline." She tipped her glass at him. "You're very good at keeping the conversation going."

Julian pointed at her as he spoke to Sebastian. "I like this one. She's a keeper."

Irritation simmered through Sebastian like escaping steam. He looked at Tessa. "You think he should come only because you don't know him like I do."

"Maybe. But it would be nice to have him there to help corroborate our story."

Julian grinned, showing off his fangs. "I can corroborate like nobody's business."

Sebastian hung on to his sanity with his fingertips. "Fine. You can come on one condition."

"Which is?" Julian asked.

"You leave us immediately so we can enjoy the rest of our dinner in peace and you behave yourself during the dinner with Evangeline."

Julian stood. "That's two conditions, but I agree because I don't nitpick the little things. Like some people. And please, what do you think I'm going to do? Try to sleep with her? Even I have standards."

He twisted on his heel and walked off, flirting with every woman he passed as he left.

Tessa pursed her lips like she was suppressing laughter. "Your brother is quite the character."

Sebastian watched him go. "I'm aware."

Thankfully, the server arrived with their steaks, saving Sebastian from further conversation about Julian.

He dug into his porterhouse, trying not to dwell on the fact that Tessa had taken to Julian so much that she'd wanted him at dinner.

Time ticked by as they ate. Sebastian couldn't get past what had just happened. He shoved a forkful of meat into his mouth and chewed. Was Julian that much more interesting than he was? Sebastian had long ago accepted that he wasn't to every woman's taste, but what did it mean that not even the woman pretending to be his fiancée preferred him?

Was Julian really such a prize?

Or was he just that unappealing?

Tessa ate her steak in small bites, very aware that Sebastian's mood had taken a dark turn. It stayed that way, too, even though their meals were more than half gone. At first she thought he'd just been upset by his brother's visit, then she realized Julian's sudden appearance was just the catalyst. She washed down her last bite with a swig of beer and stared at the vampire across from her. "You're upset."

He didn't look at her, just went on eating. "I'm fine."

"No, you're not. You forget that I can judge character and intent. And you're upset." She tried to get a deeper read on the vibes he was throwing off. "With me. You're upset with me."

"No, I'm not."

She narrowed her eyes, opening herself fully to the valkyrie senses she so rarely used. "Yes, you are. But you're mad at yourself too."

He frowned.

She put her fork down. "Want to tell me why? Because I'm absolutely clueless on this one." She wasn't entirely sure why she cared about a man this damaged and frustrated, especially when she'd done her best to avoid things that upset her all her life. They had one more day together. That was it. Unless she got the job.

He stabbed a piece of steak. "It's childish and unimportant."

"If that were true, you wouldn't be so bothered."

He went still for a long moment, then lifted his gaze to meet hers. "You prefer my brother over me and I am petty enough to care. I understand it, but I also don't wish to discuss it further."

In the name of Freya, the man was jealous. Never in her life had a man expressed that emotion toward her. "What makes you think that?"

"You want him at dinner. You smiled at him. You—look, I said I don't want to discuss it further. Please, let's just eat."

She laughed, unable to contain her amusement. "You're jealous."

"No, I'm not."

But the vibes coming off him were as green as a tree frog. "You *are* jealous. That's sort of sweet, especially considering we're just pretending to be a couple. Keep that up and Evangeline will definitely believe you."

His knuckles whitened as he clenched his fork. "I am not jealous."

"If you say so. I promise, I do not prefer your brother over you. I just thought he'd be a great distraction at dinner and would be able to help us if things get off course. Period. End of story. I'm sure he's a nice enough sort, but he seems like he'd need a very different kind of woman than who I am. He also strikes me as more concerned with things like how his hair looks or if his manscaping is on point than when the next Haruki Murakami novel is coming out."

Sebastian's eyes brightened. "You read Murakami?"

"Yes. Do you?"

"Of course."

His answer pleased her to no end. At least they could converse about books if nothing else.

The server returned. "How are we doing here? Everything all right? Can I get you anything?"

Sebastian shook his head. "I'm fine. What about you, Tessa?"

She smiled. "I'm good too."

The server left and Sebastian physically relaxed. "I apologize. I wasn't as upset at you as I was upset at myself. I should learn to accept certain things, but after this many centuries, I suppose I am who I am and there's no hope for change."

She smiled. "You hate change anyway."

"There is that."

"What would you change? If you could."

He sat back. "I imagine being less uptight would be a good thing. Being more relaxed about details, that sort of thing."

"But you handle the money for the town. I can't imagine being less relaxed about that would be a good thing."

He nodded, a small spark of happiness lighting his eyes. "No, it wouldn't."

"Anything else?"

"I could be less critical."

She shrugged. "So you have high standards."

"Evangeline finds my academic pursuits tedious."

"Do you?"

"No."

"Then why change for a woman who hasn't been a real part of your life in nearly three hundred years? And can I just say, some women find intellect very sexy."

The light in his eyes went from happy to wicked and became a genuine, silvery glow. A vampire thing, she imagined. He leaned forward. "Are you one of those women?"

She lifted one shoulder, aware that she was being coy for perhaps the first time in her life. It surprised her that it was something she was even capable of doing. "I *am* a librarian. We certainly don't dislike brains."

His gaze tapered but a smirk crooked his mouth. "Are you sure you're not a zombie?"

She snorted, a horribly unladylike sound, but the funniness of his comment was multiplied by the fact that he was actually making a joke. "Worried about your gray matter now?"

He laughed with her. "Maybe. Should I invest in some sort of metal helmet?"

"Or just go with tin foil. That could be a good look for you."

"I doubt that."

They grinned and stared at each other and in that moment, something passed between them. A sense of togetherness. Of camaraderie. And mutual respect.

He drank the last of his whiskey. "I must apologize to you again for thinking you incapable of becoming my better half. I clearly judged you based on appearance alone and that was foolish. This dinner won't be easy, but I believe everything will come out in the end as it should."

"What if Evangeline continues to take you for granted? Will you still take her back?"

His happiness faded. "As we are technically still married, I suppose I have no choice."

"But you do. You can always say no. Appeal to the council."

"It's not that simple. It never has been."

"I feel like there's more to this than you're willing to talk about."

"You're very perceptive." He let out a long sigh. "I suppose you should know. It will make things clearer, at least."

She waited patiently.

With a frown, he began. "Evangeline's father and mine were strong friends even before our marriage was arranged. I'm sure their friendship had something to do with that arrangement, but it was still considered a good match and we'd been promised to each other almost since birth."

Tessa just nodded and let him speak.

"The wedding was a few months off yet when her father was thrown from his horse. He was severely injured. There was no question that he would die, it was just a matter of when. He called for me and of course I went to see him."

"As I sat at his bedside, he confessed to me that he knew he'd spoiled Evangeline, that he'd pampered her too much and turned her into a willful, moody creature who cared only for her own pleasure. He apologized for the years ahead of me and the suffering she would bring me as a wife. He told me that if I wanted out of the arrangement, he wouldn't hold it against me. In fact, he would see to it that no censure would come to me because of the disillusion."

Sebastian straightened his knife. "I was young

and couldn't see past her beauty. I thought he was mad from the injury. I told him I would not break the arrangement. That I loved Evangeline."

"Did you?"

"Then? Yes. Fool that I was." Sebastian's face went a shade paler. "That's when he made me promise to look after her for the rest of my life. He feared that if left to her own devices, she would come to ruin."

"I vowed that I would." His eyes held a very different light now, one so distant that Tessa imagined she could see him as he must have looked before he'd been turned.

"Her father died the next day and at the reading of his will, I discovered he'd left me an inordinate sum of money." Sebastian swallowed. "He'd paid me to keep my promise."

"You don't know that."

"I do. I wish it were otherwise, but it is what it is. I have been paid to watch over her *and* I promised to do it. As I am a man of my word, I have no choice but to do exactly that. Especially since she was turned by my own hand, something I would take back if given the smallest chance. Becoming a vampire did precisely what her father feared would happen to her anyway. It ruined her. And so, I do what I can to look after her. I will until the day one of us dies."

Tessa could respect that. So few people held to

their promises these days. It was a slightly old-fashioned view of life, but one she appreciated. And he was a man from another time. How else could he respond to such a promise? "I understand."

"Do you? Because I don't think my brothers would."

"They don't know?"

"Greaves is the only person outside of you who knows. Mostly because I refuse to discuss Evangeline with my brothers or my grandmother."

"So they've asked."

"My brothers used to. Now they know it won't get them anywhere, so they've stopped. It's understood I don't wish to hear her name in my house, and they tend to abide by that. As far as my grandmother is concerned...I think she likes to pretend Evangeline is dead."

"I see." She folded her napkin and set it beside her plate. "Thank you for telling me what happened then. I feel honored that you'd share your past with me."

He laid his napkin on the table as well. "Considering what you're about to do for me, I thought you should understand how intertwined in my life she is. And why I would want her around me again."

"I get it. You feel responsible for her because of the promise. Even more so because you feel you turned her into the person she is today."

He nodded and sighed. "The truth is, I find it all very exhausting. Perhaps that's why I don't leave my house as often as most people."

"Could be."

"Speaking of, are you ready to go?"

"I am." She collected her purse. He clearly needed a change of scenery and subject.

"Shall we take a walk through town? Continue getting to know one another? Or have you had enough of me?"

"A walk sounds nice. And no, I haven't had enough of you. We still have a lot to learn about each other." Although she definitely felt like she knew him so much better than she'd imagined she would. And curiously, she liked him far more than she had when he'd shown up at Jenna's.

Amazing how one conversation could change so much.

"That we do."

They got up and he put his hand on the small of her back as they walked out. It was a sweet, intimate gesture that sent a shiver of unexpected pleasure through her.

She shifted the shopping bag of goodies to her other hand and reminded herself that this was all for show. She was not in a relationship with him, nor would she ever be. For one thing, he was a moody vampire. The vampire part wasn't so bad, but the moodiness she could do without. For another, he had enough on his plate with Evangeline. And if he'd lasted for centuries without succumbing to the charms of another woman, he certainly wasn't about to fall for a valkyrie with self-esteem issues, a dread of confrontation and a deadly temper.

She made herself smile and focus on the town as they walked toward Main Street. If she had supposedly been living here, she ought to know more about the place. "What should I know about the town?"

"We celebrate Halloween every day. It's what brings the tourists in, it's our industry. There's trick-or-treating for the children every Friday night. And every month has a larger event designed to bring in even more visitors."

"Oh? What is it this month?"

"It's already happened. New Scare's Eve. Although technically that could be considered a December event, but January is a slower month than most. Which is fine. Many of the shopkeepers take their vacations this month."

"So what will it be in February?"

"The Valentine's Day Bake Off. Also, the annual blood drive but that's more of a local event."

She cocked a brow. "And that blood drive benefits who?"

He smirked. "Nocturne Falls General Hospital. Mostly."

She shook her head. "I suppose that's a necessity."

"We only take what we need."

"And the Valentine's Day Bake Off? Who does that benefit?"

He shrugged. "Everyone who gets to taste the desserts, I suppose. All the funds raised from the entry fees go toward the hospital's cardiac ward. The contest is popular with the locals, but we get a lot of visitors in for it too. Especially women." He sighed. "Which makes it one of Julian's favorite events."

She laughed. "That seems about right. Do you and your brothers do the judging?"

"I don't. Julian has but he was banned for being too easily swayed by a pretty face or a sexy smile. And Hugh can't this year because Delaney will definitely compete."

She lifted the bag Delaney had given her. "If her entry is half as good as that truffle she gave me tonight, I'd say she's a shoo-in."

"She may well be."

"Do you at least go to it?"

He shook his head. "No."

"Might be fun to have a day out, though, don't you think? There's probably more to it than just a bake off, right?"

"Yes, there are pie eating contests, games, live music and what else, I'm not sure. Dancing maybe. But again, not my thing."

She imagined what it might be like to dance with him. She enjoyed dancing, although it wasn't something she got to do very often. The thought of being in his arms, of being pressed against his body, sent another shiver through her.

"Are you cold?"

"No, I'm fine. Just…fine." Then a new thought occurred to her. One brought on by the idea of being very, very close to him. And maybe encouraged by the beer she'd had. "If you're going to kiss me, I'd rather we get the first one over with now."

He stopped on the street. "What?"

They were just outside the entrance of a bar called DOA, which was translated on the window as Drinks On Arrival. "I was just thinking, if you're going to kiss me in front of Evangeline, I'd rather not be surprised by it or she'll know you've never done it before."

The look of shock remained on his face. "I suppose you're right, but…"

"I know. It's an uncomfortable thought. Which is why I'm suggesting we get it over with now so that if we're somehow pressed into it the night of the dinner, it won't seem so awkward."

He cleared his throat. "That's smart. And if we

can pull off a kiss that looks natural, it would go a long way toward convincing her."

"All right then."

He looked around. "Perhaps not on the street."

"People seeing us together will just strengthen the story that we're a couple."

"True." He cleared his throat again and smoothed the lapels of his jacket. "I haven't done this in some time."

Neither had she. "It hasn't changed, I promise."

"No, I guess it hasn't."

He looked at her with great intent, a soft, silvery glow gleaming in his eyes. He leaned in, closed his eyes and pressed his mouth to hers.

She closed her eyes and kissed him back.

A second later, her lips were vacant of his. The kiss was over.

It had been warm and technically a kiss, but not much else could be said for it.

He shifted uncomfortably and looked relieved that it was over. "That wasn't so bad."

"Actually..." She smiled at him, trying to ease the sting of her answer. "I know you haven't kissed anyone in a long time, but that wasn't so good."

His expression fell. "It wasn't? How not so good?"

She crossed her arms, tucking the shopping bag half under one of them. "You're supposed to be in love with me, right? We're engaged and all that. You have to…kiss me like you mean it or this whole thing has no chance of convincing anyone."

"All right then." The glow in his eyes sparked brighter. "Round two."

Sebastian had been holding back, thinking he could get away with the barest of effort. That was not, apparently, the case. But a war raged inside him, one side fighting to keep his emotions in check, the other, the side of him that was sick and tired of being alone for so long, battled to kiss this very willing woman in front of him until she forgot her own name.

He could do it, too. Or at least, he thought he could. But it would mean allowing her into his life, because there was no way he could kiss her for real and not feel something. He was a vampire, but still flesh and blood. Still capable of feeling, no matter how hard he'd tried to shut that part of himself down.

He'd been nearly three hundred years without the touch or affection or attention of a woman. Surely one honest kiss wouldn't undo the very delicate self-control he'd put into place, would it?

Tessa stared at him, her pretty blue eyes filled with doubt. "I'm ready when you are."

There was a challenge in her voice. It was enough to make his decision. He was going to kiss this woman like his life depended on it.

He threaded his fingers into her hair and brought his lips to hers.

The sweetness of her mouth combined with the warmth and softness of her lips into a glorious cascade of sensation. It showered over him like sparks, biting into his skin with a mix of pain and pleasure.

Oh yes, he remembered this. What it felt like to kiss a beautiful woman. Except this sensation was far beyond anything he'd experienced with Evangeline. Maybe it had been so long that he didn't remember it accurately. Or maybe he was just that out of practice.

Or maybe it was Tessa.

He teased his tongue along the seam of her lips. They parted and his tongue grazed hers tentatively, testing for her response.

It came a second later as she moaned softly, a sound so quiet it could have been a whisper, but it spilled from her throat as involuntarily as a breath. The sound washed over him like a balm, soothing the scars that latticed his soul. Scars left by

Evangeline. Deep down inside, a part of him broke open.

He almost wept with how much he'd missed this small intimacy. The contact. The communion of touch. To think otherwise was a lie. His throat constricted with need and his fangs ached with the craving to have even more of her. All of her.

In his head, he knew he needed to stop.

But that knowledge didn't match the desire that burned through his body.

A slave to the overwhelming need for more of her, he indulged the kiss a moment longer, lingering at her mouth like the succulent offering it was, until at her second, louder moan, he finally released her.

Her eyes stayed closed for three long seconds as she inhaled a breath that seemed to have no end. When her lids lifted, she blinked several times.

He realized his hands were still in her silky tresses. He eased them free, already wondering when he might be able to kiss her again.

She just stared at him.

"Better?" he asked. If she said no, he'd have no other recourse than to take her somewhere private for his third attempt. Because there would be a third. Sebastian Ellingham was no quitter.

She nodded and swallowed and blinked some more.

Her cheeks were flushed. He'd met her

challenge, that much was plain. He took a modicum of joy from that.

"That was..." She cleared her throat and gripped the bag of sweets a little tighter. "That was much more convincing. I think that will do. If an occasion for such a thing even arises." She laughed in a sort of nervous, giddy way that seemed very unlike her. "Probably won't, but who knows?"

"Right. If needed. And only if needed." Except, bloody hell, he was ready to do it all over again immediately.

She jerked like she'd suddenly remembered where she was. "I should probably get home."

"The car's not far from here." He got them moving toward it and imagined she was happy for the reprieve from being face to face with him. Perhaps he'd put too much into the kiss. Had he offended her? Taken the kiss too far? Damn his inexperience with women. With normal women, anyway.

Silence hung between them until he'd gotten her settled into the car and taken his own seat behind the wheel. Traffic was minimal. He drove up Main to make a U-turn at the light, buying himself a few more minutes to figure out if he owed her an apology.

She broke the silence before he'd come to a conclusion. "What time do you want me tomorrow?"

His mind couldn't quite process what she was

asking, going somewhere he doubted she'd meant. Then the teeth of the cogs caught the wheels in his brain and everything made sense. "Early is fine. I don't sleep much."

"Neither do I. Eight a.m. too soon?"

"No, perfect. Come for breakfast then. I'll tell Greaves."

"Your butler?"

"Sort of." She might not know what a rook was, but there would be plenty of time for explaining in the morning.

She nodded. "Eight it is."

She seemed happy enough. Maybe he'd misread her being upset by the kiss. He pulled into her sister's driveway and went around to open Tessa's door.

She climbed out and gave him a little nod, holding her purse in one hand and the shopping bag in the other. "Thanks for dinner. I'll see you tomorrow."

Before he could say anything, she leaned up, kissed him on the cheek, then darted toward the house.

She had her hand on the doorknob as he spoke. "Tomorrow, then. Sleep well."

She nodded, a jerky, rapid motion. "You too. Night."

Then she was through the door and gone.

He stared at the closed door. Women were

curious creatures. He was nearly four hundred years old and what he understood about them wouldn't cover a postage stamp. Not that he'd ever cared to improve upon that.

Not until now.

"How was it?" Jenna was lounging on the couch, eyes glued to the television where her favorite reality show, Real American Firefighters, was on, while eating ice cream out of the carton. She wore sweatpants with bleach stains and a NFPD T-shirt with a frayed hem. Jenna took her down time very seriously.

"It was fine." Tessa couldn't bring herself to say more than that because while she was slightly afraid of what adjectives might come out of her mouth, she was more afraid of her sister knowing the truth.

It had been the best evening she'd had in a long, long time. Finished off with a kiss so mind-numbingly amazing, she'd actually forgotten where she was for a few moments. For a man who hadn't been involved with a woman in over three hundred years, Sebastian kissed like it was his superpower. And if he was that good at kissing…

That could explain why Evangeline wanted him back.

"That's cool," Jenna answered, gaze still fixed to whatever shirtless contest was ongoing in firefighter land.

Duncan was playing with a foil ball on the living room floor. He looked up at her and cried.

"Oh, poor baby, did you miss me?" Tessa dropped her purse and the treat bag on the side table and scooped him up.

For the first time since Tessa had walked through the door, Jenna's eyes came off the half-naked men on the TV and focused on Tessa. She hit the pause button and leaned forward. "Odin's good eye, what on earth is that rock on your finger?"

Tessa had somehow forgotten about the ring. Maybe because Sebastian's unexpectedly good kiss had melted some of her brain cells. She stuck her hand out as Duncan chewed on a piece of her hair. "It's just temporary. Obviously. But if we're supposed to be engaged, I need a ring."

Jenna grabbed Tessa's hand and stared at the ring. "So it's a fake, right?"

"No. It came from that jewelry store on Main Street."

Jenna's eyes widened. "Are you freaking serious? This is real? Holy hammer of Thor. That's insane. You're basically wearing a really nice luxury automobile on your finger."

Tessa admired the stone. "Yes, and it's mine for

all of twenty-four hours. After dinner tomorrow night, it's going right back."

Jenna's gaze narrowed. "You should see if you can get him to throw it into the deal. Those Ellinghams are loaded. Maybe it could be like a bonus if things go extra good."

Tessa yanked her hand back. "I am absolutely not doing that. I'm already getting an incredible job out of this. That's enough."

Jenna sat back. "You get the job if things go well. If they don't, you get nothing."

"It will go fine. Even Sebastian thinks so." And he'd basically said the job was hers regardless. Hadn't he?

Jenna's left brow lifted. "You're giving off some majorly weird vibes right now."

"I don't know what you're talking about." Except that she did. Jenna was reading her, picking up on her happiness and growing fondness for Sebastian. That was the trouble with valkyries. You really couldn't lie to them. Tessa hugged Duncan a little closer as she grabbed her purse and attempted an escape before her sister also figured out that Sebastian's kiss had turned Tessa on. "Okay, see you in the morning. I'm going to bed."

"You like him."

Tessa hadn't even made it past the kitchen. With a sigh, she turned. "Of course I like him. He's giving me a job. Probably. And he just bought me dinner."

Jenna's disbelief was plainly evident on her face. "Yeah, but Sebastian Ellingham? He's like the Grinch without the green fur. He's Scrooge with fangs. Nobody likes him."

Tessa couldn't stop herself from leaping to his defense. "I'm sure his grandmother likes him. And his brothers. And Delaney seemed at least...tolerant of him. You shouldn't buy into rumors and gossip. Granted, he might be a bit, I don't know, set in his ways, but he's very nice when you get to know him."

"Get to know him?" Jenna's mouth came open. "You're defending him. Oh, wow, you *really* like him."

"I just think you're being judgmental and that's unfair. You have no idea what he's been through." Or how amazingly loyal he was. Or how his kiss had the power to set things on fire internally.

Jenna threw one leg over the arm of the couch. "Judgmental is a valkyrie's middle name. Speaking of being a valkyrie, I can tell you that every time I've had any contact with him, the read I get off him is true to what everyone says about him. He gives off strong vibes of wanting to be left alone, of being super concerned about details, and being generally standoffish when it comes to the opposite sex. He's a cold, cranky fish. How you can like him, I have no idea."

"Because he's not that way all the time." Tessa realized she was digging herself a deeper hole, but after what Sebastian had told her about keeping his promise to Evangeline's father, she felt for the man. He was doing his best to do what he thought was right. He deserved to have someone stand up for him. "Just cut him some slack, okay? Everyone has a story and you have no idea what's happened in his life to make him this way."

Jenna shook her head. "Fine, you like him. Just don't tell me you *like him* like him or I might lose it." She snorted. "Next thing you know you'll be kissing him. Gross."

Tessa made a small involuntary sound. She turned quickly, headed for the guest room again. Duncan meowed when she squeezed him a little too tightly. Please let Jenna go back to her show...

"What a minute. You just went red. Did you kiss him? Did he kiss you?" Jenna was off the couch and in her face. "You did. You did! No. Way. Was it gross? Did he force you?" She gasped and shoved Tessa's hair off her shoulder to peer at her neck. "Did he bite you?"

"No, he didn't bite me and no, he didn't force me. Don't even imply that." Tessa put Duncan down, tired of his squirming and tiny, needle-sharp nails, then she swatted her sister's hands away.

"And no, it wasn't gross. It was…nice. *Very* nice." It was the best kiss she'd ever had. Not that she'd had many.

Jenna jerked back. "You're not lying. I need details."

Tessa leaned against the wall. "This relationship has to look real. We're supposed to be an engaged couple. We didn't think having our first kiss in front of his ex was such a good idea. So we got it out of the way." They'd hardly gotten it out of the way. If anything, it was all Tessa could think about. Well, maybe not the first one, but the second one…oh boy.

Jenna nodded, seemingly mollified. "That makes sense. So it wasn't gross? Are you sure he didn't try to bite you?"

Tessa rolled her eyes. "I'm going to bed. I have to be at his house at eight in the morning. It's going to be a long day. Oh, and there's a box of goodies from this sweet shop we went into. Apparently, his sister-in-law owns it and—"

"Delaney's Delectables?" Jenna pivoted to look for the box. "No wonder I'm getting a pheromone spike off of you. I knew that couldn't be from Sebastian. But Delaney's better-than-sex goodies? Definitely."

"Yes, that must be what it is." Crisis averted. "The box is in that little shopping bag there. Don't eat them all."

"Yeah, okay." Jenna opened the bag, her attention well diverted. "Night."

"Night." Tessa headed for her room to the sound of rustling paper.

"Still, it's kind of weird."

She stopped with her hand on the door knob. "What is?"

Jenna lifted a truffle from the box. "You and him? It's weird."

"Why? Because you're not used to me having a man in my life? Or because you don't think of him as boyfriend material?"

Jenna's face screwed up in a curious expression. "Whoa. Are you saying you do think of him as boyfriend material? Because...wow. I mean, that whole dark and moody thing isn't really your gig, is it? I never figure you'd see anything in a guy who wasn't a total brainiac bookworm. Of course, it's all just pretend, right? But still."

"Right." Tessa offered her sister a smile. "Just pretend."

Except ever since that kiss, it hadn't seemed like pretend at all.

Nerves were not something to which Sebastian was accustomed. And yet, here he was, at seven fifty-five a.m. feeling like a schoolboy who'd just been called to the headmaster's office. He was downright jittery and didn't know what to do about it.

And all because Tessa was about to arrive.

The woman whose kiss had brought him back to life. He'd thought of very little else since that kiss because it had done exactly what he'd feared. Reminded him of everything he was missing.

Now his thoughts had turned to her impressions of him.

What would she think of his home? It was nothing like his grandmother's estate, but it was larger than both of his brothers' homes. Well, Julian lived in the penthouse at the Excelsior, which hardly qualified as a proper house so it shouldn't even be compared, but Hugh's house was large and well-appointed.

Sebastian had built his home knowing it would be his refuge. He'd allowed for things like a library, a gymnasium, a theater and a pool—indoor, of course. And because of those allowances, the house was on the large side. Plus he had a guest house.

But for the first time since living here, he cared what someone else thought. Two someones, actually. Tessa and Evangeline. In Tessa's case, he hoped she liked his home and saw it the same way he did, as a sanctuary. In Evangeline's case, he hoped his house told her that he was doing just fine without her. Maybe even showed her what she was missing out on.

Hmm. He'd never realized how petty he could be. Another trait Evangeline brought out in him. And another reason to be done with her. If only he could.

The doorbell rang and he jumped, then immediately groaned at his response. "Calm down, man. You're acting the fool."

He forced himself to relax. He cracked open the Tombstone, the local newspaper, and did his best to read it, but there was nothing on the pages as interesting as the woman Greaves was welcoming at the front door.

From the library, the conversation was easy to hear. Especially with Sebastian's heightened vampire senses.

The door opened and Greaves' gravelly accent followed. "Good morning, miss. I'm Greaves. Please come in."

The door closed. "Good morning. I'm Tessa Blythe. Sebastian invited me for breakfast. Well, for more than that, really, but you probably know all about that already."

"I do. Quite generous of you to help him out this way. May I take your coat?"

"Sure. Thank you."

"If you'll follow me, Mr. Ellingham is in the library."

Sebastian stiffened as their footsteps came closer. It was no accident he'd positioned himself in this room on this morning. He wanted her to be impressed and if there was any room in his house he thought capable of accomplishing that, it was his library.

The double doors opened and Greaves stepped in. "Mr. Ellingham, your guest has arrived."

Sebastian folded the paper and stood as Tessa walked in.

Her hair was down and she wore a simple wine-colored dress with a scoop neck that showed off her slender throat and lovely collarbones.

He'd not had such attractive company for

breakfast since Evangeline had been sharing his bed. "Good morning, Tessa."

"Good morning." But her eyes were not on him. They were on the room. Slowly, she walked deeper into the space, her gaze sweeping up the shelves to the second-story balcony that encompassed the room then back down again, lingering only briefly on the collection of antique weaponry hung around the fireplace before her inspection returned to the books.

He smiled, pleased that he'd been right. His nerves disappeared. "We'll take our coffee in here, Greaves. And tell Frauke we'd like breakfast in half an hour." He'd borrowed his grandmother's cook, not trusting Greaves with anything beyond toast.

"Very good, sir." Greaves left with a nod.

Sebastian turned to watch her. Her face was awash in abject wonder, giving him the feeling that he was being made privy to a rather intimate view of her. "What do you think of my library?"

She shook her head. "It's beautiful. And so well stocked. It reminds me of the library at Harmswood."

"It should. I used this one as a model, expanding the school's version to handle all the academic books as well."

Her gaze finally met his. "You designed that library?"

"I gave my input. Architecture has always been

119

a bit of a hobby but I can't take the credit for that space. All I did was make some sketches that were then turned into the final plans by a man much more skilled than I."

She looked around again. "If I had a room like this, I would never leave it."

They were so alike. The realization brought him inordinate pleasure. "I rarely do."

Greaves returned with their coffee service, setting it up on the side table. "Anything else, sir?"

"That will be all, thank you."

Greaves left them alone again.

Sebastian lifted the silver carafe. "How do you like your coffee?"

"In a vat. I might be a little addicted." She smiled and walked toward him. "Is there cream and sugar?"

"There is." He filled two cups. "Americans do like their java, don't they? Cream is in the little pitcher and the sugar cubes are in the covered dish."

She gave him a strange look. "So do you still think of yourself as a British citizen? I was under the impression that you'd been in the United States for quite a while."

"I have been. All my family has. Technically, I suppose I'm more American than British now. We've lived here far longer than we lived in England. Still, it's hard to change one's mindset."

She fixed her cup. "Especially when you don't like change."

He smiled as he added a single cube of sugar to his coffee. "Precisely."

She lifted her cup and took a sip, sighing as she swallowed. "Shouldn't you be drinking tea, then?"

His smile expanded. "Yes, but that just proves I *can* change."

She grinned back.

"I'm glad you like the library. It's my favorite room."

"How could it not be?"

"Did you sleep well? Or did all that steak and chocolate keep you up?" Or thoughts of the kiss, which had visited him even in his dreams.

"I slept like a baby." She drank some more of her coffee.

"Good. Today will be arduous. That rest will serve you well."

Her stomach rumbled and she put a hand to it, looking dismayed. "Sorry about that."

He laughed. "Not to worry. Breakfast is just around the corner. How about a tour of the house while we wait? Get you started on where everything is? The guest house we'll do after breakfast."

"Sounds good."

"Excellent. Bring your coffee, if you like."

She set her cup back on the tray and smiled up

at him. "Already gone. I can wait for breakfast to have the second cup. Lead the way. This place is really something from the outside. I can't wait to see the rest."

He hesitated, captivated for a moment by the glow of pure interest in her eyes. He realized she wasn't going to judge him based on his house. She wasn't that kind of person. But then, why would she be when her valkyrie senses could tell her exactly what his motives were? Could she sense he wanted to impress her? Did she know that she'd made him nervous? And that those nerves were now gone?

Could she sense that his desire to show her his home had suddenly been replaced by a very different need? One that had nothing to do with his house and everything to do with kissing her again. And again.

She frowned a little. "Is everything okay?"

"Everything is fine." He put his cup on the tray beside hers. "I was just thinking we should test something first."

"What's that?"

"Your reaction."

Her frown returned. "To what?"

"To this." He pulled her into his arms.

Tessa gasped as Sebastian's mouth closed over hers. Her first thought was that she had no idea what the test was.

Her second thought was that she didn't care.

She leaned into him, letting him kiss her and reveling in the fact that he'd wanted to do it again. And that she hadn't been the only one to take pleasure in the moment they'd shared last night.

Her hand settled on his chest. His very hard chest. She hadn't touched a man this intimately in many years. The thrill of it zipped through her, hot and wicked.

She shuddered with overwhelming pleasure just as he released her. She breathed open-mouthed, trying to catch her breath. "Th-that was a test?"

He nodded, eyes gleaming silver-bright for a moment. Then he quickly looked away, suddenly concerned with the position of one of his gold cuff links. "Yes. I'm sorry to say you failed."

She got a hold of herself, straightening and shunting the pleasurable feelings he'd filled her with to some safe part of her brain where she could dissect them later. "I failed? What was the test?"

He tugged at the cuff of his shirt. "To see how you'd react to a spontaneous show of affection."

Was that what that was supposed to be? Because it had felt like a blatant display of lust. But then, what did she know? He was the first man she'd kissed in ages so her ability to compare was pretty low. "I see. And I reacted with too much surprise?"

"Precisely. If we're a couple, those sorts of things should be more commonplace. More expected. Don't you agree?"

He had yet to make eye contact with her since the kiss. She decide to try a test of her own. "So that was *just* an assessment of my reaction?"

He finally looked at her. "Yes. That's what I said. Merely a test."

She bit the inside of her cheek to keep from smiling and giving herself away. He was lying. She didn't need her valkyrie senses to figure that out. He'd wanted to kiss her. The test excuse had been just that. An excuse. "Just checking."

He made a small noise of agreement.

She crossed her arms, feeling a jolt of power at her new knowledge. "I'll try to do better the next time."

He started, then quickly covered with a fake cough. "Very good. Well, we should get on with the tour or our breakfast will be cold by the time we return."

"Let's go."

But as beautiful as his house was, it was difficult to pay attention. All she could think about was that he'd wanted to kiss her. And had.

Was Sebastian falling for her? Maybe just a little bit?

She'd never considered the possibility of a

vampire as a partner, but maybe that was just short-sightedness on her behalf. A vampire was immortal, so they'd be immune to...death. That would make him the perfect mate for her, considering.

She stared out a window, lost in memory, her fingers absently caressing the scar on her knuckles.

"*Tessa*."

She jumped and looked at him, tucking her hands behind her. "Sorry, what?"

He frowned. "Have you heard a word I've said? This is important. If we've been seeing each other for over a year, you have to know the layout of my house."

"Yes, sorry, this is your...den?"

"My office."

She glanced around. Of course it was. Why else would there be a desk in it? She moved to stand beside it, trying to ignore the wall of weaponry on proud display. The man liked his blades, apparently. In that respect, they were very different. "I got a little distracted."

"By what?"

She frowned right back at him. "By your *test*."

He straightened. "I see."

Ooo, that felt judgy. She crossed her arms and leaned against his desk. "And you pretending that's all it was didn't help."

He shifted uncomfortably. "It *was* a test."

"You're lying again. Did you forget I can tell intent? Maybe on some level you meant it as a test, but the truth is, you wanted to kiss me."

His Adam's apple bobbed but he said nothing. After a long silence, he finally spoke. "I have been alone for a very long time. I apologize if I've offended you. That was certainly not what I meant to do."

"You didn't offend me." She trailed her finger along the wood grain on his desktop, unable to look at him as her feelings about the kiss came to the surface. Her cheeks burned as hot as Brokkr's fabled forge. "I wasn't upset by the kiss. At all."

He took a step toward her. "I'm happy to hear that."

She looked at him. "I hear a *but* in your voice."

He sighed and brushed a strand of hair back behind her shoulder, his smile tentative and a little sad. "I don't want to lead you on. My desire for a woman's touch shouldn't be confused with an interest in a relationship. That's not the case. I have an obligation to Evangeline, regardless of what anyone thinks, and I will uphold it. There is no place in my life for another woman."

His words stung far more than they should have. She'd known the man for a day, had no reason to feel anything for him, and yet...she felt like he was breaking up with her. She made herself smile. "I completely understand."

She didn't. Not at all. But difficult decisions were one of the many threads that made up a valkyrie's tapestry.

He nodded. "Thank you."

He lifted his hand and gently caressed her cheek.

She grabbed his wrist and pulled his hand away. "You can't do that. You can't tell me you don't want to lead me on and then touch me with that kind of tenderness."

"We are supposed to be an engaged couple. If I cannot be tender with you, how am I supposed to be?"

"During the dinner and in front of Evangeline is one thing. But beyond that, it can't happen. No more *tests*. And don't tell me I need to be comfortable with you touching me or kissing me. I'll be fine, you'll see."

He stiffened as if rebuked, which she guessed was exactly what she'd done. But he couldn't expect her to not respond to his attentions. He nodded. "Of course, you're right."

He might think she was a mouse, and maybe in many ways she was, but she was a mouse with a heart and she wasn't about to sacrifice it for his sake.

Job or no job.

Tension colored the rest of the morning and afternoon, until at last they separated to prepare for the evening ahead. Sebastian stood in his quarters, pondering the day. He understood where Tessa was coming from and actually agreed with her. He shouldn't kiss her or touch her or pull her into his arms. Not when he couldn't promise her more than that. It wasn't fair to either of them, but especially her.

But knowing that did nothing to quell the desire in him. He was inexplicably drawn to her, against all his common sense and better judgment. Was it because she was the first woman he'd allowed into his life since Evangeline? Or was it because, with every passing moment, Tessa seemed more and more the complete opposite of Evangeline, and therefore, his perfect match? Tessa definitely made him feel alive in ways Evangeline never had. And never would. Or was it because Tessa seemed more and more perfect for him with every passing moment?

He had no idea the reason. All he knew was that dwelling on it only made him want to kiss her again to test his theories.

But she'd specifically said no more tests.

He sighed, frustrated with himself, with his life, with his pledge to the late Lord Heathcote, Evangeline's father. The money the man had left Sebastian remained untouched in numerous accounts all over the world. He'd moved it periodically as time had demanded, but once settled into a new account, there it sat, collecting interest and serving as a reminder of what rash promises could cost.

That money was a millstone about his neck. He would never be rid of it or Evangeline. Never be free to attempt happiness with another. This was his life. His burden to bear.

And people wondered why his mood was always so dour. Who wouldn't be dour in his shoes? Which were currently a pair of John Lobb oxfords in black to complement his charcoal gray suit. At least his outward appearance didn't match his mood.

As far as he knew. He frowned at the reflection in the mirror, inspecting his attire. He'd dressed for dinner early, knowing that his brothers would arrive well ahead of seven p.m. so they could talk.

The sun set around six p.m. in Nocturne Falls in January, meaning Evangeline could arrive any time after that, but it had always been her fashion to arrive late so that she could make a grand entrance. He didn't imagine tonight would be any different.

Satisfied with his appearance, he headed downstairs. He'd borrowed Frauke again to prepare dinner. The woman was a bit of a terror, but if Greaves had been left in charge of dinner they'd be eating tinned soup and crackers. He stuck his head into the kitchen.

Everything smelled wonderful. He picked out the scents of beef and wine and roasting potatoes. A good winter meal. Frauke's back was to him as she stirred something on the stove. She had earbuds in. No doubt listening to one of her operas. He let her be, heading next to the dining room where Greaves was putting the finishing touches on the table.

The man looked up as Sebastian walked in. Greaves stood back from the table and gave it a nod. "I was never a butler or a footman, but I think it'll do."

"Well done, old man. It looks very nice." Hard to set an ugly table with good crystal and china and the heirloom silver.

"Much appreciated. Can't recall the last time you used this room."

"Neither can I." Dinner parties were not something he did. "Have you seen Tessa?"

"She's in the guest suite getting ready."

"Fine. I'll be in the library. Having a stiff drink. Send my brothers in when they arrive, will you?"

"Very good, sir."

Sebastian went into the library, closing the doors behind him. He tried to shake the tension from his muscles and failed. He'd been so sure about tonight's outcome until the moment earlier in his office with Tessa. Now, that certainty was gone. What if he touched her and she reacted poorly? Or grabbed his hand again to keep him away?

Evangeline would see that for what it was in an instant.

He poured a generous drink. This whole thing was foolishness. He should just confess all to Evangeline and be done with it.

Except she would then continue to act toward him as she always had. Or worse, if that was possible. He needed some leverage with her, especially if she truly wanted to live as husband and wife again. It was the only way he'd get her under control enough to fulfill her father's wishes that she be protected.

With every passing year, Sebastian was astonished that Evangeline remained alive. How she hadn't yet been discovered as a vampire with all her reckless living, he had no idea. Daily he checked news sites around the world for reports of a woman suddenly going up in flames as the sun hit her. That would be just like Evangeline, to be caught outside at dawn.

Just like her to do something he couldn't protect her from. Something that would make it impossible for him to keep the promise he'd made. He knew that her decision to leave him meant the only protection he could really offer was financial, and he'd done that, but it wasn't what her father would have wanted.

Sebastian wonder what the man would think of his daughter now. He downed the whiskey in a single swallow and poured himself another one as the last one burned a pleasurable path down his throat. If Evangeline did accidentally incinerate herself, he would at least be free. He closed his eyes at such a horrible thought, but the truth remained. Evangeline was the reason he couldn't even entertain the idea of a woman like Tessa.

Sweet, pretty, intelligent Tessa. He'd called her a mouse and yet, she'd stood up to him today. He'd been so wrong about her. She wasn't plain or simple. She was a rare jewel of a woman with a keen mind, a sharp wit and the kind of beauty that went beyond her pretty face and blue eyes.

A soft knock at the library door turned him around. "Come in."

The door opened and Tessa stepped through,

shining brighter than any gem he'd ever seen. "I hope this dress is all right for dinner. I borrowed it from my sister. The shoes too. I was sort of surprised she owned anything this nice, but I'm glad she did."

"So am I. You look…perfect." And she did. The slim black dress was simple, but showed off her gorgeous figure and the black lace pumps were a little naughty, a nice contrast to the strand of pearls around her throat. She'd left her hair down, creating a new desire in him to run his hands through it. The blazing diamond on her finger stood out like a beacon.

She looked classy and sexy and just slightly unattainable. Perfection. His heart clenched at the sight of her. His fake fiancée.

"Thank you. You look very nice too." She stayed by the door, hands clasped and looking rather unsure of herself.

He realized she must be racked with nerves. He lifted his glass. "Would you care for a drink? Might help take the edge off."

"I don't think that's a good idea. I can't risk losing control. What if I slip up and do something wrong?"

The worry bracketing her mouth cut him. She was doing this for him. Bearing this stress, all in the hopes of winning a job. "You won't do anything wrong. You can't. Whatever happens tonight, happens. The job is yours, Tessa. No matter this evening's outcome. You've already done more than enough for me. Come on, have a drink and relax a little. One won't hurt. And it might take the edge off."

She walked toward him, eyes rounding a little. "You mean that, about the job? You're definitely giving it to me?"

He nodded as he poured her a whiskey. "Yes. You've earned it. And I don't mean just because of this favor you're doing for me. You're exceptionally qualified."

"Thank you." She hesitated, then leaned in and kissed his cheek.

Her perfume teased his senses and he smiled wryly. "Was that a test?"

"No. That was just a thank you. Although I suppose I shouldn't be kissing my boss."

"I'm not your boss yet." He handed her the glass, then picked his up and knocked it against her. "Cheers."

"Cheers." She took a cautious sip.

The doorbell rang.

Sebastian smiled, doing his best to ease her mood. "That will probably be one of my brothers."

Delaney's and Hugh's voices rang out from the foyer. Greaves showed them into the library a few minutes later.

"Hi, Tessa." Delaney gave Tessa's arm a

squeeze. "How are you feeling? You look fantastic."

"Thanks, so do you. I'm feeling okay. A little nervous." Tessa lifted her glass. "This is helping."

"I'm sure it is." Delaney laughed. "How were the chocolates? Are they all gone?"

"Not yet. Of course, that's assuming my sister didn't eat the rest for breakfast."

As the two women chatted, Hugh sidled up to Sebastian. "You ready for this?"

"Yes. One way or the other, things have to change between Evangeline and me."

Hugh nodded. "That's for damn sure."

"Whiskey?"

"I'd rather have wine. You have any red?"

"Not in here."

Before Sebastian could ring for Greaves, the doorbell sounded again.

Julian strode into the library a few moments later. "Isn't this cozy? Evangeline not here yet?"

They all answered him in unison. "No."

"All right then." He poured himself a glass of whiskey. "What's the plan?"

"Reinforce our story. Whatever we say, go with it. Keep the conversation light. Steer Evangeline away from any probing questions," Sebastian said. "But above all, if anything goes wrong, protect Tessa."

Delaney made a worried face. "You think if

Evangeline finds out this is all a ruse, she'll try to hurt Tessa? What kind of woman is your ex-wife?"

"Wife," Julian corrected. "They haven't actually gotten a divorce."

Hugh glared at his brother. "After this many years of separation, it's a formality."

"True. But Evangeline would probably disagree with you." Julian sipped his drink and went off to join the women.

Hugh gave Sebastian a nod. "Tessa won't come to any harm. Evangeline's outnumbered."

"Numbers won't keep her insults at bay. She won't lay hands on Tessa, but she will try to eviscerate her with words if given the chance."

Delaney linked her arm through Tessa's. "Then we just won't let that happen, will—"

The doorbell rang again and everyone in the library fell silent. Sebastian's entire body tightened with resolve.

Evangeline had arrived.

The dining room was beautiful, the food was delicious and five of the six guests at the table were firmly on Tessa's side.

None of that kept her from feeling like a woman on trial. Was this how the dying souls on the battlefields felt when her valkyrie sisters came to collect them?

If so, it was horrifying, and confirmed her decision to live her life as far removed from her lineage as possible.

Evangeline was tremendously beautiful. Tessa knew some of that was due to her being a vampire. The turning magnified a person's human beauty. Evangeline must have been stunning as a mortal. Her skin was as perfect as a picture in a magazine, her eyes bright and full of mystery, her hair dark brown and glossy except for a few streaks of red.

Compounding the matter, she was dressed impeccably in a cobalt blue dress that hugged her perfect body. Her make-up was equally perfect and she seemed to be unflappable, with the right response to every question and comment.

Evangeline was the kind of woman who made the world her playground and turned those around her into staff.

Tessa felt like a pretender. Well, more of a pretender than she already was. Getting ready for dinner had been as simple as changing her clothes and accessories, adding a little more makeup and running a brush through her hair. Something told her Evangeline had exerted quite a bit more effort than that.

She took a breath and reminded herself that this was not a competition. This was just a game in which the goal was to make Evangeline believe Sebastian was capable of attracting another woman and to therefore remind Evangeline that he was not to be taken for granted.

With that in mind, Tessa stopped staring at her potato gratin and lifted her head to smile lovingly at her bogus betrothed.

It wasn't hard to do. She was, sadly, a little smitten with him. It was a rare man who valued books and learning the way he did and had the means to indulge those passions. That alone would have been enough to sway her. But then there were his dark good looks. He was the vampire version of Mr. Darcy and if she was supposed to resist that, then someone needed to tell her how.

But if she thought about the kissing, her bones went to jelly and her brain to mush and the heat of desire warmed her to the point of combustion.

She hadn't realized the extent of her loneliness until just this moment. Freya help her, she was a sad thing. And, to make matters worse, she missed Duncan. Snuggling that little fur ball was a tremendous stress reliever.

Jenna would roll her eyes and proclaim Tessa had finally become the stereotypical cat lady librarian, but the truth could not be ignored.

Nor could the man seated at the head of the table.

Sebastian listened as Delaney described the

dessert she'd brought, some red velvet cake with raspberry filling that was a test for the cake she was going to enter in the Valentine's Day Bake Off.

Tessa smiled. She liked Delaney and not just for her skills with sweet things. She was a kind, happy woman who Tessa imagined was also a fiercely loyal friend. And Delaney and Sebastian's brother Hugh were very clearly in love. It was charming how he watched her, a proud gleam in his eyes.

Tessa wondered if a man would ever look at her that way.

Maybe Duncan would.

She snorted at the thought, then quickly covered her mouth with her hand.

Evangeline, seated mercifully at the other end of the table, raised her brows and directed her gaze at Tessa. "What was that?"

Tessa swallowed. "Nothing, sorry." She lifted her goblet of water and drank, hoping that would end the questioning.

It didn't.

Evangeline tipped her head while her eyes remained on Tessa. "Will you be entering the bake off?"

Tessa put her water down and shook her head. "I'm not a baker by any means."

"Where do your talents lie?"

Sebastian reached over and took her hand. "Tessa is a librarian. In fact, she's about to become the Dean of Library Studies at Harmswood Academy."

Evangeline smiled and looked dutifully impressed. "Well, how about that. Congratulations. I've never had much time for reading. All those dull, musty pages. Not for me. Not when there are so many other more interesting things to do. But now I see why Sebby is so attracted to you. He loves dull things." Before anyone could say a thing, Evangeline laughed. "Books, I mean."

Tessa's valkyrie temper nudged at the base of her spine. She forced herself to smile. "Of course."

Sebastian's hand tightened over hers. She looked at him in time to see a muscle in his jaw twitch. "Watch your tongue, Evangeline."

She rounded her eyes and blinked at him as though she didn't have a clue why he might be angry. "I said I meant books."

He grunted at her, the sound a mix of disbelief and irritation.

She grinned and lifted her wine. "Quite the leap to defend your paramour. A very nice touch. Definitely the way a man should act."

The muscle in his jaw twitched again. "What is that supposed to mean?"

She grinned over the rim of her glass. "Nothing at all. I do find it rather convenient that you've rallied the troops. You're the one who invited me to dinner, after all."

Despite Julian's lazy slouch in his chair, there was something dark simmering in his gaze. His dislike of Evangeline, Tessa guessed. He leaned a little farther away from the vampiress before he spoke. "We're here because your reputation precedes you, Eva."

She drained her wine, then set the glass down. "What reputation is that?"

Someone else snorted and Tessa realized it had come from Hugh. "Evangeline, don't play coy. My brothers and I have known you for nearly four hundred years. You were willful and spoiled as a child, given to tantrums and diatribes that lasted until your demands were met. None of that changed as you grew up and when you became a vampire, the turning did what it always does. It took the strongest of your characteristics and magnified them. Unfortunately, in your case, those characteristics weren't all good ones."

Hugh shook his head as he continued. "For once in your self-centered, indulgent life, do the right thing and let Sebastian be. He's found happiness. You ought to try to do the same."

Evangeline stared at him. An icy glaze narrowed her eyes for a moment and then she seemed to catch herself. She smiled and straightened in her chair. "I will ignore your insults but only because I'm concerned for Sebby. I just want what's best for him."

Julian barked out a laugh. "If that's the case, give the man his dissolution already."

She snapped back, "What's best for him is me."

Sebastian grunted again.

Evangeline's eyes went liquid and her gaze turned to Sebastian. "Is that what you want, my darling? A dissolution? To end us once and for all?"

All eyes shifted to Sebastian. Tessa watched, knowing this was a pivotal moment for him. He'd said that getting Evangeline back was necessary for him to keep the promise he'd made, but his actions toward Tessa had said he'd prefer to be free.

She put her hands in her lap and interlaced her fingers, squeezing them together. Maybe she shouldn't have pushed him away. Maybe she should have given in to her own feelings and let him touch and kiss her all he—and she—had wanted.

If he chose Evangeline because Tessa had denied him, she would be complicit in his unhappiness. Because there was no way he could be happy with that woman.

No. Way.

Tessa couldn't imagine spending any length of time with her. Thank Freya this dinner was almost over and the charade with it. Any longer and she wasn't sure she'd be able to keep her dangerous temper under control. The woman was just flat out infuriating.

Sebastian lifted his chin, his mouth firmly set until he finally spoke. "A dissolution would be bloody brilliant."

Sebastian couldn't believe the words coming out of his own mouth, but Evangeline's presence at dinner had put a very hard line under the truth of who she was. And always would be.

Compared to Tessa, she was, well, there was no comparison. Unless you went with something like black and white. Winter and summer.

Angel and devil.

Evangeline's mouth gaped open.

Sebastian folded his napkin. "I'm not saying I would abandon you, Evangeline. We've been connected this long, we can certainly remain...acquainted. But you've been out of my life for centuries, except when it suits you. Which is most of the time."

She sputtered a few words. "But...I—"

He held up his hands. "I'm willing to continue helping you should you find yourself in need of something, because I imagine you have few friends willing to extend themselves for you that way." Also, he was obligated to help her and would be for the rest of his life so why fight it? "That need would be mostly monetary, the same as it's been these last centuries, but this more personal relationship of ours, such as it is, has been over for a very long time. Let's make it official. Let me—and Tessa get on with our life. I can have my solicitor draw up the necessary dissolution papers in a day then we can send them off to the council and be free to live our lives."

Spending time with Tessa had made him realize just how deeply he was suffering at Evangeline's hands. There was no reason he couldn't fulfill his promise to her father but live his own life as well. Having her sign dissolution papers would finally bring this ridiculous relationship to an end. They would be completely divorced in the eyes of the council and there could be no repercussions for either of them after that, even if he was still technically her sire.

Her mental and emotional hold on him would be gone. She would become just another item in his budget to be accounted for.

Evangeline finally found her voice. It held an edge of weepy disbelief. "I came here to make amends and resume our life together and this is how you repay me?"

"I'm not repaying you, Evangeline. That implies a debt I owe you and if it's cost analysis you want, I assure you your side of the ledger is rather lacking. I'm merely attempting to move on with my life."

Anger shimmered in her eyes. "I don't believe you. I think you're trying to force me into groveling. Trying to get me to beg you to take me back." She sniffed. "That's not who I am, Sebastian, and you know it."

"I do." Indeed, if she *had* groveled and begged, he might have taken her back no questions asked. But she hadn't. And he'd told the fortuitous lie that had brought Tessa, and the bright light of reality, into his world. "I promise I'm not trying to force you into anything. Again, this isn't about you. It's about me. My life." He looked at Tessa. "My happiness."

"Good for you," Hugh said.

"Rubbish," Evangeline spat out. "You can pretend all you like, but I know you, Sebastian. I don't believe for a moment that you're planning on getting married. This is a game and I, for one, am done playing it."

Sebastian laughed. "You're done playing? Games are all you know."

She reared back in her chair. "Is that what you think? Fine. I have a new game for you. Give me one week, living in this house with you. Let me see the two of you together, twenty-four hours a day.

Convince me that you're truly in love and I'll give you your dissolution, no questions asked. I'll sign with a smile. I'll even pay to file the papers with the council."

Her words settled over him like a pall. Tessa would never agree to that. She'd never move in with him, not after today. Asking her to keep this charade up for a week with Evangeline in the same house was too much. A bridge too far. "I wouldn't even let you live in my guest house."

Tessa spoke before he could say anything else. "I'm game if Sebastian is game."

Sebastian cleared his throat to cover his surprise. "Be that as it may, Tessa and I need a moment to discuss this."

Evangeline pursed her lips as though she'd won something and looked directly at Tessa. "He's afraid that having me around all the time will be too much of a temptation for him. Then your poor little dull librarian's heart would get broken."

Tessa rose out of her chair and muttered, "Something might get broken, but it won't be my heart."

"What was that?" Evangeline asked over the sound of Julian snorting with amusement.

"Nothing." Tessa glanced at Sebastian. "I'll be in the library."

Without waiting, she strode off. Sebastian stood,

frustration souring his mood further. "You're unbelievable, Evangeline."

She smiled lazily. "I am, aren't I?"

He went after Tessa.

She stood, waiting in the library. Fingers interlaced. Face masked with distress. "She is...awful."

"I know. I'm very sorry. Obviously, I'm going to tell her this preposterous idea of hers is not going to happen—"

"Absolutely not. You have to agree to this. It's your chance to get your life back. And like I said in the dining room, I'm agreeable. As much as anyone can be in this situation."

He stared at her, trying to be sure he'd heard her correctly. "I don't think you understand what you're saying."

"Of course I do. I'm going to have to move in here with you for a week."

He shook his head. "Nothing makes sense to me right now. Why are you all right with this? With her?"

"I'm not all right with her, but this has nothing to do with Evangeline." A cautious smile curved her mouth. "It has everything to do with you. You stood up to her tonight. And it feels like something has changed within you. Like you've finally figured out that you want to be happy and that you can be, if you remove her from your life. I know you still want to keep your promise to her father and I won't try to dissuade you from that, but if you want your life back, then I want to help you."

"I don't know what to say."

"Say yes."

No one outside his family had ever done anything like this for him before. Or shown so much concern for his well-being. "I am amazed that you would do this for me. What do you want in return?"

"Nothing." She shrugged. "You're giving me a job. A great job. That's plenty."

His heart swelled with affection for her. So many people came to him with their hands out, but not Tessa. She was giving him something that had no price. A chance at happiness. "You can keep the ring."

She jerked back. "What? No, that's far too much. And I don't have any use for it. Please, just let me do this. I'm not trying to get anything out of you. Evangeline's done that enough, I think."

A true statement. "This isn't going to be easy."

"No, it won't be. I'll have to run back to my sister's and collect my things."

"You can do that in the morning, once Evangeline succumbs to daysleep. She'll be out cold for at least five or six hours." He raked a hand through his hair, worry filling him at the thought of everything that could go wrong. "I don't like this idea at all."

"Neither do I, but despite what she said about not believing us, she's doubtful. I could read it in her and a valkyrie's instincts are never wrong."

"Is that why you're doing this? Because she's on the fence?"

Tessa's smile returned. "I'm doing this because...I like you, Sebastian. I see a kindred spirit in you. And it makes me sad to think you've already spent so much of your long life burdened by responsibility for a woman who doesn't love or respect you. I understand living a life that feels constrained by something you cannot control, but you have a chance to change that and I absolutely think you should."

Emotion clogged his throat. He was unaccustomed to anyone wanting to help him, something he knew he'd fostered by his insistence on Evangeline being an off-limits subject. "Thank you," he managed.

She nodded. "We should go out and tell her the good news."

He snorted. "I'm not sure I'd call it good, but yes. In a moment." He caught her hand and kissed her knuckles, wanting to do more, but restraining himself. If this worked, he would be indebted to Tessa for the rest of his life. Unlike with

Evangeline, however, that was a debt with which he felt comfortable.

She allowed him to hold on to her for another second, then eased her hand out of his. "Come on. I'm sure she's chomping at the bit to move in here and cause trouble."

Sebastian sighed. "Amazing how well you know her in such a short span of time."

Together they walked back into the dining room, which was uncomfortably quiet. Evangeline's gaze held the determination of someone prepared to fight for what she wanted. It was not an unusual look for her.

Sebastian paused just inside the door, Tessa at his side. Knowing full well he was taking advantage of the situation, he slid his arm around her waist and settled his hand on her hip. The warmth of her seeped through his skin, a tease of what he couldn't have. At least not yet. But it was still worth it. "Tessa and I have nothing to hide. You want to see us together for a week, fine. But then you will sign dissolution papers and we are done. My family serves as witness to this. Agreed?"

Evangeline smirked. "Agreed."

"Witnessed," Hugh said.

"Witnessed." Julian pointed at Evangeline. "You're not getting out of this."

She steepled her fingers against her chest. "I

have no intention of getting out of it. I'm a woman of my word."

Hugh barked out a laugh. "Bollocks."

She glowered at him before looking at Sebastian again. "Tell Greaves to get my things out of my rental car."

Sebastian's brows lifted. "Get them yourself. He's my rook, not a servant at your beck and call."

"I'm a guest," Evangeline shot back.

"You're an interloper. I've agreed you can stay the week, but don't for a moment think you're a guest. *Guests* are invited."

Tessa slipped her arm around Sebastian's waist and out of the corner of his eye, he saw the side of her mouth quirk up. This was going to be a very interesting week indeed.

While Evangeline carried her bags in, loudly protesting Sebastian's inhospitable treatment the whole time, Sebastian and Tessa said goodbye to their guests, then Tessa retreated to the library with her phone to text Jenna with an update.

Jenna was about as understanding as expected, but didn't give Tessa any more than the usual amount of grief, agreeing to help her sister in the morning with whatever needed to be done.

That accomplished, Tessa went back out to find

Sebastian. He was in the kitchen with Greaves, both of them leaning against the counter. The cook had already left, but someone had made coffee. The rich aroma permeated the space. Sebastian sipped a cup.

Tessa glanced around. "Just you two in here?"

Sebastian nodded. "Yes. She's upstairs in the guest suite."

Tessa stiffened. "My things were in there from when I changed for dinner."

Greaves shook his head. "I took care of that, miss. I put your belongings in Sebastian's quarters."

"Thank you." Relief swept her. This was going to be a very long week, but she'd agreed. Too late to turn back now. Not that she would change her mind. Sebastian needed this. And on a deeper level, helping him felt like it might balance her darker valkyrie side a bit. All that proclivity for death and destruction needed a few good deeds to level the scales. Something to appeal to the valkyrie's nature to protect.

"Thank you, miss." Greaves put his hand on a large white box sitting on the kitchen counter. "Would you like a slice of cake and some coffee? Dinner never made it as far as dessert and it would be a shame to let Miss Delaney's cake go to waste."

"Sure, why not?" She took a seat at the old wooden farmhouse-style table. It matched the rest of the rustic kitchen that had no doubt cost a fortune to look that way. Then she stood again. "I guess I should get myself some coffee before I get settled."

Greaves held a hand up and moved toward the pot. "I've got that, miss. I'll bring you the cream and sugar, too."

"Thank you." She sat back down and folded her hands on the table, looking up at Sebastian. "Jenna's going to help me in the morning. Won't take much. One trip. I'll go first thing as soon as you tell me it's okay."

"Greaves will drive you."

"It's okay. I can drive myself."

Greaves brought her coffee over, along with the sugar. He made a second trip with the creamer. "But you wouldn't be if you were living here. Let me, miss. It's what I do."

"But Sebastian just told Evangeline you were a rook, not a servant. I certainly don't want you to go out of your way—what is a rook, exactly?"

Greaves smiled. "Sort of a vampire's butler. And I'm happy to help the woman who's helping Sebastian. Whatever you need."

"All right." She shrugged. This was not a life she was used to.

Greaves went back to the counter, opened the cake box and turned to look at her. "Large or small?"

She frowned. "Um…"

He winked at her. "Slice of cake."

She considered the evening. "Large." Now was not the time to deny herself anything.

She glanced at Sebastian. "Aren't you joining me?"

He held his cup in front of him. "I rarely eat—"

"Sweets. Yes, I know." She patted the table top in front of the chair beside her. "Tonight you do. Sit."

He made a curious face, but did as she asked, settling in beside her. "Happy?"

"Yes."

That seemed to appease something in him and he smiled. "Greaves, apparently I'm also having cake."

"Very good, sir."

Two generous slices appeared shortly after on china plates, along with silver forks and cloth napkins. The cake looked like red velvet with fresh raspberries and buttercream in the layers.

She picked up her fork, which was surprisingly heavy, but that was because it was sterling. She contemplated the setting before her. "Do you always do things so formally?"

Greaves made a soft noise.

Sebastian shot him a look as he answered. "You mean because of the china?"

"And the silver and the crystal and the cloth napkins. All of it. It's lovely, don't get me wrong, but it's sort of formal for every day."

He seemed to think that over for a moment. "It's just how things are. Although I never eat in the dining room. I usually eat in here."

Lonely was the first word that popped into her head, but she kept that to herself. She smiled. "We can eat in the dining room tomorrow if you like. Unless you prefer not to."

He forked up a morsel of cake. "I prefer not to when I'm alone. As long as you're here, the dining room will be perfect."

Greaves cleared his throat. "About breakfast…"

Sebastian put his fork down. "Ah, yes. That will be a problem."

"What?" Tessa asked.

Sebastian cocked a brow. "We order most things in. Greaves is a wretched cook."

Greaves shook his head. "I burn water."

Tessa laughed. "I can cook."

"You're a guest," Sebastian said.

She laid her hand on his arm. "Technically, I'm the lady of the house. If I want to cook, I will."

Greaves chuckled.

Sebastian leaned back, his amused expression rather charming. "As you wish."

The kitchen door swung open and Evangeline swanned in. "As who wishes what?"

Tessa stuffed a bite of cake into her mouth. It was the perfect excuse to be quiet.

Sebastian sighed. "I take it you're settled in?"

"Yes." She put her hands on her hips and surveyed the room. She'd changed out of her snug blue dress and into a long satin nightgown with a matching robe and feathered slippers.

Tessa wanted to roll her eyes at the choice of outfit, but didn't. At least the cake was delicious. Delaney knew what she was doing with flour and sugar, that was for sure.

Evangeline took a few steps toward the counter, then backtracked and sat beside Sebastian. She waved her hand in Greaves' direction. "I'll have coffee and cake too."

Greaves arrowed a look at Sebastian.

Tessa stood, ready to diffuse the situation. As much as she appreciated Sebastian's willingness to stand up to Evangeline, they were going to be living in the same house for the next seven days. Battles had to be chosen carefully. "I'll get it."

Greaves looked mortified. "No, miss, I've got it. You sit and enjoy your cake."

Evangeline's brows rose and she leaned back in her chair. "Really? You would have waited on me?"

Tessa took her seat. "You're a guest in our house, no matter how that came about."

157

Evangeline looked at Sebastian. "Your fiancée has a better attitude than you do."

Tessa lifted her cup. "Most people have a better attitude than Sebastian." She smiled at him, trying to play the perfect fiancée. "But I love him anyway."

Saying those words caused an uncomfortable feeling to ripple through her. Like she'd just signed some sort of irreversible pact that left her vulnerable. She knew the words were just for show, but they weren't the kind of words that should be played with. Love was…bigger than that.

He smiled at her. "And how lucky I am that you do."

Evangeline rolled her eyes. "Oh, spare me."

Greaves put Evangeline's plate and cup in front of her without saying a word, somehow managing to look down his nose at her the entire time.

Tessa was developing a soft spot for the gray-haired gentleman. "Evangeline, you must remember what it was like to be so madly in love that you thought your partner could do no wrong."

Sebastian's mouth puckered like he might be trying to suppress a snort.

Evangeline stirred a heaping teaspoon of sugar into her cup. "We weren't in love. Our marriage was arranged. For the good of the country and the peerage and all that."

"I see." Tessa put her fork across her plate, her cake gone in an embarrassingly short number of bites. "That's sad. For both of you. I hope you find your own happiness someday too."

Evangeline started to say something, but Tessa wasn't interested in anything more the woman might have to add. It had been a long day and her patience was wearing thin. She squeezed Sebastian's hand and smiled at him. "I'm going up to bed, sweetheart. I hope you don't mind."

His eyes glowed softly. "Of course not. I'll see you soon."

"Rather early, isn't it?" Evangeline asked.

Tessa stood and Sebastian got up along with her. "No," he said. "She's not a vampire. She keeps human hours and so do I."

Evangeline's eyes narrowed. "You didn't used to."

"Times change." He ignored her to pull Tessa close and kiss her cheek. "I'll be up shortly."

"Miss?"

Tessa turned. "Yes?"

"Do you mind if I walk with you?" Greaves asked. "We still need to go over that shopping list."

She hoped that was Greaves' way of helping her find Sebastian's room. She had no idea where it was. She was sure it had been on the tour, but she'd been a little distracted today and knowing the location of Sebastian's bedroom wasn't information she'd thought she'd need again. "That would be perfect."

They walked out of the kitchen and toward the great room in silence. When they approached the stairs, Greaves spoke.

"I wasn't sure you'd know your way."

"I don't." She vaguely remembered something about it being on the second floor, but as they approached the landing, she realized she had no clue if she should go left or right. "Thank you. I owe you one."

He gave a small shake of his head as he directed her to the right. "You owe me nothing, miss. You're doing this man a great service. That woman has kept him in a dark place for too long."

"I sensed that."

He pointed at the set of double doors at the end of the hall. "His quarters. Do you need anything else before you turn in?"

"No, I'm fine. Thank you."

He hesitated. "May I ask you something, miss?"

"Sure."

He tucked his hands behind him and took a deep breath. "Do you like Sebastian?"

She nodded. "I do."

"Do you think you could ever...care for him?"

She smiled. She already did in some small way. "Yes, I think I could. But I don't know if he's ready or open to that."

"No, I suppose not."

She watched the man's tender expression. It matched the emotion coming off him. "You love him, don't you? In your own way."

Greaves sniffed. "Been with him nearly four centuries. He's all the family I have. We've been through a great deal. And I am his rook, after all." His gaze shifted toward the stairs. "But that woman…she's been the worst of it."

She nodded. "I can imagine."

He straightened. "I've bothered you long enough. Have a good night, miss."

"Thank you, Greaves. You too." She watched him go for a moment, then opened the doors and went in.

The room was as neat and masculine as Sebastian, but the object that stood out the most was the one thing she hadn't really thought about.

The bed.

And the fact that there was only one.

11

Sebastian freed himself from Evangeline as soon as possible. He made a quick trip to his office to make sure his desk drawers were secured, then he locked the door and went upstairs.

He found Tessa standing in the middle of the room, staring at his bed.

He understood instantly. He closed the doors behind him. "I'll sleep on the couch by the window. Unless you'd rather not have me in the room."

She turned. "No, that's fine. And very generous of you."

"If one of us is being generous, it's you. I know I've thanked you, but that seems so insufficient against the reality of what you're doing for me."

She smiled and shrugged. "It's okay, really."

"Did Greaves show you around? Where the bathroom is?"

"No, he just dropped me off at the door. It was

nice of him to come with me. I wouldn't have found it on my own." She tucked a strand of hair behind one ear. "He's a good man. I like him."

"He is a good man. Been with me since before I was turned. Hugh's rook was his valet too."

"And Julian's rook?"

"He doesn't have one. For all his catting around, he's a rather private sort. Likes to be alone more than he lets on."

"That's interesting. Of your two brothers, he's the hardest to read. It's like he's covered in a fog that hides his true intent."

Sebastian loosened his tie. "Can fae magic interrupt your abilities?"

She nodded. "Possibly. That's old magic and earth bound."

"That might be what it is, then. Hugh told me Julian had Willa make him a charm. She can put fae magic into the pieces she makes if the customer requests it. Supposed to help him with the ladies or something. Anyway, maybe it's what causes the fog."

He pulled his tie free. She hadn't moved from the center of the room. "Is everything all right?"

She glanced down at her dress. "I don't have anything to sleep in."

"Ah." He thought for a moment. "I must have something, but I'm not sure what to offer you."

"I don't suppose you have any souvenir T-shirts

lying around?" She laughed. "You don't seem like the type to wear anything that qualifies as casual."

"No, I'm not."

"What do you normally wear to bed?"

"Pajamas." Although he rarely wore the top. He didn't like to feel confined under the covers. He motioned to her. "Come on, they're in the closet. I'll show you."

He headed into the walk-in with her behind him.

"Wow, this might be bigger than my last apartment." She did a slow circle as she looked around. "Also, you have a lot of suits. And shirts. And shoes."

"A well-dressed man is prepared for anything."

She gave him the eye. "I thought you rarely left your house?"

"I don't."

"Then what exactly do you think is going to happen?"

"I…yes, I see your point. I like to look presentable. Whatever I'm doing." He opened one of the drawers of the built-in dresser and extracted the first set of pajamas on the stack. He held the top out to her. "You can have the top, I'll wear the bottoms."

She took it, shook it out and held it up to herself. She looked down, presumably to check the length. "Okay, that will do."

He held his hand out toward the door. "The bathroom is all yours. It's the door next to this one. I'll change in here."

"Thanks." She hugged the pajama top to her chest as she left.

He heard her gather up her things, then the bathroom door opened and closed. He undressed, putting his shoes, belt and cuff links away before hanging up his suit and throwing his shirt and socks in the hamper.

The soft sounds of her movements in the other room filtered through. He tried not to think about her undressing.

And being just a few feet away.

He pulled the pajama pants on, then looked at himself in the full length mirror on the back of the closet door. The chain about his neck that held the amulet responsible for his daywalking ability stood out against his skin. If he left it on, she might ask about it and he didn't want to lie to her, but taking it off wasn't something he wanted to do either.

The amulet had kept him safe from the sun for so long he couldn't imagine being without it. The magic it contained had changed his life.

Much in the way Tessa was about to change it again.

He left the chain on. If she asked, he'd tell her. After everything she was doing for him, he felt safe trusting her with such a valuable secret. And maybe she wouldn't ask. She wasn't the type to pry, either.

He took a pillow and blanket from the linen cabinet that was part of the closet and went back into his bedroom to make up a bed on the leather chesterfield sofa. It sat beneath the bank of windows overlooking the back garden. It was one of his favorite places to sit and read and a rather comfortable spot, but he'd never slept there.

As he spread the blanket out, the bathroom door opened.

He turned. "How'd the top work for…"

His pajama shirt skimmed the tops of her thighs, displaying legs that were pale and gorgeously muscled and so long he lost himself staring at them. He couldn't recall the last time he'd seen so much of a woman. The expanse of alabaster skin was positively enthralling.

Tessa cleared her throat.

He picked his head up to meet her gaze, hoping he hadn't inadvertently drooled on himself. Her hair was bound in a messy knot atop her head and her face was scrubbed clean, leaving her cheeks pink. She looked like a wild creature. A forest nymph. He wasn't sure he'd ever seen a woman more beautiful.

"Hello," he whispered.

Only as the word left his mouth did he realize how inane he must sound.

She smiled. "Hi," she whispered back. She tugged at the shirt's hem, trying to lengthen it and failing. "It's a little short, but it will do."

"It looks good on you. I've never seen a woman in my clothes before." It was infinitely more arousing than he'd imagined.

"Really? Is that why your eyes are glowing? I know it's a vampire thing, and I can sense that it's strong emotion, but I can't quite pinpoint what emotion it is specifically. It's almost like your vampire reaction fogs up my ability to read you a little."

It was overwhelming desire, but he wasn't interested in sharing that. But then, he didn't have to share what he was feeling for her to know, did he? She had to been sensing some of what he was feeling. He turned away, using the prepping of his makeshift bed as an excuse to hide his chagrin. "It's not always voluntary, but one can learn to control it."

He heard rustling and glanced over his shoulder to see her climbing into his bed. It was a traditional tall bed with a heavy wood frame, and as she maneuvered under the thick down comforter, he caught a glimpse of the white cotton underwear that covered her firm backside. White cotton. Of course that's what she would wear. It was practical and unadorned and perfect. His throat went dry.

If his eyes had been glowing before, they must

be positively on fire now. He forced his head around. How was he going to spend the entire night in the same room with her? Already her soapy-clean fragrance permeated the space and in such quiet, listening to the rhythm of her beating heart was its own kind of seduction.

He closed his eyes. The image of her cotton-clad backside peeking out from under his pajama shirt appeared. He opened them back up again.

She sighed. "I wish I had my book."

He risked a look at her again. Thankfully, this time she was under the covers. "I could run down to the library and get you something. Or there's a copy of Forbes on the nightstand, but I don't imagine that would hold much interest for you." Or he could crawl in bed next to her and give her something else to do besides read.

She squinted at him. "Your eyes glow a lot."

He forced himself to get control. "It's all the…stress." That was the best he could do.

"I'll skip the magazine. I'm plenty tired and have to be up early, so it's just as well."

He nodded. "I'll get the lights then."

He strode across to the switch and turned them off, but enough moonlight snuck through the curtains for his vampire eyes to see the room as though nothing had changed. She watched him from bed, probably unaware just how well he could see her. "Good night, Tessa."

"Good night, Sebastian."

He slid beneath the blanket and settled in, throwing one arm behind his head. From the way he was positioned, he could see her perfectly. In his bed. He couldn't stop watching.

She closed her eyes and turned onto her side, her face away from him. If he lay behind her, she would mold to his body seamlessly. Spooning, they called that now. He barely remembered what it felt like to hold a woman that close.

His body ached with need to the point that physical pain bloomed in his chest. Finally, he twisted away, made himself close his eyes, and prayed for sleep.

It was the only way he was going to stay out of that bed.

Tessa stared at the wall, or what she could see of it. Valkyrie sight was good, but not as sharp as a vampire's eyes. Close, though, and the moonlight trickling in helped. She took a deep breath, then let it out slowly, trying to cleanse the emotions of the evening so that sleep was a possibility.

But sleeping when there was a half-naked vampire just steps away was not going to be easy.

Especially when that vampire was giving off waves of desire. She'd asked him about his eyes hoping he'd confess to it, but he hadn't and she'd realized a second later that he was trying very hard to control himself.

So she'd let it be. Because she was trying very hard to do the same thing.

She was glad the sight of her naked legs had distracted him when she'd come out of the bathroom. That had saved her the embarrassment of being caught staring at him. No doubt her mouth had been open and eyes wide. She knew she'd blushed.

Sebastian without his shirt was…wow. It wasn't like she hadn't seen a man's chest before. She did go to the community pool during the summers. And there was television and social media and the covers of romance novels, which she devoured in between the literary stuff librarians were expected to keep up with. But being in the same room with a half-naked man? Who had also kissed her? To the point that she'd thought parts of her would catch on fire?

That was a very different thing.

And now she was in his bed. It smelled of him, dark and spicy and sort of woodsy. Like the pages of a much-loved, leather-bound book.

He'd been in this bed. Right where she was now. Probably wearing this exact shirt.

She swallowed as an uncontrollable shiver ran through her.

Her lips parted and the urge to call him to her was so strong she pressed a hand over her mouth. No, no, no. Getting involved with him in a purely physical way would never end well. She wasn't that kind of woman anyway.

She sighed and wished Duncan were here. At least then she could snuggle his furry little butt. If he'd stay still. When he slept, he went out pretty hard. And since they'd been in Nocturne Falls, he'd taken to spending part of the night with her and part of the night with Jenna. He was probably curled up on her pillow making biscuits in her hair right now.

Tessa's eyes blinked open. She hadn't cleared bringing Duncan here, but he was her cat. And kittens needed a lot of attention. It wouldn't be fair to leave him at Jenna's when she was gone so long on her shifts for the sheriff's office.

She already knew Sebastian wouldn't like it. Look at his house. It was immaculate. But after what she was doing for him, he was just going to have to suck it up and deal with it. She wasn't going to spend an entire week away from her baby.

Not even for that ridiculously handsome man. There was only so much sacrifice she was willing to make.

Maybe she'd bring Duncan and then tell Sebastian about him after he was firmly ensconced in Chez Ellingham. The whole ask for forgiveness rather than permission thing. It wasn't her way. Her way was usually planning and by-the-book and all forms in triplicate. But what if he said no? They couldn't have that argument in front of Evangeline.

She huffed out a breath. Evangeline. The woman was under this same roof. Probably snooping around right now.

"Sebastian?" She said his name quietly, not wanting to wake him if he'd already fallen asleep.

The quickness of his reply indicated he had not. "Yes?"

There was an eagerness in his voice that surprised her. Had he been expecting her to ask him something? If so, what? She'd think about that later. "Aren't you worried that you-know-who might be riffling through your things while you're asleep?"

"She might be, but anything of importance is behind locked doors. My desk drawers and filing cabinets are locked as well."

Tessa rolled over to lay on her back. "Couldn't she pick those locks?"

"I suppose she could, if she's learned to do that. But Greaves is probably keeping an eye on her. And even if she gets into my office, she'd have to pick the locks on my desk drawers as well."

She smiled. "You're a smart man to have that double security even in your home."

He laughed softly. "You say smart, my brothers say overly cautious."

"But you're protecting them, too—and the town. I approve."

"Thank you."

They both went quiet again. Sebastian spoke a minute later. "Are you comfortable?"

"Yes. Are you?"

"Yes. This couch is surprisingly adequate as a bed. Considering what it cost, it should be."

Note to self, do not let Duncan claw the bedroom furniture. "Good. I'd feel bad if you were miserable."

"And if I was?"

She smiled up at the ceiling. His words seemed very flirty. "We'd have to figure something else out for you."

"Something else?"

"A different place for you to sleep." Like next to her in this very large bed.

Because that would lead to sleeping. Sure.

He chuckled softly. "I'm not sure how well I would sleep in that situation either."

Her eyes widened. It was like he was in her head. Vampires couldn't read minds, right? She'd never heard of that being a thing. The best she could do for a response was laugh nervously, but it came out a strangled noise that made her sound like she was choking on something. She quickly cleared her throat and changed the subject. "We should go out to dinner again tomorrow night."

"What about Evangeline?"

"You agreed she could live here for a week. I can't imagine that includes accompanying us on all the things that couples do. Like dinner, movies, walks in the park…"

"You're a brilliant woman, you know that?" She could hear the smile in his voice.

She smiled right back. "Thanks. I take it that means yes to dinner?"

"That means yes to anything you want."

Her smile widened. She'd be sure to remind him of that when she brought Duncan back to his house in the morning.

Sebastian opened the day's paper, a third cup of coffee on the table beside him. He should be in his office working, but he wasn't in the mood to crack the books just yet. Tessa's breakfast had been simple but very good. Cheese and mushroom omelets. A far greater accomplishment than Greaves could have pulled off.

Sebastian smiled. The two of them should be back soon. They'd been gone forty-five minutes already.

Evangeline still slept like the dead and would for at least four more hours. According to Greaves, she'd only just gone to bed as dawn approached.

Greaves was a light sleeper, but also a terrible snoop. For once, Sebastian was glad of it. The man had stayed up to keep an eye on her just as Sebastian had guessed he might. Because of that,

Sebastian was giving him the remainder of the day off so he could get some rest.

Sebastian's ears perked up at the sound of the mudroom door opening. It was at the far end of the house near the kitchen and led in from the garage. He set the paper aside and went to help Tessa with her things.

He met them in the kitchen and came to a sudden stop. "What is that?"

Tessa paused mid-sentence in her conversation with Greaves and turned to face Sebastian head on. "What is what?"

"That…thing in your arms."

She frowned at him. "I know you don't get out much, but do you really not know that this is a kitten?"

She held the ball of claws and fluff up so he could see it better. "See? Whiskers, a tail, fur—all the usual kitten parts."

"I know what it is. What's it doing in my house?"

She hugged it to her chest again. It mewled, a rather pitiful sound that Sebastian refused to let sway him. "Duncan is my cat and since I'm living here for the next seven days, so is he."

"No."

Her brow wrinkled. "It sounded like you said no."

"I did. I don't want that thing in here, tearing up

my house, scratching on my antiques and generally treating the whole place like his…toilet. No. The cat goes back to your sister's."

Greaves had the good sense to stay out of it. He lifted Tessa's bags. "I'll just go put these in your quarters, miss."

She shook her head. "Put them back in the car, Greaves. If Duncan goes, so do I."

Greaves stayed right where he was.

Sebastian huffed out a breath. "You can't be serious."

"Have fun explaining to Evangeline where I am."

"Tessa, please, you have to understand. Those animals are…"

"Are what?"

He grimaced and told the truth. "I don't like them."

She tipped her head. "Why?"

"Because they're—"

"You're scared of cats."

"No, I am not." Maybe a little. It was irrational, but one had chased him from the stables when he was a boy and he'd never quite gotten over it. Hugh had inherited one when he'd married Delaney, but thankfully that enormous beast seemed to sleep all day and was rarely around when Sebastian called.

"You are. I can see it. I'm sorry, but Duncan is

just a baby. He's not going to hurt you. And this is a great chance for you to get over that fear."

Sebastian crossed his arms. "You're forcing my hand. I have no choice but to agree. I find that very unfair."

She smiled. "I think that's sort of how actual marriage works. Give and take and compromise. Isn't this fun?"

"No." His good mood had fermented. "Keep it away from me."

"Duncan is a he, not an it, and he sleeps with me."

Sebastian scowled at the tiny, furry beast, instantly jealous. "On the bed? My bed?"

"Yes."

"No."

She pointed a finger at the ceiling. "Greaves, back to the car."

Sebastian threw his hands in the air. "Greaves, take her things up to my room. She and I will work this out but apparently, the animal is staying."

"Very good, sir. I'll return for the rest of Duncan's things in the car, then, miss." Greaves departed for the upstairs.

"Thank you, Greaves." Tessa looked at Sebastian and her grin widened in blatant satisfaction. "And thank you."

"Don't thank me yet. This is going to cost you."

Her smile faltered. "How so?"

His mood meant his social graces mattered less. That sense of recklessness made his body thrum with energy. "I demand a goodnight kiss every evening and good morning kiss upon waking."

She swallowed, but took a step toward him. "That hardly seems equal to having this innocent little kitten living here for the rest of the week."

"You're the one who brought up give and take. Am I the only one who should compromise then?"

"No." She gave him a skeptical look. "Fine. Two kisses a day."

"As many kisses as are required, but one will be mandatory at the beginning and end of each day."

She hugged the beast closer. "Then Duncan gets the full run of the house. And you can't complain about it."

"I absolutely can complain about it. But I shall also try to remember that as you are my fiancée, I do things to make you happy. The creature is one of those."

"His name is Duncan. Say it."

Sebastian sighed. "Duncan. Happy?"

She kissed the beast on the head. "Want to hold him?"

"Not even remotely. Put him down."

She twisted slowly back and forth, like she was rocking the beast to sleep. "His litter box isn't set up yet. He might pee on one of your fancy antiques."

Sebastian's lip curled. "That's exactly what I was—"

"I'm teasing you. Lighten up."

Greaves came back in. "I'll get Duncan's things now. Where shall I set up his box, miss?"

"In the laundry," Sebastian said.

"In the upstairs bathroom," Tessa replied. "He'll be in that bedroom most of the time. Although we should have a second box on this floor too. That one can go in the laundry room. His food and water can go here in the kitchen."

"I'll run to the Shop-n-Save and get another box this afternoon and buy some more food for him. Dry or canned?"

"Both and it has to be for kittens. He's still growing."

"Good to know. I may have to visit the pet shop in town to make sure I get the right kind. But I'm happy to do it."

"Thank you, Greaves."

"My pleasure." Greaves went out to the garage and came back a short while later with Duncan's bag of toys, his carrier, and his covered litter box.

Sebastian frowned. The rook was entirely too accommodating toward this furry nightmare. "I'd better not smell that animal's business."

Greaves raised a brow. "I imagine he feels the same way about you, sir."

Tessa snorted in laughter and gave the cat another kiss on the head.

Sebastian stared at her as Greaves left. "I cannot believe I ever thought you were a mouse."

She shrugged one shoulder. The cat swatted at a strand of her hair. "I've been underestimated many times."

"I'm sure."

"If you'll excuse me, I'm going to take Duncan up and get him settled."

"You owe me a kiss."

"I'm taking Duncan upstairs, not going to bed."

Sebastian wanted her more than he cared about what time it was. "This morning's kiss. You're one short."

She shot him a look he couldn't quite read, but her pulse increased ever so slightly. "Fine. But I'm not putting Duncan down."

"I'm not kissing you with that animal sandwiched between us."

Her brows lifted with a very *whatever* sort of expression. "I guess you'll have to wait until tonight then."

Before he could respond, she walked out of the kitchen, the cat cradled over one shoulder like a baby.

Sebastian shook his head in disbelief as she left. Thwarted by a wretched feline. Who was now going to be sharing his bedroom. What exactly had Tessa done to him to make him this addled?

Tessa held her laughter until she reached the bedroom, then let it out in one unladylike snort.

"Sorry, miss?" Greaves popped out of the bathroom, a litter scooper in one hand.

"Nothing."

He went back in, returning a second later without the scooper. "Litter box is all set up. Little Bit must be hungry, don't you think?"

"I'm sure. He can always eat."

Greaves clasped his hands in front of him. "I could take him downstairs and feed him. There were a few cans left in the supplies we picked up from your sister's, I believe."

"There were. I put that bag on the counter in the mudroom." She held Duncan out to the rook, suspecting that what he really wanted was to hold the kitten. "Here you go."

Greaves took Duncan very carefully. The rook's face broke out in an enormous smile. "He's so soft. And little. I'm afraid to hold him too tightly."

"He's pretty durable." She started unpacking her bags, which sat on the bench at the foot of the bed. "Not saying you don't have to be careful with him, but you're not going to hurt him if you're gentle."

Greaves lifted Duncan to see him eye to eye. "Hello there, little man. Welcome to the house. We're going to take good care of you."

Duncan swatted at Greaves' nose.

The rook laughed. "You want to play, do you? We'll play. I promise." He looked at Tessa. "We've never had any animals. Hunting dogs, years ago, but nothing like this." Greaves cradled Duncan against him. "I'll play with him a bit, get him fed, then make that run to the store. Have to make sure he's got everything he needs."

Tessa smiled as she shook out her clothes and laid them on the bed to be hung up. Greaves was clearly smitten. "Thank you so much."

With a nod Greaves headed for the door. He passed Sebastian on the way in.

"Was that my rook holding that animal?"

"That animal's name is Duncan. And yes." She shook her head. "You're like a dog with a bone. Duncan's not going to ruin anything or steal your breath while you sleep or—"

"Fortunately, breathing is an option for me."

Tessa narrowed her eyes. "Aren't you lucky?" She stared at the rest of her things. They were a tepid mix of navy, black and ivory. Nice. Serviceable. But Jenna was right. Boring. "I'll need a little closet space. Very little, really. And a drawer. One should do."

"Is that all you have?"

"No. The rest of my stuff is at my sister's. I didn't see the point in bringing everything. I just brought the good stuff."

One of his brows lifted with skepticism. "That's the good stuff?"

She put her hands on her hips. "I'm a librarian, not a fashion model."

"Understood, but still." He picked up one of her silk blouses. "Was this a hand-me-down from a great-aunt or something?"

She snatched it out of his hand. "I like simple, serviceable clothing. Things that don't go out of style. I can't afford to buy new things all the time. My clothes have to last and need to be classic pieces that transcend fads."

"Your new salary will be more generous."

"It can't be worse." She frowned at her clothes. Serviceable didn't really cut it anymore. Not while living in this house with all its beautiful things. She was going to look like she was on staff, not engaged to the owner. She let out a long sigh.

He made a curious expression. "You're unhappy with a better salary?"

She crossed her arms. "I'm unhappy because my things aren't acceptable for the woman who's supposed to be your fiancée. Or the dean of library studies, frankly."

He sat on the edge of the bed. "You could go

shopping if you wanted. There are places on Main Street. Women's boutiques."

"I could." But that would require money she didn't have. Her boring wardrobe would have to suffice. "Maybe later."

"Why not now?"

She lifted her gaze to his. "Because I can't afford it."

His voice was gentle and kind when he answered. "I can."

She sat on the end of the bed and stared at her clothes, laid out and waiting to be put away. "No. I don't want to spend your money."

"But I've put you in this position. It's only fair you use my money. Which, according to our ruse, would very soon be our money. And I promise you, the woman in my life would have the best I could supply her with. The complete benefit of my economic status. Please, Tessa. You're here because you're helping me. Consider this a head start on your new dean's wardrobe."

"I don't like it. It feels…unsavory."

"I understand. I'm sorry I've put you in this position, but I have."

"Only because I agreed to it." The hem on the navy skirt needed tacking again and her charcoal slacks were starting to pill. She let go of her stubbornness with a sigh. "Okay. I'll go shopping. Is there a place in town?"

Sebastian nodded. "Greaves can take you. He's going out anyway."

She stared at the bed, unable to look at him while she said what needed to be said. "I'll take the money. But this is just a loan until I get on my feet."

"All you have to do is tell them to bill me."

She lifted her head. "What's it like to be you? To have all this money and reputation and status?"

He dropped his gaze, running his finger along the fabric of the comforter. He was silent for several seconds. "If I'm honest, it's lonely."

Her heart broke a little for him. That was what she'd suspected. She stood and walked around to his side of the bed. "Not this week, though, huh?"

He laughed softly, looking at her. "No, not this week. And I have you to thank for that."

She stood there, studying him. His face was kind and open when he smiled. Very different from the face he usually wore.

"What?" he asked. "You're staring at me for reasons I can't fathom."

She touched his cheek, still smooth from his morning shave. "I was just thinking."

"About?"

"How I owe you that kiss."

A deep, predatory gleam lit his eyes. "Does that mean you're going to pay up?"

"Yes." She leaned in and did just that.

13

With Greaves and Tessa gone again, Sebastian finally headed to his office. Work had to be done. Normally it was something he looked forward to. It gave him a purpose, something that on many days felt lacking. But with Tessa around, work was the less interesting choice. With her out of the house, he might as well take up his pencil again and get something done. He smiled as he started to unlock the door.

He looked harder at the lock. There were small scratches in the brass. Like someone had tried to pick the lock and failed.

Evangeline.

He shook his head and finished the job she'd started. As he went inside, it was impossible to be upset over Evangeline's actions. Not while Tessa's kiss still lingered on his lips. It was the most pleasant feeling he could recall since…the last time they'd kissed.

Yes, his life was sadly lacking in companionship. Tessa's presence had made that markedly clear.

He settled in behind his desk and pulled out the budget for the wedding chapel. If he didn't finish this soon, Julian would be hounding him again.

Time passed as he worked. The budget didn't seem quite as egregious as he remembered, but he went at it with great intent. He scratched through some items, suggested new ones in a few other places, and the world around him fell away. All he saw were numbers and figures and dollar signs. Supply and demand. The future of Nocturne Falls.

Until needles dug into his leg.

"What the—" He jerked back in his rolling chair to see Tessa's furry beast clinging to his pant leg. He threw his pencil onto the desk. "Get off me, you foul creature."

The cat hung there, swaying on the gabardine like he wasn't sure what to do next. Then he scrunched up his eyes and let out a long, plaintive meow that sounded absolutely dreadful.

"These are Savile Row's finest, you wretched thing." Sebastian unstuck his claws and scooped him up. The little creature was soft as silk. Sebastian held him at arm's length. The cat meowed again. "Why are you crying? What do you need? I don't know how you work, but if something happens to you while you're under my care, Tessa will never forgive me. We can't have that, can we?"

The cat just stared at him.

Sebastian set him on the desk. "Stay." Then he bent to inspect his pants. They seemed to be unaffected by the attack. A tribute to fine British tailoring, no doubt.

His pencil rolled off the desk and fell to the floor beside his shoe. He looked up to find the cat pawing at the corner of his ledger. "That's enough of that now. Behave."

The animal lay down, rolled over with his feet in the air and looked at Sebastian from an upside down position.

"That's no way to view the world." Sebastian extended a finger and scratched the beast's chin.

Duncan closed his eyes for a moment, then captured Sebastian's finger between his paws and gnawed on the end, his baby teeth making no headway against Sebastian's callused skin.

"Hey, now. None of that." Sebastian pulled his hand away. "I'm the only one in this house allowed to bite people and I haven't done that in ages." Although the thought of sinking his teeth into Tessa's pretty neck had its own appeal.

The cat rolled over and got to his feet. He was no bigger than a handful and mostly fluff.

Sebastian scratched his back. The little cat turned and head butted Sebastian's hand, eyes closed in pleasure. Sebastian obliged with more chin scratches, which seemed to go over well. A ragged purr tumbled out of the animal.

Despite his best efforts, Sebastian smiled. A little. "I suppose you think we're friends now. We're not. You're a guest in this house and on a very serious probation, so watch yourself."

Duncan laid down on the corner of the ledger, curled up and closed his eyes.

"Cat. You can't sleep there. I'm working."

The kitten took a deep breath, licked his paw once, then went to sleep.

"Well, that's just perfect." But Sebastian made no move to disturb the animal. Instead he cautiously eased the papers out from under the beast and shifted everything to a more available area on the desk.

He shook his head as he went back to work, both amused and surprised at himself for *almost* liking the little creature. But Tessa clearly loved Duncan and he knew it would make her happy if he could be more tolerant of the animal. He would try. Letting the thing sleep on his desk was certainly a start. That had to be worth some sort of credit.

Sebastian fell into his work again, occasionally pausing to pet the cat or watch as his paws twitched with a dream. Did cats dream? Sebastian had no idea. The thing could be plotting world domination for all Sebastian knew.

At last, he reached the end of the budget. He wrote up a quick summary of the report, then sent a text to Julian to say he was ready to discuss it. Before Julian replied, there was a knock on his office door.

Duncan didn't budge. Apparently the cat was a sound sleeper.

Sebastian looked up. "Come in."

The door opened and Tessa poked her head in. "Just wanted to let you know we're back and—" Her gaze shifted away from his face. "Is that Duncan sleeping on your desk?"

Sebastian pressed his lips together in a stern expression. "He was pestering me so I put him somewhere I could watch him."

An uneven smile lit her face. "Pestering you. Uh-huh. Good job on the kitten watching then."

Sebastian changed the subject before she could rib him further. "Did you find anything you like?"

"Many things. Greaves is helping me take them upstairs. He also did a little shopping at the pet store while I was in the boutiques."

"What does that mean?"

"You're now the proud owner of a cat bed, a month's supply of catnip mice and a cat tree. Also, Duncan is not about to go hungry anytime soon."

"What on earth is a cat tree?"

"Let's call it something for Duncan to scratch on besides your antiques."

"Hmm. In that case, I approve."

"Good. We'll be upstairs. Bring the baby when he wakes up."

"You mean carry him? I don't—" His phone chimed. "Wait a moment." He checked the message. Julian, ready to go over the budget. "Actually, I need to go see Julian and discuss this wedding chapel business with him. Will you be all right here by yourself?"

In other words, alone with Evangeline.

"Sure. Greaves is here. How much longer is our guest likely to sleep?"

"Another hour or two, I'd think. I'll be back before then, I promise."

"Okay. But I think I'll take Duncan upstairs with me now then." She came in and picked the cat up. He stayed asleep, even as she cuddled him against her.

"He's a good sleeper."

"He's a baby. It's what they do. Play hard, sleep hard."

For a moment, Sebastian pictured her with a human child in her arms. His child. He blinked the fantasy away. It wasn't one he had a right to. "We're still on for dinner out tonight, yes?"

She looked up at him and smiled over the cat's

head. "We'd better be. You bought me a new dress today."

Tessa carried Duncan upstairs to the bedroom. Greaves had laid all her packages on the bed and was already working on putting the cat tree together.

The rustling of the box and the paper the pieces were wrapped in brought Duncan to life. He squirmed in her arms so she put him down. He ran over and started attacking the paper. She laughed. "Looks like you have a helper."

"Very good. Hello, little man." Greaves gave Duncan a scratch on the head before resuming the assembly.

"Oh, and just so you know, Sebastian's gone to talk to Julian about the wedding chapel project but said he'd be home before you-know-who wakes up."

Greaves nodded. "Thank you for letting me know." He hefted a section into place and began working the bolts through the guide holes.

"You need help with that? Looks heavy." It was much larger than she would have chosen, but when Greaves had come to pick her up, he'd insisted it was the one. After that, there was no going back. The trunk on the Rolls hadn't closed because of it and had to be held down with some packing twine. That alone probably would have upset Sebastian, but when he saw this thing in his bedroom, she was pretty sure he'd have something to say.

"No, I've got it. Being a rook means I have considerably more strength than I did when I was fully human. Thank you though."

"You're welcome. How exactly did you get to be a rook? I don't really understand what it means. Valkyries and vampires don't mix that often so I'm not fully up on all these vampire things. I suppose there's a book I could read…"

He smiled. "I'm a rook because Sebastian bit me on two consecutive nights. It's as close as a person can get to being a fully turned vampire without actually becoming one. Another bite on the third night and I would have been turned, but stopping on the second left me as a rook. This way I have the privileges of both sides. I have more strength, more speed, and sharper senses but I'm not affected by the sun either. It's given me a life far better than the one I'd imagined I'd live."

"Even taking care of Sebastian the way you do?"

"Even so." He started attaching a carpeted bed to one of the arms. "Just like Hugh's rook, I've been with Sebastian since he was human. I know the man better than anyone outside his family and I can tell you, he's one of the good ones. He can be difficult, but he bears a lot of weight on his soul."

"Because of Evangeline."

Greaves nodded. "And because he feels responsible for his family. With the death of his father, Sebastian became the Duke of Sinclair and—"

"He's a duke?" Tessa had no idea. But it made so much sense. Of everyone she'd ever known, Sebastian certainly seemed like the most likely to be nobility.

"Yes. Although I don't think the title would still hold up after so many years. But he knows it and because of that, he's taken on the care of his family. Their financial status is all thanks to his careful investments and close eye."

"Wow." She sat on the bed, crinkling the edge of one of the shopping bags.

"You'd better put those clothes away before they get wrinkled." He stiffened. "My apologies, did you want me to do that?"

"Absolutely not." This life. So different than what she'd known. She'd grown up with money, but as an adult, her own finances hadn't been so generous. Which was fine. She managed. That's what adults did. She went to the closet, got some empty hangers and went to work. But the thought of finances made her cringe at how much she'd spent and now had to repay Sebastian. At least the clothes were beautiful, well made, and much chicer than her current wardrobe. They'd serve her for a long time.

When the clothes were hung and the cat tree finished, she and Greaves watched Duncan play on it. He climbed for a bit, swatted at the dangling toys, then went into one of the cubbies and passed out.

"Well, I guess he likes it."

Greaves smiled. "A purchase well made."

"Let's hope Sebastian thinks so when he sees it."

"He'll grump and fuss, but he'll be fine."

"You know him better than I do."

"Indeed I do, but that will change." He brushed a stray carpet fiber off his white shirt and put his jacket back on. "Care for some lunch?"

She raised her brows. "I thought you couldn't cook?"

"I can't. But I have an entire binder of take-out menus and am a deft hand at ordering."

She laughed. "Got it."

They went down to the kitchen. Greaves pulled out the binder and handed it to her. "There's Italian, including pizza, Chinese, Thai, American sort of fare—wings, burgers, subs, that sort of thing. Let's see…Mummy's Diner is quite good for, well, diner food."

"That one I know is good. I had a burger there with my sister." She flipped to that menu. "I could go for a Greek salad. If there's something from there that you'd want too."

"Don't worry about me. I'm happy with the blue

plate special, whatever it is. Meatloaf, fried chicken, hot turkey sandwich. It's all good."

"You might have just talked me out of that Greek salad. What's the special today? Do you know?"

"No, but I'll call the house phone when I get there."

"Wait. You have to leave to pick this up? This isn't delivery?"

"No, miss, I'm sorry. Would you rather I stay then? I understand not wanting to be alone in the house with Evangeline. I'm sure there's something in the house we can eat."

She'd seen the fridge when she'd made breakfast. It was pitifully bare, except for the take out containers. Greaves and Sebastian lived like bachelors. Which they were. "No, I'm sure it'll be fine."

"You're worried about her." It was a statement, not a question.

Tessa shrugged. She didn't want to upset the normal routine. "She's asleep. How much trouble can she be? Go. Get us some lunch. I'll be fine."

"You're sure?"

She wasn't. "Absolutely. But let's exchange phone numbers first. Then you'll have my cell and I'll have yours."

"Very good."

She gave him her number, which he entered into

his contacts, then she took his down. "I'm going to run upstairs, check on the baby, and grab my cell phone. I'll keep it with me so I can answer as soon as you call."

"All right. I'll be quick." He headed out through the mudroom.

She went back up to the bedroom. Duncan was still fast asleep. She took her phone out of her purse only to realize she didn't really have a place to put it. A second later, she was changing into the new jeans she'd bought. Skinny jeans. Jenna would be proud. She added a cute printed top and one of the new cardigans that went with it.

She tucked the phone in her back pocket and went to check herself out in the mirror. Wow, what a difference an outfit could make. She looked less like someone's mom and more like a fun girl to hang out with. Which she totally was. She was really starting to see why Jenna had bugged her to dress more currently for so long.

She owed her sister a spa day after this was over with. Nocturne Falls had to have a spa, didn't it?

She checked on Duncan one more time, then went down to the library to peruse the books some more and see what Sebastian considered worthy of being in his collection. Her phone rang as she was looking at an impressive shelf of first editions.

"Hi Greaves. What's for lunch?"

"The special today is open-faced roast beef

sandwiches with mashed potatoes or French fries and glazed carrots. I feel it's only fair to mention they have coconut cream pie on offer today as well. It's very good, if I do say so."

"I'm in. On everything. Mashed potatoes for me with the roast beef."

"Excellent. I'll order and be home forthwith."

"I'll be waiting." She hung up and went back to the books, picking out a volume of world mythology that looked interesting.

"All alone, are we?"

Tessa's blood chilled at the sound of Evangeline's voice. She hugged the book to her chest as she turned to see the woman standing in the doorway. Blocking the exit, essentially. Tessa decided not to answer the question, countering with, "Good afternoon. I hope you slept well."

That sounded like a thing the woman of the house would say, right?

Evangeline smiled. "Your concern is touching."

"We wouldn't want you to be uncomfortable." Even though Evangeline was putting off all sorts of defensive vibes right now.

"I think Sebastian might argue with that." She strolled into the room, wearing the same silky black nightgown and feathered slippers she'd had on the night before. Apparently, she thought being a vampire entitled her to dress like an aging movie starlet. "Speaking of, where is my husband?"

Tessa bristled but did her best not to show it. She tried to think of Evangeline like a noisy patron who needed shushing. Start with tact first. With that in mind, Tessa chose her words carefully. "Sebastian should be home any moment. He had a meeting with Julian this morning."

Evangeline stopped just short of the sunbeam Tessa stood in. "And Greaves is out, too, isn't he? Probably getting you lunch. The man never did learn to cook, did he?"

A good guess or the woman had been eavesdropping. Not surprising. But her defenses seemed to be dropping now that she knew Sebastian wasn't around. "Yes, he's picking up lunch. He should also be back soon. Is there something I can help you with?"

Evangeline leaned her back against the shelves and studied her long, pointed fingernails. They were painted deep red. "I'm fine. Thank you."

Those nails were such a cliché, Tessa thought. But the fact that the woman was frustrated with something came through loud and clear.

Evangeline stretched her fingers out, admiring the polish. Or whatever. "Aren't you worried about Sebastian?"

Tessa held the mythology book in front of her like a shield, which wasn't an item valkyrie were equipped with unless they were headed into battle. Even then, it was more for show. Valkyrie were fairly invincible. That fact gave her some comfort. "Worried about him in what way?"

Evangeline stopped looking at her nails and turned her gaze to Tessa. "He's out there in all that…" She waved her hand at the light streaming through the windows and genuine fear radiated off the vampiress. "*Sun.*"

Tessa glanced toward the sunlight. It was a bright, beautiful day outside. She couldn't imagine being afraid of something so ordinary. "I guess he's one of those vampires who is immune."

Evangeline snorted. "There's no such thing as a vampire who's immune to the sun."

"Well, he is."

"He's not. None of us are."

"Oh." Evangeline wasn't lying, Tessa could tell. So how was Sebastian able to brave the daylight then? "Maybe he's…staying in the shadows."

"I suppose." Evangeline smiled. "That's a pretty cardigan you've got on." She reached out to touch the sweater, moving her hand into the sunbeam surrounding Tessa. Smoke curled off her finger and her skin started to bubble. With a soft cry, she yanked her hand back and pressed it to her chest. "Damn sun. Do you see what I mean about sunlight and vampires?"

Tessa recoiled. "Yes. Are you all right?"

"I'll heal." Evangeline hugged her hand against her body, pain and fear blocking Tessa's abilities to read anything else off her. "But Sebastian had better be careful or there will be nothing left of him. Nothing ruins a wedding like having your fiancé turned into a pile of ash."

Tessa shook her head. "Why would he go out in the sun if it's that deadly?"

Evangeline glared at her. "Do you think that was some trick I just pulled? Did you see my hand? Do you want me to show you again?"

"No. Please don't. I'm just saying Sebastian is a careful, cautious man. He wouldn't take that kind of risk."

"Well, maybe you should talk to him about it."

Tessa nodded, trying to appease Evangeline's anger. "Maybe I should. I'd hate for anything to happen to him."

Evangeline sighed and seemed to relax. "So would I. I know you two are in love. I see that now. But you must understand that I will never stop caring for Sebastian in my own way. We've been a part of each other's lives too long for me to just forget him."

"Of course."

Evangeline's gaze softened. "Please make sure he's not taking any sort of unnecessary chances."

"I will." Tessa doubted Evangeline's concern but maybe that was petty. It was possible the woman genuinely didn't want harm to come to Sebastian.

Evangeline smiled. "I know he's in good hands with you. I see the way you look at him. You love him, don't you?"

"Yes. I wouldn't have agreed to marry him otherwise." Good thing vampires couldn't read people the way valkyries could or Evangeline would know what a lie that was. Tessa cared for Sebastian, but love? That wasn't something she was ready to commit to. Yet.

Evangeline's smile dissipated and real concern filled her eyes. "If you could talk to him and let me know that everything is okay, that he's not risking death every time he steps outside of this house, I promise I will leave before the week is out so that you two can get back to your life. Dissolution papers signed."

"I can't promise he'll tell me—"

"Surely he doesn't keep secrets from you, the woman he's committed to spend the rest of his life with."

"No, of course not. I'll see what I can find out." Tessa knew as she spoke the words that she wasn't about to do anything for Evangeline. She would talk to Sebastian about him going out in the sun, but it would strictly be because Tessa wanted to be sure he was all right. If Evangeline really wanted to know that as well, she could talk to Sebastian on her own.

"Thank you. That's all I want. To know that he's

protecting himself. You should want to know that too."

"I do." Especially because Evangeline was reading very truthfully. She was genuinely concerned about Sebastian. Probably because if anything happened to him, her constant flow of cash would dry up.

Evangeline leaned in conspiratorially, as though they'd just become friends. Which they had not. "Make sure he's not relying on cheap magic to protect him. I lost a good friend in Paris that way. Went up like a bonfire." She shook her head and sniffed. "Terrible way to go. I wouldn't wish it on my worst enemy."

Tessa grimaced, an image of Sebastian on fire flashing through her mind. "I'll keep that in mind." Just like she'd continue to ponder Evangeline's curiousness about Sebastian's well-being.

"Miss? I'm home." Greaves voice rang out from the other side of the house.

Tessa swallowed, thankful for the interruption. "My lunch is here. If you'll excuse me."

"Of course. I'll be in the theater for the rest of the day. Greaves told me about it last night and I can't resist. It's not often you get a theater to yourself so I'm going to indulge and catch up on some movies. That'll keep me out of your hair for a while, too. I'm sure it must be a huge bother having me here."

"It's no bother, really."

"All the same, I have movies to watch." With a little nod of her head, Evangeline left.

Tessa stared after her, the fiery image she'd conjured up still lingering. Why would Sebastian go into the sun if it could kill him? The answer was, he wouldn't. Sebastian wasn't the type to take chances like that, which meant he must have a way to protect himself when he was outside. Curiosity burned within her. She had to know. After all, she cared about him and whatever happened between them after this, she knew they'd remain friends.

Unless he wasn't around to be friends with.

As Evangeline disappeared out of sight, the urge to protect Sebastian strengthened in Tessa. What on earth was Evangeline up to? She wanted to know that as much as she wanted to know how Sebastian didn't go up in flames during daylight hours.

What Tessa did know was that if Evangeline was headed to the theater, she wouldn't be in her room.

Tessa went upstairs, straight into the guest room. She stood at the door, filled with the sort of bravery she hadn't felt since her days at battle camp.

She stepped into the room. Evangeline's things were everywhere. Neatness wasn't high on her priority list apparently. Tessa had no idea what she was looking for, but there had to be some clue in here as to Evangeline's true motives.

She found Evangeline's purse. If the woman was hiding something, it might be in there. But a quick riffle through determined the handbag held nothing but the usual stuff. Tessa glanced toward the door every minute or so, hoping Evangeline really was ensconced in a good movie.

Tessa stood and looked around the room, trying to think like a vampire. A traveling vampire.

Her gaze shifted to the suitcases. There were three of them in descending sizes, matching hard shells on rolling wheels. Sleek black carbon. Very modern. The largest one looked big enough to hold a person.

Tessa went closer. Did Evangeline ever use it to take shelter from the sun? In a pinch, it might do. She stared at the thing, wondering what else the suitcases might be used to hide.

She stuck her head out of the room to look for Evangeline. No sign of her.

Tessa grabbed the big suitcase, unzipped it and had a look. The bag was lined with charcoal nylon printed with the company's logo. And it was empty.

She moved on to the medium one with the same result. Nothing inside. With another check for Evangeline, Tessa unzipped the smallest one, probably a carry on. It was empty too.

She sighed in frustration and was about to zip it back up, when something white caught her eye.

The edge of a piece of paper.

It stuck out from a hidden zipper in the lining. Tessa ran her fingers over that part of the nylon. There was definitely something under it.

She released that zipper and freed the paper caught in it. Then she reached in and pulled out a thin sheaf of papers. They all had dates scrawled on them. A span of the last ten years or so. And each paper held a copy of a newspaper article that had been clipped from the Nocturne Falls Tombstone.

Every article was about something happening in town. Many of them were about the charity events that Sebastian had told her about. One showed the dedication of the new blood bank. Another the opening of a business. But all of them had two things in common. They were all accompanied by pictures.

And all the pictures had Sebastian in them.

Sebastian's meeting with Julian went well. His brother was in an odd mood. Almost contemplative, which wasn't a state Sebastian was used to seeing Julian in. Whatever the reason, it had made Julian easier than usual to talk to and they'd agreed upon a budget in less an hour, which was probably a family record.

Nocturne Falls was about to get its first wedding chapel. Technically, it was already operational, but once the grand opening took place, it would be in full swing. New businesses were always good for the town, and while Sebastian had his doubts about the necessity of this one, Julian felt strongly that it would succeed.

Sebastian hoped that was true, but with the budget done, his part was over. It was Julian's to deal with now.

Sebastian pulled into his driveway, past the

main entrance and into the first garage. He locked the Aston Martin, a habit even though the car was inside, and went into the house.

He heard Tessa and Greaves in the kitchen. He passed through the mudroom and joined them. Both had slices of custard pie in front of them and a Mummy's Diner shopping bag sat on the other counter. "Don't tell me you're having pie for lunch?"

"No," Tessa said. "We had actual food first."

Greaves tipped his head toward the refrigerator. "There's a steak sandwich in the icebox if you're hungry."

Sebastian glanced at their empty take-away containers. "What did you two have?"

"Open-faced roast beef sandwiches," Tessa answered. "They were so good. That diner is a winner."

"It's very popular with tourists and locals. We order from there often enough." Sebastian checked the floor. "Where is that small furry thing you like to call baby?"

She grinned. "He's upstairs. Possibly sleeping. Possibly shredding your ties." She shrugged. "Hard to say."

He frowned at her. "I believe Duncan and I have come to an understanding. If he shreds those ties, it's at his own peril." He gave her his sternest expression. "If I have to banish him to the guest house, I will."

She laughed, then rolled her eyes. "I wish you could banish someone else out there."

A sense of concern filled him. "Did something happen while I was gone?"

"Nothing major. I'm just making conversation." She shot a quick look at Greaves, then went back to her pie.

Sebastian got the sense that she wanted to talk but not in front of the rook. "I have a few things to finish up in my office. Tessa, when you're done with your pie, come see me."

"I'm done now. I'm stuffed." She closed the clamshell container it was in. "I'll save the rest for later."

"I'll clean up and put things away," Greaves offered. "You two go talk."

"Thanks." She smiled up at Sebastian, but something darker lingered in her eyes. "To the office, then?"

He grunted a response, his mind already calculating what Evangeline might have done.

She walked with him. "Everything go all right with Julian?"

"Very well. We came to an agreement on the budget. There's a lot of heavy lifting yet to do, but that's on him."

"Are you worried he won't get it done?"

Sebastian unlocked the door. "No. When it comes to his pet projects he makes them happen.

Despite my distaste for my brother's Casanova ways, I must admit that when he sets his mind to something, he accomplishes it. Unfortunately, I believe that's his approach to women as well."

"He probably hasn't met the right one yet."

Sebastian pushed the office door open for her. "How would he know? He doesn't keep any of them long enough to find out."

"That could be a problem."

He went in behind her, then shut the door and locked it so they wouldn't be interrupted. "What didn't you tell me in the kitchen?"

She turned, and took one of the chairs across from his desk. "I'm not sure where to start."

"The beginning is always the best place."

She laughed softly. "I suppose it is." Then she sighed and her smile disappeared.

Instead of going behind his desk, he sat next to her. "Did Evangeline do something to you? Threaten you? Because I will not stand for that."

Tessa waved her hand. "No, nothing like that. But she did get me thinking about something. It might not be a bit of a personal matter."

"What? You can ask me anything."

She folded one hand over the other, her fingers tracing the scar on her knuckles with the sort of absentmindedness that told him that scar had been there a long time. "How is it that you can go out into the sun and not be harmed?"

The question took him back. That wasn't what he'd thought she was going to ask at all. Something about his past with Evangeline, yes, but not this. "I...just can."

Her mouth bunched up on one side. "That's not the truth."

He sighed. He'd thought about telling her if she asked, but meeting with Julian had reminded him that the secret wasn't his alone. "It's not something I'm supposed to share with you. Or anyone."

She nodded slowly. "I see. And that's fine. You don't owe me."

He made a noise deep in his throat. "Except that I do. Can I ask why you're so curious?"

"Well..." She glanced at the windows. It was one of those bright winter days with not a cloud in the sky. "I realized today how dangerous it can be for your kind. Evangeline accidentally put her hand into the sun today and it was awful. Smoke and blisters on her skin. I swear she would have burst into flames if it had touched her a second longer."

"She would have."

Tessa shook her head and grimaced. "She was worried about you being out there, but seeing that made *me* worry for you. And I'll probably keep worrying every time you go out during daylight."

"The only thing Evangeline worries about is me not being around to pay her bills."

"That's what I assumed as well. I can tell you she read true during our conversation."

He studied her. Concern bracketed her eyes. It was very sweet and a little touching. "You don't need to worry about me. I promise. That's all I can say."

She nodded and looked away, her expression less than convinced. "I understand you not telling me. I know I'm not anything to you, except a soon-to-be-employee, but I like to think we've at least become friends. I don't have a lot of those and I can't help but care about you."

"I care about you too." More and more every day. "I'd like to think we're more than just employee and employer. After this, how can we not be?" Indecision warred within him. He wanted to tell her, to stop her from worrying, but his family's secret was a secret for a reason. The amulets that protected them could very easily be used against them. Not that Tessa would ever use them against him. She just wasn't the type. "All I can tell you is that I'm not in any danger."

Her mouth pulled taut into an unhappy line. "You say that, and you read true, but I hope whatever reassurance you have that you're safe wasn't given to you by someone who wasn't as truthful."

"It wasn't." He hesitated. "I will give you this much. I have the help of some magic. Old and very trustworthy magic. Does that make you feel better?"

She shrugged with no real commitment. "I guess."

"You don't put much stock in magic?"

"I'm a valkyrie. I have magic of my own so that's not the issue. I just know that magic can be counterfeited. It can also seem powerful for a short time then fade away. Have you been using this magic awhile?"

"Yes. We all have." Well, that was more than he'd meant to say. "Bugger."

She stared at him, slightly amused. "I wasn't trying to get your secret out of you, I'm sorry. Just a reassurance that you're not taking unnecessary risks."

"Don't worry about it. I trust you. And you don't know the half of it, so—"

She squinted at him. "It's that amulet you wear around your neck, isn't it?"

"Bloody hell." He shoved a hand through his hair. "Yes, but you can't tell a soul."

She grinned. "Or what?"

He couldn't imagine her telling anyone, but if she did, it could be ruinous. "You'll end up on my grandmother's black list and you do not want that. She'll force me to fire you. At the very least."

Tessa's smile disappeared. "You shouldn't have told me that was it."

"If I'd said it wasn't the amulet, you would have seen I was lying."

"I won't tell anyone. I swear on my sword."

"You have a sword?"

She scrunched up her nose like she'd just revealed something she hadn't meant to. He knew the feeling. She sighed. "All valkyries do."

"So you must know how to use it."

She nodded reluctantly. "I do."

The thought of her wielding a sword seemed very out of character, even if she was a valkyrie. Sebastian pictured her with a medieval blade, a fierce look on her face and a suit of whatever kind of armor a valkyrie might wear.

It was rather erotic.

He cleared his throat. "Do you still train, then?"

Her gaze took on a distant, haunted look. "No. Typically valkyries do—my sister does all the time—but I've sort of put that life behind me."

This side of her intrigued him. Especially since she seemed to want nothing to do with it. "Why? It's who you are."

"Being born valkyrie doesn't define me. I've chosen a different path, that's all."

Now it felt like she was the one holding something back, but he let it slide. If she wasn't ready to tell him the truth, so be it. They didn't owe each other their deep, dark secrets. Although he had told her about the promise to Evangeline's father. "Did you bring it with you?"

"My sword?"

"Yes."

She crossed her arms. "It seems we both have a secret."

"I'd say fair enough, but you know mine." And she seemed to be keeping two: one about the sword and one about her past.

"Only because I guessed it."

He gave her a look. "You're enjoying this, aren't you?"

"A little."

He sighed. "Fine. Don't tell me. I'll figure it out."

"You won't. But enjoy trying."

"I believe I will." He glanced toward the door. "Where is Evangeline, by the way?"

"In the theater. She said she wanted to catch up on movies and stay out of my way."

Sebastian frowned. "She really said that?"

Tessa nodded. "And she meant it, too. As far as I know, she's still in there."

"Maybe the years have softened her a little."

"You'd know better than I but I'd say she really has been missing you."

His brows pulled together. "What makes you say that?"

She traced a pattern on the arm of the chair.

"Well..." she sighed. "I did something today I'm not super proud of."

Now that was surprising. "What?"

Her mouth bunched up on one side. "I snooped in Evangeline's room."

It was so unexpected, he barked out a laugh. "What? You? Why, Miss Blythe, how positively criminal." He laughed again when her cheeks went red.

She put her hands on the arms of the chair. "It's not funny."

"It's hilarious. Find anything interesting?"

"Actually, I did. Photocopies of newspaper articles from the Tombstone. Some of them may have been online stories that she printed out." She waved her hands like that wasn't important. "Anyway, all of the articles had pictures and every single picture had *you* in it." She jabbed a finger at him. "She's been checking up on you. Seeing what you're doing. She misses you."

"Maybe." He wasn't convinced. "She might also be trying to estimate how much I'm worth these days."

"Then why make copies of the pictures?" Tessa shook her head. "She wants to be able to see you."

"Good point. Doesn't seem like something she'd do, though."

"Well, like I said, you know her better than I do." Tessa looked over at his desk. "I should let you get back to work."

"I'm done. Finishing that budget and seeing Julian were all I really needed to do today."

"So what are you going to do until dinner?"

An idea had begun forming when she'd mentioned the sword. "I'm so glad you asked."

This was a room Tessa remembered from the tour. It was hard not to remember a space this big. Also, what house had a gym with an area set up especially for fencing?

The door swung open and Sebastian walked in, looking impressive in his fencing whites. They set off his dark eyes and hair and the gleam of the mask tucked beneath his arm gave him an air of debonair danger. He grinned, lighting his face in a way that sucked the air from her lungs. "Ready to duel?"

But his handsomeness did nothing to quell her nerves. "I-I guess. This isn't the kind of sword fighting I know."

"That's all right," Sebastian said. "I'll show you the basics. I have a feeling you'll pick it up quickly."

Her nerves wound tighter. She squeezed her

hands together. "I don't know. I'm not much for fighting."

"It's not really fighting. It's more of a sport. A game, really." He narrowed his brows. "Either way, fencing can't be that unusual a thing for a valkyrie to do."

"No." But the last time she'd held a sword, things had gone very badly. Not so much because of the sword, but because of her temper. That was why she did everything possible to live a life where her temper was never riled. A simple, plain, boring life.

That was the price she was willing to pay to never experience another day like the one that had shown her who she really was. And how much damage she was capable of doing.

Greaves pushed through the doors of the gym, arms filled with white clothing. "I brought the jackets that seemed the closest in size, miss. We'll find one that fits."

"Oh, good." She sighed. She couldn't get out of this without explaining her past to Sebastian. Or making herself look silly for not wanting to try something most people would probably think was fun. Sebastian obviously did. And she liked him too much to want him to see either of those things. Plus, what if she told him the truth and he decided she was unfit to be around the students at the academy?

No. This was something she had to keep to herself. She pasted on a happy expression as Greaves held up one of the fencing jackets. "That looks small."

"It has to fit snugly. Loose fabric could hinder your movement and get caught on a foil. Give it a try. Step into the croissard, then put it on like a regular jacket."

"So that strap goes between my legs?"

He nodded and his face went a little red. "It's so the jacket protects the delicate bits."

"I see." She took off her cardigan and stepped one foot through the loop, then put her arm in and shrugged the jacket on. It wasn't a perfect fit, but it was close. "There's no way this would fit you, Sebastian. Who did this belong to?"

"One of the Harmswood students. We have a fencing team and I used to tutor some of the students here."

"Used to?"

He wiped a smudge off the face plate of his helmet. "I stopped a few years ago."

"Why?" Greaves helped her zip the jacket, which made it fit even closer.

Sebastian shrugged. "There is no real reason. I just...didn't want to."

Greaves grunted. "Because you're a recluse, that's why."

She expected Sebastian to refute that, but he just sighed.

"I suppose that's part of it." He lifted his brows. "It's easier not to engage sometimes."

The truth of the words struck her. "I get that. I really do."

Greaves handed her one of the masks. "To protect your pretty face and neck."

"Thank you. You sure I'm going to be all right in my jeans?" Sebastian was fully kitted up, making her wonder why she wasn't.

Sebastian nodded and answered her. "For one thing, I promise to go easy on you. I certainly don't want to hurt the new dean of library studies. The only real target area is the torso anyway. For another, if you like it and want to spar again sometime, we'll make sure you have knickers and everything."

"All right." There wasn't going to be a next time, that much she knew already.

"Greaves, you have gloves for her? We don't want to add another scar to those knuckles."

She froze for a second, then bent her head and put the mask on, covering her face as fast as possible. Why she'd assumed he hadn't noticed the scar on her hand, she had no idea. It wasn't like she'd done anything special to conceal it. Maybe it had been wishful thinking that he hadn't seen it. The stupid thing was enough of a reminder for her.

She didn't want it to become a source of questions, too.

Greaves handed her a pair of gloves and she yanked them on, happy to cover the mark left by another's blade. The mark that had driven her to nearly kill.

"Ready?" Sebastian asked.

"I guess so."

Sebastian put his mask on. "Greaves, our foils."

The rook retrieved them from a case on the wall, returning with two gleaming blades. He handed one to her, then one to Sebastian.

Sebastian slashed the narrow blade through the air a few times as if testing it. The metal sang as it cut the air, a sound she hadn't heard in person in a very long time. The foil's song was higher pitched than that of the weapons the valkyrie and berserkers used, but it was familiar all the same.

She shivered and shoved back at the memories threatening to invade. "What first?" She needed to do something besides stand there.

"Watch. I'll show you the opening moves." Sebastian went through a series of stances and showed her how to attack and lunge and parry. He demonstrated how to feint and disengage.

Despite her trepidation, she concentrated and did her best to understand and remember. It was only mildly similar to what she'd been taught in battle school. It seemed to her that the best comparison of the two styles of fighting would be a junkyard mutt and a show dog. Her style was designed to get things done brutally and efficiently, while his style was all about sportsmanship and elegant skill. She had been trained to go for the kill, damn the finesse, and she had no idea how to use that training now to engage in friendly swordplay.

It only marked how different—and brutal—her training had been. This was a sport. Her training had been about life and death.

Sebastian pulled upright. "What do you think? Does it make sense or was that too much too fast?"

She shook her head, the confines of the mask impeding her peripheral vision a bit. "No, I think I got the gist of it."

"All right, then." He lifted his weapon. "Greaves, you're refereeing. Make sure she doesn't demolish me."

The rook smiled. "Very good, sir."

They took their opening stances.

"Come at me, Tessa, and I'll show you how to cease parry and circular parry."

"Okay." She tentatively stuck the foil toward him.

"Oh now, you can put more effort into it than that. Come at me. Like you're angry."

She hesitated, cocking her head to the side. "But I'm not." And she didn't want to be.

"Pretend I've changed my mind about giving you the job."

"I don't know…"

"And that while you were out, I got fed up with Duncan and took him to the pound."

"You wouldn't dare." A surge of anger filled her and she lunged the way he'd demonstrated, going straight for his chest.

He swept his blade around, spinning hers away. "Very good! That was a circular parry."

She straightened and let her blade hang at her side as she took a deep, calming breath. "I don't want to—"

"What's going on in here?" Evangeline walked in, finally wearing street clothes instead of lingerie. Not that her street clothes were that much more modest. Skintight jeans, a low-cut black lace shirt embellished with small crystals and knee-high black leather boots. She looked like a very modern vampire, sleek and dangerous and, Tessa admitted reluctantly, sexy.

Sebastian pulled his mask off. "Fencing. Did it look like something different?"

Greaves snorted.

Tessa pulled off her mask too. "I thought you were watching movies."

"The last one just ended and I'm tired of sitting. Plus this looks like more fun." She put her hands on her hips. The burned one was completely healed. "I want to play."

"We were just finishing." Tessa shook her hair

out. She was happy to be done. She wasn't keen on the way fencing made her feel. Evangeline's interruption gave her the perfect excuse to take a breather. She held her foil toward the woman. "Here you go."

Evangeline didn't take it, sticking out her lip instead. "And here I thought we'd get a chance to fight for our man." She looked directly at Tessa, her eyes sparking with challenge. "Unless you don't think he's worth defending."

"Of course he is." A frisson of valkyrie ire traveled through Tessa with the speed of light, sending a fresh bolt of energy down her spine. The jolt startled her, but the anger wasn't misplaced. Evangeline was a real pain in the keister whose only real skill seemed to be wearing tight clothes and pushing people's buttons. As much as Tessa hated to fight, this was the perfect controlled opportunity to put the woman in her place, something that should have already been done.

But Tessa wasn't going to be the one to do it. Not if her freshly hatched plan went off like she thought it would. She pulled her mask back on. "One fast bout."

Sebastian's brows lifted but he nodded at Greaves. "Get Evangeline in a jacket."

15

"I don't know about this." Sebastian had not expected Tessa to agree to Evangeline's provocative request, and while he was flattered that she had, he couldn't help but sense some tension in her. He didn't want her doing something with which she was uncomfortable.

"Afraid I'm going to hurt your fiancée?" Evangeline cooed.

"Frankly, yes. I don't trust you."

She put a hand to her throat. "I'm wounded."

Tessa snorted. "Not yet you're not. Let's do this."

Sebastian shot Tessa a look. "You're sure?"

She nodded but with her mask on, it was impossible to read her eyes.

If she was afraid of Evangeline, she wasn't showing it. He doubted Evangeline would do anything to Tessa in his presence, but that didn't

226

mean she was harmless. If Tessa was worried, it would be understandable. Evangeline had a rather intimidating personality.

But considering how he'd had to prod Tessa to get her to attack him, he wondered if there was something more that made her hesitant to be the provocateur. Based on their conversation in his office, he'd say it was something from her past.

Something to do with that scar she was always running her fingers across.

He'd never been well acquainted with a valkyrie before but she was nothing like what he'd expected. Certainly nothing like what he knew of her sister, the deputy. Tessa wasn't eager to fight, not quick to anger, and certainly not a fan of confrontation.

Suddenly, Tessa seemed very much like a woman who chose control as a method of self-preservation rather than because she was just naturally a pacifist. What had happened to her that she deemed it necessary to rein in her life this way?

Greaves finished helping Evangeline into a jacket and gloves and was handing her a mask.

Sebastian got his attention with a nod. "Greaves, we'll both referee this one."

Greaves nodded back, clearly understanding this wasn't just an ordinary bout. There was no chance he wasn't keenly aware this was another of Evangeline's games, but Sebastian wasn't about to tell Tessa what to do and he certainly wasn't about to forbid her to do anything.

She was a grown woman. If she wanted to do this, that was her decision. And one he would unquestionably respect.

He would, however, do whatever he could to make sure she wasn't hurt in any way. He mapped out the rules as Greaves equipped Evangeline with a foil, speaking very distinctly in her direction. "The torso is the only viable target. Any other touches or hits will not result in points. Blatant hits to other parts of the body will result in disqualification. First to three legal touches wins. Do you understand?"

"Yes." Evangeline rolled her eyes, then pulled her mask on and faced Tessa. "This will be over quickly if we're only going to three."

Sebastian wasn't aware of Evangeline ever having any training in this particular discipline, but she seemed awfully confident. Of course, that was her standard approach to life. He'd never known her to assume she was going to lose at anything.

But this sort of assumption when she had a weapon in her hand? He didn't like that at all. "This is a game of skill and turns, Evangeline. Not brute force and damage."

She looked over at him as she stepped onto the piste, the strip that defined the boundaries of the action. She splayed a hand over her heart. "Brute force? Damage? What on earth do you think I'm about?"

He knew exactly what Evangeline was about. That was the problem. "Tessa, a moment please."

She walked to him and lifted her mask. "Yes?"

"You don't have to do this."

"I know. I want to."

"She can't be trusted."

The right corner of Tessa's mouth lifted. "I know that too. Don't worry. I can handle anything she dishes out. *Anything.*" There was a dark fire in her eyes that made him suddenly wonder if Evangeline was the one he should be worried about.

Desire coiled through him at the thought of Tessa as the dangerous one. He smiled and shook his head. "All right."

He backed away as Tessa returned to the mat to face Evangeline. The woman he'd spent his life taking care of and the woman who could take care of herself. The contrast wasn't lost on him.

Evangeline waved her foil at Tessa. "How nice that Sebby's worried about you, but we're just going to have a fun little match, aren't we, Theresa?"

"Tessa," the valkyrie corrected brusquely.

Greaves snuck a look at Sebastian. He shook his head in response. It wasn't a tone either of them had heard her use before, but Sebastian couldn't blame her. Evangeline knew very well what Tessa's rightful name was. The game play had begun.

"How silly of me to forget. Sorry, Tess." Evangeline tested the tip of her foil against her glove, bending the whip-thin metal into a curve.

Tessa took her position perfectly, proof that she was not only an able student but a fast learner with a slant toward perfection. "Tess-AH."

"Tess-ah," Evangeline mimicked. "My apologies. Small details like that don't always stick in my head."

She was attempting to rile Tessa, but Sebastian couldn't tell if it was working, because the masks hid the women's eyes, making it impossible to read either of them. But Evangeline was certainly riling *him* with her little jabs.

Perhaps Evangeline had some natural proclivity toward fencing. She certainly knew how to cut a person with words. He'd been on the receiving end of her verbal sparring for years.

Evangeline took her spot, approximating an opening stance with as much precision as a chain saw being used to trim topiary. Tessa, on the other hand, looked like she'd been fencing all her life.

Pride spiked in Sebastian. The valkyrie had style and grace. Two of the many things Evangeline lacked.

Greaves stood at the center of the piste. He glanced at both of the women. "Since you are already en-garde, we will proceed. Are you ready?"

Both of them nodded.

He nodded back and stepped off the strip. "Fence!"

Tessa inched forward, cautious and definitely anticipating whatever Evangeline might do. It was a good call, since Evangeline came out with a thrust.

Tessa defended with the circular parry Sebastian had last demonstrated. He smiled and nodded, his pride in her growing.

Evangeline retreated, swatting wildly with her sword.

Tessa feinted left, then quickly jabbed Evangeline in the ribs on the right side.

"Halt," Greaves called. "Point to Tessa. Back to your starting positions."

"Point? What? How?" Evangeline pulled off her mask. "I can't see in this thing." She tossed it away. "I'm not wearing that. It's messing up my hair anyway."

Sebastian narrowed his eyes. "You must wear it. It's for your own protection."

She fluttered her lids as she rolled her eyes. "We're playing a game. Neither one of us needs protection. Especially when the only spot we're trying to hit is below the neck and above the belly button. Right, Tessa?"

Tessa eased her mask off. "I suppose."

"See?" Evangeline said. "Tessa doesn't want to wear a mask either."

"She didn't say that." Sebastian looked at his lovely pretender. Her face was aglow with exertion and perhaps a little frustration. "Do you want to wear the mask?"

She shrugged half-heartedly. "I'm okay either way."

"Good," Evangeline interjected. "No masks."

"Then this bout is over." Sebastian put his hands on his hips. "This is my gym. My house. What I say goes."

Tessa lifted her eyes to him. "I'm fine with it and I'd like to continue."

He shook his head. "It's not your call to make. Either one of you could accidentally injure the other. I won't be responsible for that."

Evangeline heaved out a sigh. "You're such a spoil sport, Sebby."

"Really," Tessa said. "It's okay. We'll be careful, won't we, Evangeline?"

Evangeline nodded. "Oh, yes, absolutely."

Sebastian pinched the bridge of his nose. "I don't like this."

Greaves raised his brows. "Should we continue? This is highly irregular."

"In many ways," Sebastian growled. "Yes, continue."

At least this way he could watch Evangeline's eyes and expression.

Greaves got them into place again, and a second later, proclaimed, "Fence."

Evangeline advanced slowly this time, her tongue protruding slightly from between her lips. It was a look he knew, one she adopted when she was concentrating. He'd found it adorable at one time. Now it just reminded him of days gone by, wasted at the altar of duty.

Tessa's face, however, was pure warrior. Her thousand-yard stare and the steely set of her jaw surprised him for a moment, but then he realized he was seeing her in her truest form. She was a valkyrie, trained for battle. Even if her weapon was a foil and the battle was merely defeating an overconfident vampiress with a penchant for manipulation.

It was a rather stirring sight.

Evangeline poked at Tessa, who easily sidestepped and took the opening to plant the point of her foil in the center of Evangeline's chest.

"Halt," Greaves called. "Second point to Tessa."

Evangeline let out a loud, exasperated sigh. "That's not fair. I didn't have a chance to defend myself."

Sebastian crossed his arms. "That's fencing, Evangeline. You must be diligent about every move."

She made a face, but got back into position.

Tessa did the same and Greaves called "Fence" once again.

This time, Tessa attacked first with a tentative lunge. Not much of an effort. Maybe testing Evangeline or trying to prod her to strike back and leave herself open. Evangeline swatted the foil away with an easy parry.

Then she snapped the foil through the air and caught Tessa squarely on the side of the head.

Tessa grabbed her ear and went down on her knees, cringing in pain. She hissed out a breath as she dropped her foil.

"Halt," Greaves cried. "Halt!"

"Bloody hell, Evangeline. You did that on purpose." Sebastian charged forward, his hands on Tessa the instant he was beside her. "Are you all right? Let me see." He looked over his shoulder at Evangeline, anger boiling in his gut. This was exactly what he'd been afraid Evangeline would do. "No apology? Nothing to say for yourself? You'll never change, will you? Get out. I'm done with you."

She dropped her foil to the piste and yanked her gloves off. "You throw me out and I'll never sign those dissolution papers."

"Out of my sight now. I'll deal with you and your foolish demands later. Greaves, remove her if she doesn't start toward the door immediately."

Greaves headed for Evangeline without waiting, and took her by the arm.

Sebastian turned back to Tessa as Evangeline's protests faded with Greaves efforts. "I'm so sorry. Let me see your ear."

The door closed behind them and the gym grew quiet.

She moved her hand. A welt marred her fair cheek and her ear was red, but there was no blood that he could see or smell. For that much he was grateful. He had no doubt the scent and sight of Tessa's blood would enflame desires that had no place here.

He sat on the piste beside her and moved a strand of her hair out of the way, her cheek like satin beneath his fingers. "How badly does it hurt?"

She shrugged one shoulder, her breathing as steady as her pulse. Both of which surprised him. "I'll live."

He leaned in and feathered a gentle kiss over the mark, then tipped his head against hers trying to quell the anger still roiling in his gut. "I'll throw her out. She hit you on purpose. I don't care what she says about signing the papers."

"Yes, you do." She leaned away from him. "And you should." She smiled, a small, understanding expression that made him feel undeserving. "But I'm glad you stood up to her. You need to do that

235

more often, I think. Show her you mean business. And what you're capable of."

He studied her, amazed that the bright red mark cutting her cheek did nothing to diminish her beauty. "You could have taken her, couldn't you?"

Tessa glanced away and shrugged. "Maybe, maybe not. I'm out of practice."

He picked up the foil she'd dropped. "And this isn't your kind of weapon, I know." He pushed the blade away, the desire to see her valkyrie sword strong in him, but now wasn't the time to ask her about that.

"No, it's not. I'm not much on any kind of weapon, really."

He pulled her gloves off and then held her hands in his, rubbing his thumb over the scar. "How did you get this? Please tell me."

She swallowed and a deep shuddering sigh passed through her. A few long moments later, she spoke. "I was sixteen. My third year at battle camp. All valkyrie and berserkers spend their summers there as soon as they turn fourteen."

She shook her head. "I was…full of myself. And I guess with reason. I'd won every tourney in my age group the last two years and that summer seemed to be shaping up to be more of the same. I lived to spar. I took on every comer. I even bested one of the visiting instructors. Fighting was my life."

That was the last thing he'd expected to hear. "Really?"

She laughed bitterly. "Yes. There was talk of my becoming an instructor. And more talk of moving me into the Ragnarok Guard, the contingent of valkyries and berserkers who go into battle all over the world wherever assistance is needed, with intentions of grooming me for a commander position."

He looked at her with this very impressive new information and saw her very clearly as the warrior she was. "So what happened?"

"One of the berserker commanders sent their best to meet me in a match. He was good. My equal, it was whispered to me. But Varren was a year older and immense. A mountain of a man even at seventeen."

"I knew who he was, had seen him fight. I was thrilled to get a shot at him." She flattened her hand on the mat and stared at the scar. "For several minutes, we tested each other. Then I went at him, ready to do some damage and make him know my name. We fought hard. I knocked him down. He was on his feet instantly and retaliated. That's when he drew first blood, slicing me across the knuckles."

She balled her hand into a fist. "It was like something broke inside me. My rage took over. The idea that someone had dared to draw my blood…"

She took a slow inhale. "They had to pull me off him. I almost killed him. Would have, I guess. The berserkers, they say they experience something like what I felt when they're in battle. Blind fury. They welcome it. It's what makes them invincible. But it made me feel like I'd lost myself."

She sniffed and bent her head. "Like I was a monster."

A small, dark spot appeared on the knee of her jeans and he realized she was crying. He took her hand. "Oh, Tessa. I'm so sorry. I can't imagine—"

"You shouldn't have to. No one should. It was awful. I lost control and it almost cost Varren his life." She looked up at him, eyes wet. "I never want to feel that way again."

"Which is why you work so hard to control yourself."

She nodded. "I might have been born a valkyrie and that's not something I can change, but I don't want that to define who I am." She pulled her hand out of his. "Not with this...thing inside me."

"But you didn't lose control today."

She got to her feet. "Because I work at it. I'm always working at it."

He stood beside her. "I'm sorry I made you fence. That must have been uncomfortable for you."

She shrugged. "You didn't make me. I chose to participate."

"Did you also choose to test Evangeline?"

She made a face. "You figured that out, did you?"

He nodded. "It was clear how much more skilled you are than she. Like watching a...kitten and a tiger. You scored twice against her so easily. Why didn't you just take the third point and end it?"

She tipped her head back. "Because Evangeline wouldn't have been satisfied with that. Would she?"

"No. Losing to you would have pushed her to do worse."

"And I wanted to see what she'd do. And how you'd react."

"You were testing me." His brows lifted. "Did I pass?"

"I was hoping you'd stand up to her, and you did. And it was a better alternative to her losing to me, because then we'd be wondering what she'd try next."

"She'll still try something." He grunted, "Which is why I'm calling this charade over."

"Before it's finished?"

"She *hurt* you."

Tessa's fingers coasted over the welt on her cheek. "In an hour or two, this will be gone. Don't let this be the reason you don't get closure. Evangeline needs to sign those papers so you can be free."

"You really want me to let her stay? To keep up this game?"

"Until it's truly done, yes."

He let out a long sigh. "All right. But you tell me differently and I will personally escort her to the town limits."

Tessa smiled. "I appreciate that."

He leaned in and kissed her forehead. "Why don't you rest for a bit? I would still very much like to take you out for the dinner I've promised you."

She nodded. "Don't worry. That's still happening. It'll be good for Evangeline to see us together. And a rest sounds nice. I'll be upstairs if you need me."

He watched her go, thinking about all she'd told him and just how formidable an opponent Tessa could be. He'd never been so glad to have someone on his side. Nor had he ever underestimated anyone quite so much.

Tessa had only entered Sebastian's bedroom when she realized she was no longer alone. She turned to find Evangeline in the doorway. A tiny ripple of fear passed through her. Was the woman going to try something now that Sebastian and Greaves were downstairs? Tessa decided if that's what Evangeline had come for, she wasn't going to find the same Tessa she'd just faced. "Can I help you? I came up here to rest, not continue sparring with you."

Evangeline's brows arched in surprise. "I'm not here to spar. I wanted to congratulate you."

Hah. Tessa crossed her arms. "On what?"

"On thoroughly captivating Sebastian." She leaned against the door jamb. "I know you love him, but I wasn't sure how he really felt about you until today. I honestly thought he'd be in love with me for the rest of my life. I was sort of counting on it when I came back here, but clearly I was wrong."

Tessa didn't know what to make of that. "Thank you. I suppose. Why were you counting on it?"

Evangeline sighed. "I thought we could be...us again, I guess. Life as a vampire was enormously fun at first. There's a sense of freedom and possibility that you can't imagine."

"No, I suppose not." Life as a librarian, valkyrie or not, was filled with schedules and events and work to be done.

Evangeline chuckled. "My life as a human was completely mapped out for me. As the daughter of a marquess I was expected to act a certain way, attend certain functions." Her eyes arrowed into Tessa. "Marry a certain man. Any decisions not made by my father for me, my mother happily commanded. What I wore, what friends I kept, what parties I attended."

She shook her head. "I suppose that sounds rather trivial to you, but it wasn't. I lived my life in a gilded prison. Realizing I had freedom and power as a vampire was the most intoxicating cup I'd ever drunk from."

For the first time, Tessa felt like she understood some of Evangeline's actions. "I bet it was. What did you do first?"

"You mean after I broke Sebastian's heart?" She sighed. "I went to Paris. I'd been there before, of course, but I'd had my mother and several chaperones. As a vampire, I finally experienced the real Paris. Oh, it's a marvelous place when you have the sort of power and influence of our kind."

"I can only imagine."

A horrified look marred Evangeline's beautiful face. "Do you mean you haven't been? Has Sebastian never taken you? What on earth have you two been doing all this time?"

"Getting to know each other. Living our lives. We'll travel after we're married." That seemed like a reasonable answer.

Evangeline made a rude noise. "Not if you don't stay on him about it you won't. He gets very stuck in his ways. That's a good part of why I left him. Life with him was more of what I'd experienced with my father. Everything was a foregone conclusion. Which house we'd summer at, what parties we'd throw, who would be invited, what would be discussed…"

She waved a hand through the air. "Fancy dresses and parties might seem like fun, but even they lose their luster after a while. I wanted to do life on my own terms. For once. You must understand that. To live as you want, not the way it's expected of you."

Tessa nodded slowly. "I understand that very much. And I can see why you did what you did. Doesn't mean I approve." She didn't. Especially not of the cheating part. But this wasn't about what she thought right now. "Leaving your husband was a pretty drastic measure, but that was your decision to make."

"Thank you for understanding. And not judging too much."

"It's not my place to tell you how to live your life. But you can't expect me to keep silent about the parts that affect Sebastian, either."

"I'd expect nothing less from you. After all, you love him. It's almost mandatory that you speak up." Evangeline's smile took on a feline quality. "So what am I doing that you'd like to comment on?"

"I think you know the answer to that."

"Tell me anyway."

Tessa narrowed her eyes. "Sign the papers and let him get on with his life. You've seen us together enough to make your decision. Why wait out the week?"

Evangeline went quiet for a moment, making Tessa think she'd gotten through. "Did you speak to him about his going out during daylight hours? That's still a concern of mine."

"I did. And I assure you, he's protected." The woman was certainly fixated on that. "Anything else? If not, I'd like to rest before my fiancé takes me out for dinner."

Evangeline pursed her lips as if tasting that news and finding it sour.

Then Duncan came skittering out of the closet at full speed, ricocheting off Evangeline's boot and shooting back across the room and up the cat tree.

Evangeline shrieked. "What is that creature?"

Tessa bit her lip to keep from laughing. "It's my cat, Duncan."

"A cat? In this house?" Evangeline wrapped her arms around her torso protectively and grimaced. "Are you part witch? How did you get Sebastian to agree to that?"

Tessa lifted one shoulder. "I guess he loves me."

Evangeline's lip curled as she stared at Duncan with the same look most people reserved for disease-carrying vermin. "If that's not proof, I don't know what is."

Sebastian retreated to his office, still too angry at Evangeline to deal with her at the moment. Going over some numbers would calm him down and help him suss out what the proper next step was.

But his mind kept going back to Tessa and her story. Reconciling her past with who she was now wasn't that hard. He'd seen glimpses of the warrior within her the first night they'd been out together. No woman turned around and walked away from a man who was making her unhappy without having some sort of backbone.

He'd just never guessed Tessa's was made of steel and grit and Norse magic.

Knowing what he did about her now only made him like her more. She'd chosen a very deliberate path for herself. One that wasn't easy. He admired that kind of determination. It spoke to her strength of character and fortitude. She'd decided not to be defined by the parameters of her kind.

He frowned. But then so had Evangeline when she'd turned her back on being his wife to pursue the vampire life of instant gratification and endless pleasure she thought existed beyond the walls of their manor house.

It wasn't the same, though. Not at all. He couldn't imagine Tessa shirking responsibility in favor of her own selfish desires. Her agreeing to be his fake fiancée was proof of that.

No, Tessa was the kind of woman he should have married. Not a narcissistic status-seeker, but a woman who understood duty and responsibility and sacrifice.

Bloody hell. That was the life he lived now and he was miserable. What kind of life was that for anyone?

Tessa deserved so much more than that. She deserved rich experiences and happiness and to be loved by a man who understood how amazing she was.

He swallowed. He knew very well how amazing

she was. But he didn't dare let himself love her. He wasn't what she deserved. Especially after he let Evangeline hit her with the foil. How unfair that the woman he'd spent his adult life protecting had been the cause of his failure to protect Tessa.

Blast it, he wasn't what any woman deserved. Evangeline had shown him that rather clearly. And continued to do so.

Evangeline strolled in and plopped down in the chair across from his desk, putting an abrupt end to his musings. "A cat, Sebastian? I wouldn't have believed it if I hadn't seen the beast with my own eyes."

He scowled. If thinking about Evangeline brought her into his presence, he must find a way to strike all memory of her. "I didn't realize I'd forgotten to lock the door."

She made a face at him. "Yes, well, here I am. What are you going to do with me? Are you going to throw me out?"

"Are you going to sign the papers?"

She kicked her legs up over the arm of the chair and leaned sideways in it. "Eventually. Probably." She traced the seam of the leather. "Are you sure you want to marry Tessa?"

He shook his head at her nonsense. "Unequivocally, yes. What are you playing at?"

"Nothing. Just making conversation." She pointed a lazy finger at him. "You should take her around the world for your honeymoon. Make a grand gesture out of it. See the places you and I never made it to."

Just like Evangeline to assume what he would and wouldn't do. "How do you know we haven't already?"

She shrugged. "You're right. I don't. Except that I know you and you were never one to vacate a residence unless the season dictated it. But please, tell me I'm wrong. Tell me where you and Tessa have been."

He frowned. Anything he said would be a lie. But what was one more on top of the many he'd already told?

Evangeline studied her nails. "Paris is lovely in the spring. You should put that on your itinerary."

"We've already been. Last year. It was remarkable." He'd tell Tessa about this new wrinkle as soon as he was free of Evangeline.

"Really? Paris? How wonderful. I'm so happy for you. I'm glad you've found a woman who's spurred you to travel and experience new things. Tell me again why you haven't married her yet."

He launched halfway across the desk. "Because you refuse to release me from our marital bonds. We'd already be married if not for you."

"I see." She nodded, something swirling in her gaze. "I'll tell you what. Let's take a trip tomorrow night to that new wedding chapel Julian was talking about. You two get married and I'll sign the dissolution of relations for the vampire council as soon as the ceremony's done."

He stared at her. The lie about Paris seemed inconsequential now. Tessa would never go for this. He swallowed. "I don't think Tessa will agree to that. I imagine she'll want a proper ceremony, with friends and family and—"

"You imagine?" Evangeline leaned forward. "You're engaged to a woman you've been seeing for over a year and you haven't talked about the kind of ceremony you're going to have?"

"I, well, I've left that up to Tessa."

Evangeline smirked. "Typical male. Say, if you're so in love with her, why haven't you contacted the council and told them that I left you? With proof of infidelity, you could have had your dissolution."

He couldn't tell her about the promise, but he could tell her something. "Because I never bothered to get proof. I knew what you were doing. Why would I want to actually see my wife cheating on me?"

"And maybe you were holding out hope that I'd come back. That we would reconcile."

"Maybe. But that changed when I met Tessa." How true those words were.

"That's all I needed to know." She got to her feet. "I'd suggest you talk to Tessa about my offer because it's got an expiration date. I either see you two get married tomorrow night—no, *tonight*, or I'll write to the vampire council and tell them of your infidelity and how as my sire you've thrown me over for another woman."

Cold sluiced down his spine. "You wouldn't." And now she knew he couldn't do the same because he'd just told her he didn't have proof of her betrayal. The cold turned to anger. Evangeline was the same conniving shrew she'd always been.

She gave him a casual glance over her shoulder as she walked toward the door. "Wouldn't I? Think hard before you make up your mind, Sebby. Think hard."

Tessa's mouth hung open. Pretending to be Sebastian's fiancée was one thing. Actually becoming his wife was well more than she'd signed on for. "She wants us to get married in front of her? Tonight?"

Sebastian rubbed a hand over his eyes. "It's so out of left field. She's never once mentioned bringing the council into this in all the years I've known her. She's just playing games."

"Really? Because that sounds pretty serious to me." It also sounded like Evangeline was seriously jealous of what she imagined Sebastian and Tessa had, which just confirmed Tessa's suspicion that Evangeline really did want to be part of Sebastian's life again. Why else would she have all those newspaper articles with his pictures?

"It is serious. That's why she's only now

brought it up. I promise, she's just pushing me. Trying to see if this is truly real."

"And if we don't get married?"

He frowned. "She's threatened to contact the vampire council. It's probably a bluff. I doubt she—"

"If she did, what would that mean in layman's terms?"

His frown deepened. "She could bring charges of neglect against me as both her sire and her husband. Infidelity would be part of that. It wouldn't be pretty."

Tessa sat on the bed and wrapped her arms around her knees. "How does that work with vampires? With valkyries and berserkers, everything is pretty much settled by combat." Which was one more reason not to cause trouble.

"The vampire council operates like a human court. Their rules and guidelines were established ages ago. Well before any of us were turned. They're meant to protect all of us. Vampires, that is. And as I am Evangeline's sire, I have certain responsibilities toward her, but those are compounded by the fact that we were married at the time of her turning. She can claim that I forced her to be turned, that I coerced her into it, that she agreed out of duty and not because it was what she truly desired. She might even say she feared what I would do if she refused."

"Is any of that true?"

"No, of course not. She welcomed it with great enthusiasm. And if I hadn't turned her, the chances were great that the plague killing off all those around us would have taken her too. That's why my grandmother turned us. To save us from it." He grunted. "Evangeline was as much a party to the turning as I was."

"Have any of your brothers dealt with this?"

He shook his head. "Julian wasn't married at the time my grandmother turned us. Hugh was, but his wife didn't survive the turning."

"How awful." Tessa cringed at the thought. "He seems happy now."

"He is. Delaney has done wonders for him." Sebastian's gaze softened for a moment, as if he was comparing Tessa to the woman his brother had married.

She shook it off. Whatever Sebastian was thinking, it had to be tainted by Evangeline's demands. "So what are the consequences if she levels these charges against you?"

He sat beside her on the bed and stared at the intricately woven rug that covered the hardwood. "It will be a long, drawn-out affair, but if the council finds them to be true, the consequences would be…steep."

"In plain terms, please."

"Best-case scenario, I could be jailed for a period of time."

"And worst case?"

A shudder wracked him. "I could be forced to face the dawn."

Her mouth came open again. "What?"

He nodded. "The council doesn't take these things lightly."

"Your life could be forfeit because she's unhappy?"

"It's more than that. But yes. Neglect on part of a sire, where it causes hardship or loss of quality of life for the turned, is a grave offense."

She couldn't believe what she was hearing. "But you have your amulet. You'd be safe, right?"

He smiled weakly and reached out to brush a strand of hair off her cheek. "When one is put out to face the dawn, it's in the same state that one enters into the world. The amulet must be on me to protect me."

Rage, both welcome and unwelcome, tripped through Tessa. The surge of emotion forced her to her feet. She turned to face him. "Are you sure she's bluffing?"

"No, but that's what this feels like. She wants me to admit this is all a ruse and that I still love her. That I'll take her back."

Tessa nodded. "I think that's exactly what she wants. So what if you do admit this is all a lie?"

Duncan jumped onto the bed, meowing for attention. Sebastian reached out and scratched the little cat. "She will never let me forget it. Not for a second. And she will forever hold it over my head."

Tessa imagined his life at the mercy of Evangeline. Nothing about it seemed pleasant.

He leaned his elbows on his knees and put his head in his hands. "I rarely muck things up so badly. And I never lie. Which is obviously where I went wrong to begin with. Perhaps I should just come clean and face whatever consequences are due me."

Tessa snorted. "After all this? Unless that's really what you want."

He picked his head up. "It isn't."

"Then I guess we're getting married. But I'm telling you right now, this has to come to an end with her. She cannot keep up this hold over you."

His mouth opened and he shook his head. "You can't mean you're willing to go through with this."

"I am. But only if it means you're finally going to be free of her."

"Thank you seems rather insufficient." He nodded. "She's promised to sign the papers dissolving our relationship and releasing me from my responsibilities as her sire. Once she does that, the council won't care what her complaints are."

"And you're sure she'll sign as soon as we marry? I expect it to happen immediately."

"As do I. And yes, she'll sign. She has no

choice." His gaze narrowed as his eyes filled with uncertainty. "You're sure you want to do this? We'll be married, you know. There's no pretending this time. She'd figure that out."

Tessa nodded. "I know. And yes." She shrugged and tried to smile. "It's not how I thought it would happen, but it's just temporary. After a little bit, we'll divorce and you'll be free to finally live your life."

He almost smiled. "Yes. Free." He stared into space for a long moment as a look of resignation filled his gaze. Finally, he met her eyes again. "There won't be any way to keep this quiet. Everyone will know we've gotten married."

That would make her dating life fun. Not that she'd ever had much of one before. "Can't be helped, I suppose."

His gaze shifted to the floor. "When it comes time for us to divorce, I will shoulder the blame. It's what most will believe anyway. You can tell people what you like. That I was impossible to live with, that I was boring. Unkind. Whatever story suits you."

Tessa recoiled at the idea. "I absolutely will not say any of that. You are none of those things."

His limp smile broadened slightly. "Tessa. Sweet Tessa. How is it you think so differently of me than everyone else does?"

She blinked at him, her anger fading. "Who's

everyone else? Evangeline? You're basing your opinion of yourself on one woman? One awful, horrible, rotten woman?"

Her heart ached for him. For this amazing man who'd sacrificed his own happiness out of a sense of duty and a promise older than the country they lived in. She walked forward toward the bed until her legs bumped his. She put her hands on his knees, pushing them apart until she could stand between them, then she cupped the hard lines of his jaw and brought his face up. "Sebastian Ellingham, you are the dumbest, smartest man I have ever known."

"I don't think—"

She held him fast, staring into his dark eyes. "That's your problem. You don't think. But you also think too much. I find you very easy to live with. And you're certainly not boring. As for being unkind? Duncan is proof enough of that lie."

He pressed his lips together like he was trying to stop himself from arguing with her.

She bent and kissed him, a soft gentle touch of her mouth to his, before straightening again. "What you might also be is a little blind."

He frowned. "Blind?"

Nerves tripped through her, but she was past caring about consequences. She was a valkyrie. If she couldn't find the courage to speak her mind, what hope did anyone else have? "Yes, blind.

Before you stands a woman who you can't see is falling in love with you. And I know I'm not your type, but if I can fall in love with you, then that should make you realize that someday, you'll find another woman who—"

"You...you. With me?"

She sucked in a ragged breath. "Yes. Don't worry. I'm not letting the marriage go to my head. I know it's part of the—"

He came off the bed in a graceful burst of energy to pull her into his arms and kiss her soundly. He wrapped her in his embrace, holding her close. His kiss was wild and a little rough and she swore she felt the scrape of his fangs over her bottom lip.

Warmth suffused her and put an end to her jangling nerves.

At last he broke the kiss, leaning back to look into her eyes as his blazed with the glow of his kind. "I feel the same way toward you. And I don't know how or why you're falling for me, but I promise you, I will endeavor to be worthy of your affections. You are absolutely my type. I just didn't know it until I met you. I'm sure I don't deserve you. Or this sort of result from my mangled machinations, but thank you for being so kind and understanding."

She stared at him. "Are you saying you care about me?"

"Irreversibly."

"Even knowing what you do about my past? My temper?"

He kissed her again, a gentle, brief press of reassurance. "You were sixteen. Have you done anything close to that since then?"

"No." But she hadn't drawn her sword in all that time, either.

"And even if you do, what harm could you bring me? I'm an old, old vampire. Very dangerous in my own right." He cocked an eyebrow. "You don't know me that well yet. I might have a little temper of my own."

"Do you?"

"I suppose. If provoked enough. Who doesn't?"

"Yes, but my temper almost got a man killed."

"*Almost* means it didn't. And I'm willing to take my chances if the reward means I get to spend more time with you. And build a real relationship. Look, this marriage will be in name only. I'm not going to expect anything different, if you understand what I'm saying. In fact, once Evangeline is packed off, I'd very much like for us to attempt as close to normal a relationship as possible. Dating and all that. I've never actually done it, but I suppose it can't be that difficult if my brothers can manage it."

She laughed softly. "Okay, I'd like that too."

He held on to her. "Maybe...if it's not too

forward of me to suggest it, you could stay here?"

"You mean live here? In the house?"

He nodded. "You'd have your own room, of course."

It was a very sweet offer. Not to mention the perks of being close to him and having access to that incredible library. "I don't know. That might be a little awkward with you being my boss and all."

He hid his disappointment poorly. "Yes, I guess it would be."

"I might be talked into the guest house, though."

His eyes lit up again. "It's yours. It's not very much space, but if you want it, it's yours." He smiled. "I will insist you come for dinner at least three nights a week, however."

She laughed. "You mean take out?"

"I'll hire a cook. I've been meaning to do it for ages."

She raised her brows. "I doubt that."

"Well, Greaves has suggested it. He'll be thrilled." Sebastian smiled. "I like this plan. And if you run out of space over there, you can always move back in here."

"Just how small is the guest house? Will Duncan's new cat tree fit?"

Sebastian's smile flattened. "Hmm. It hadn't occurred to me you'd be taking him with you."

She narrowed her eyes. "Did you think I would leave my cat here?"

"He is rather settled in."

She rolled her lips in. "For someone who didn't want him here at all, you're suddenly very attached to him."

They both turned to look at the kitten, who was attacking something only he could see on the comforter.

Sebastian nodded. "He's…good company."

"You have Greaves."

Sebastian gave her a look. "My rook hardly compares. And he's never half as entertaining as the little beast."

He leaned in and kissed her again. "I feel as though I owe you my life, Tessa. You're doing so much for me. I will be in your debt for an eternity."

"No. I don't want that. You've already had that with one woman."

"True. But what you're doing for me isn't something that's easily repaid."

She smiled. "It's what friends do. And we're friends now, so…" She patted his chest, a little embarrassed by his sharp focus on her. She knew she was doing him a huge favor, but she couldn't imagine *not* doing it. There was too much at stake for him. "I'm pretty sure I remember a bridal shop in town. I don't know if they can supply me with a dress on such short notice, but I should probably give them a call."

"The woman who owns it, Corette, is engaged to Hugh's rook, Stanhill. She'll make it happen. She's a witch and if she has to use her magic, she will. I'll go down to my office and call Corette now and tell her you're on your way. I'll make sure she knows I'm taking care of the charges, too."

Tessa didn't argue. She wouldn't be buying a wedding dress if not for this new drama. "And I'll call my sister and see if she wants to go over there with me."

Sebastian hesitated. "Is she going to give you a hard time because of this?"

"A little, but nothing serious. She's pretty good that way. And really, what can she say? She's the one who offered me up in the first place."

"True." He tipped his head. "I'm sorry we're not going to dinner tonight. I'll make up for that as soon as I'm able."

"I'm going to hold you to that."

He gave her a quick kiss and left smiling. She pulled out her phone and sat on the bed next to Duncan. She gave him a little scratch on the head and he immediately started gnawing on her thumb. She pulled her hand away to tap her sister's number.

"Deputy Blythe," Jenna answered.

"Are you still on duty?"

"Hey, Tessa. Sorry, I didn't look at the caller ID. Yep, on duty until six. You need me?"

"Sort of. There's been a new wrinkle in the *situation*."

"Oh boy. What now?"

Tessa took a breath. "How would you like to go wedding dress shopping with me?"

Sebastian called Corette, filled her in on what was happening, then asked Greaves to drive Tessa into town to Corette's shop. Once they'd gone, he closed his office door and made another phone call.

"Ellingham residence."

"Stanhill, it's Sebastian. Is my brother in?"

"Yes."

"Good. I'm on my way over."

"I'll let him know."

As much as Sebastian loathed leaving Evangeline in his home alone, it couldn't be helped. The talk he was about to have with his brothers couldn't happen where she could hear it. And Greaves was just dropping Tessa off at the bridal shop. He'd be home again until she called him to be picked up, so Evangeline would be unattended for only twenty minutes tops.

Sebastian locked his office and drove to Hugh's, calling Julian's cell on the way.

"Hello, Sebby. Please tell me you're not calling because you suddenly decided to change more things in the budget."

"I hate that name."

"Sorry, I do know that. Guess I heard Evangeline say it one too many times. Apology accepted?"

"No, but if you meet me at Hugh's in the next ten minutes, I'll give you far less grief about it than you can imagine."

"I can manage ten minutes." Julian hesitated. "Does this mean I'm getting the catering team?"

Sebastian nearly drove off the road. "Catering team? A wedding chapel doesn't need a catering team."

"That's too bad. My schedule just filled up. I don't think I'm going to be able to make it to Hugh's on such short notice after all."

"We'll talk about it." There was no way Sebastian was going to approve additional funds for catering at a wedding chapel. Not with all the capable restaurants in town. But now was not the time to hardline that issue with Julian. "I need you at Hugh's. It's imperative I talk to both of you."

Julian's voice finally took on an edge of concern. "Did something happen to Tessa? What's Evangeline done now?"

"Show up at Hugh's and I'll tell you."

And to Julian's credit, he did, arriving eight

minutes after Sebastian. Once they were seated in Hugh's living room and Stanhill had started pouring a round of whiskeys, Sebastian explained what had occurred.

His brothers blinked at him.

Hugh was the first to speak. "You can't seriously mean to do this."

"Tessa's agreed to it. I wouldn't be going through with it otherwise. And what's my alternative? Let Evangeline go to the council? That's all well and good until the outcome is in her favor."

Julian shook his head. "But truth is on your side. She's the one who abandoned you."

Sebastian nodded. "I know that. We know that. But you know what she's like. She's very convincing. And I have no physical proof that she ever cheated on me."

"We'll testify on your behalf," Hugh said.

"I appreciate that but as convoluted as it sounds, marrying Tessa is easier. And it might be the only way to get Evangeline to sign the dissolution papers."

Julian swirled his glass, turning the amber liquid within into a miniature cyclone. "Sounds like you have your mind made up, but have you really thought this through? What if Tessa gets a grand idea about what this means? What if she turns into another Evangeline?"

"She won't. She's nothing like Evangeline. And

we've talked about it. She's doing this to help me."

Hugh snorted. "And the job you offered her has no part in this? Do you think she'd be so agreeable if the position of dean suddenly evaporated?"

"I'm not about to rescind that offer. But yes, I think she would be. She's...not like any other woman I've ever known."

Julian let out a loud, "Oh." He shook his head. "I see exactly what's going on now."

"What?"

Julian's eyes sparkled. "You like her."

"Of course, I like her. She's whip-smart, funny, kind and doing me an incredible favor. What's not to like? She's the anti-Evangeline if ever there was one."

Julian smirked.

Hugh glanced from Julian to Sebastian. "Is that true? You can't be in love with the woman. You've only known her three days."

"I'm not in love." Not that he would confess to his brothers. "But I do like her. And what if I was in love? That's my business."

Hugh stood, leaving his drink behind on the coffee table to pace toward the French doors that led into his garden. "Sebastian, you deserve happiness more than any of us, but to tie yourself down again before the first entanglement is even over is ludicrous."

"I'm not tying myself down to Tessa. I am, at

most, starting a relationship with her." Sebastian massaged the back of his neck, trying to keep his emotions at bay. "I appreciate your concerns, I do, but I came here seeking your assistance, not your judgment on my life."

"We're not judging you." Julian looked suddenly very much like the little boy Sebastian still remembered him as. "But you're our brother and that gives us some right to be concerned. That's all. We don't want you mucked up again just as you're about to be free. But if you care about Tessa, truly care about her, then I say good for you. You've been alone a long time and that can't have been easy."

Julian's words couldn't have surprised Sebastian more if his youngest brother had suddenly announced he was joining the priesthood. Julian was the last of them he'd expected to understand.

Even Hugh turned to stare at his playboy brother with an expression that said he wasn't sure what he'd just heard. "This is one of those rare occasions when Julian is right. I cannot imagine my life without Delaney. To think how long you've been without that sort of companionship…" He shook his head. "We'll do whatever you need. That goes without question."

"Thank you." Sebastian took a sip of whiskey, then set the glass aside. "I would like you both to be at the chapel when Tessa and I marry."

"Done," they said in unison.

Sebastian nodded, thinking to the future. "I also need you to make sure Evangeline doesn't leave until she signs my life back to me. And you may use any means necessary to ensure that outcome."

Ever After was a gorgeous store dedicated to the icon of womanliness that was the wedding dress. Yes, there were racks of other kinds of formal gowns, but those were tucked away in little alcoves, just like the small corner that held the tuxedos.

The wedding dress, in all its pristine, fairy tale wonder, was front and center. And there were more of them than Tessa could make sense of. Maybe part of her snow-blindness wasn't just the billows of white fabric surrounding her, but the whole idea that she was actually in a shop like this.

And not because she was a bridesmaid.

Sure, this wedding wasn't about her spending the rest of her life with the groom, although anything was possible, especially now that she and Sebastian had decided to see where things might go, but that didn't mean she wasn't a little excited about the process.

Regardless of the circumstances, she was still here to purchase a wedding dress. Happy little nerves danced through her. No sign of Jenna yet, but she'd be here.

"Hello there. You must be Tessa." An older but very handsome woman extended her hand. "I'm Corette. Sebastian said to expect you."

Tessa nodded and shook the woman's hand. "Yes, I'm Tessa. Thank you for doing this on such short notice."

Corette gave her a knowing look. "Fortunately, I didn't have any other appointments. Although I still would have worked something out. It's not good business to disappoint the Ellinghams."

The door behind them opened with a soft chime and Jenna strode in, wearing her uniform. She grinned at Tessa. "Okay, you're here. For a second I thought I might walk in and find out this was some elaborate joke."

"No joke," Tessa said. "This is happening."

Jenna shook her head good-naturedly. "So I see." She looked at Corette. "How does this wedding dress shopping work?"

"Normally, I'd have a rack of dresses already pulled, but that's after I've already had a phone consultation with the bride. In this case, Tessa, why don't you tell me what you have in mind?"

"Um…" Tessa blinked. She'd pretty much thought she'd be single for life after she'd removed herself from society in order to avoid intense situations that could result in her temper spiraling out of control. "Whatever I can take with me, I guess, since I have to have it for tonight."

Corette smiled. "Yes, that is definitely a consideration for us today. It also means a floor sample is the best I can do, but I promise I won't show you anything that isn't in excellent shape. Now, about the dress. What sort of style do you like?"

Jenna snorted. "Style and Tessa aren't two words that often go together. Although, I have to say, sis, you're looking pretty good at the moment."

"Thanks." Jeans were Tessa's new best friend. They made you look good and held everything in. She could see why they were so popular and she was getting over the idea that they were unacceptable for anything but farmers or ranch hands. They could be dressed up very nicely.

Corette tried again. "How do you want to look on your wedding day?"

"Pretty," Tessa answered without thinking. She put her hand to her mouth. "Oh, that sounds shallow, doesn't it?"

"No." Corette smiled gently. "That sounds like a

bride. Let's take your measurements and I'll pull a few things to get us started."

Twenty minutes later, Tessa had been fitted into a bustier and was being zipped into her first gown. Corette used a few large plastic clips to secure the extra fabric in the back and form the dress to Tessa's shape perfectly.

Corette turned her to face the mirror. "What do you think? Would you like to show this one to your sister?"

Tessa's lips parted, but words escaped her. She'd never seen herself in a fancy dress before, let alone a wedding gown. It was like looking at another version of herself in the mirror. Someone who might as well have been a stranger.

"It's...lovely." And it was. Staggeringly so. "But it's a lot of skin, isn't it?"

"Most wedding dresses are strapless these days, but this has the single shoulder strap, so it actually covers more than most."

Tessa's fingers went to the strap and the delicate embellished flowers that covered it. They trailed down the bodice, ending at the waist. Other than that, the dress was unadorned. The soft, shimmering fabric hugged her body in a very becoming way.

"Maybe you don't like the ruching?"

"I don't even know what that is."

Corette patted the small pleats that covered the

dress. "It's the way the fabric is sewn with these small gathers. Ruching can conceal a multitude of body issues, not that you need help with that. Maybe it's too much? Would you prefer something simpler and a little more body conscious?"

"More body conscious? No, I like this. I'm just not used to seeing myself in anything like this, that's all."

Corette nodded. "I understand. Let's show Jenna. See what she thinks."

"Okay."

Tessa walked out to where Jenna was sitting. The area had a bank of mirrors flanking a raised platform. She stepped up onto it and faced her sister. "What do you think?"

Jenna stared over the top of the bridal magazine she'd been looking at. "Holy Loki. Is that really you in that thing? You look like a supermodel."

"I do not."

Jenna nodded vigorously. "Yeah, you do. Wow."

The phone rang. Corette clasped her hands. "I'll just leave you girls alone for a moment." With a smile, she left them.

Jenna got up and approached Tessa. "I'm serious. You look amazing. I'm afraid Sebastian's going to see you in this and decide not to divorce you. You might end up stuck with him."

Tessa couldn't help but smile. "Would that be so bad?"

"Sebastian?" Jenna snorted. "I think—wait, you're serious?"

"Yes." She lifted her chin. "I like him. And he likes me. In fact, when his ex is out of the picture, I'm moving out of your place and into his guest house."

"Is that so?"

"It is." Tessa braced for the argument. "Nothing you can say is going to change my mind."

Jenna hooked a hand on her duty belt in front of her service weapon. "All I'm going to say is, good for you."

"Well, that's not very—what?" Tessa stared at her sister. "You're okay with that?"

"Sure." Jenna shrugged. "You're a grown woman. You can make your own decisions. He might not be my choice, but who cares about that? Does he make you happy?"

Tessa let out a breath. Thoughts of Sebastian warmed her through. "Yes. Very."

"That's great. And very important." Jenna's fingers strummed her belt as she waggled her brows. "How's the sex?"

Tessa choked on air. "We haven't done that yet. We've only known each other a few days!"

"Okay, just checking. Have you kissed at least?"

"Yes." Tessa pursed her lips. "And that's also very good."

Jenna smiled. "Maybe this will turn into

something then. I will say, as eligible bachelors go, you couldn't have picked a better one."

"Because?"

Jenna started ticking things off on her fingers. "Money, power, great house, great car, really hot if you go for that sort of English lord thing he's got going on, and let's not forget immortal."

"I prefer that he's smart, likes books and is kind. To me and Duncan. Being handsome doesn't hurt."

"Neither do any of those other things, let's be honest."

"Maybe that's how most women think, but I'm not most women."

"No, you're not." Jenna's smile flattened a little. "Did you tell him about…you know? What happened?"

"Yes." Tessa stared at the platform under her feet. It was carpeted in soft ivory shag. "He's okay with it."

"He's a good match for you then. Especially because if something were to happen, well, he's a vampire."

"And basically invincible."

Jenna sighed. "You know, there might be a way to deal with this temper issue. I've said it before, but if you hadn't just up and walked away, maybe—"

Tessa groaned. "Could we change the subject?"

"Yes, you're right. Now isn't the time." Jenna's

smile seemed forced for a moment. "Back to this killer dress. Sorry, bad choice of word. This *fabulous* dress. Turn around, let me see the whole thing."

Tessa spun, facing the trio of mirrors for the first time. The dress was really amazing. Fairy tale beautiful, despite all the skin it revealed, which wasn't that much, it was just more than Tessa was used to.

Behind her, Jenna nodded. "I love this dress. Looks stellar on you." She stepped onto the platform to stand at Tessa's back. "But the best part is the strap doesn't interfere with your sword."

"That's not a consideration—"

Jenna ran her finger down the exposed bit of Tessa's spine, making her sword sing out.

Tessa shivered and turned, the bladesong as uncomfortable today as it had been right after she's almost killed Varren. "I haven't needed my sword in years. I'm certainly not going to need it at my wedding. Or ever again."

Jenna held her hands up as she stepped down. "I didn't mean to upset you. I was just thinking like a valkyrie, that's all. I know you won't need it."

Tessa cupped her hand over the back of her neck, feeling the hilt of her weapon. It vibrated under her touch. Ready to fight. Ready to kill. She pulled her hand away. "It's just not who I am anymore, Jenna."

"I know." Jenna's smile was weak and a little sad. "Forget I said anything about it."

"I should get a dress that covers it." Tessa glanced over her shoulder into the mirrors. Her sword was plainly visible. It looked like a very realistic, and very large, tattoo. Hard to believe she'd ever been proud of it.

"Why? Only you and I can see it, unless there are berserkers or other valkyries in town. Which I don't think there are. Anyway, it's no big deal."

Tessa looked away. "I suppose you're right."

"So are you buying that dress or what?"

"It's the first one I've tried on."

Corette returned. "I apologize for my absence. Did I hear you say you're ready to try on another dress?"

"I don't know." Tessa bit her lip. "Does anyone ever buy the first dress they put on?"

Corette nodded. "It happens more often than you think."

Tessa took a breath as she looked herself over one more time in the mirrors. "Then I think this is my dress."

Jenna clapped her hands and exclaimed a rather uncharacteristic, "Yay!"

Corette smiled. "Excellent. Let's do the alterations then and I'll box it up for you."

"Alterations? I didn't think you'd have time for that."

Jenna made a face. "She's not going to send you down the aisle with those plastic clips up the back."

"No, I am certainly not going to do that." Corette joined Tessa on the platform and began pinching spans of fabric at Tessa's sides and under her bust. She checked the length, which Tessa thought was perfect, then stepped back, narrowed her gaze and wiggled her fingers at the dress, finishing with a dramatic flourish.

Tessa swore she saw the shimmer of magic dancing in the air like dust motes in a ray of sun. Then the dress shifted. And tightened. And went snug all over. The plastic clips popped off the back. "Oh!"

Tessa glanced over her shoulder at the discarded clips before looking at Corette again. "Sebastian said you were a witch. I didn't think I'd get to see you use your magic, though."

Corette gave a coy smile. "I don't do that for everyone, but in emergencies, it's nice to be able to help."

"Very cool," Jenna said. "Very, very cool."

"Just one more thing," Corette said. She went to a low, ivory storage cabinet against the far wall and lifted a cloud of white free from one of the drawers. She shook the gossamer fabric out as she came toward Tessa, rejoining her on the platform. "Your veil."

"It's lovely."

She fastened the little clear combs into Tessa's hair and arranged it around her shoulders. The delicate tulle had minute crystals fastened onto it, matching the sparkle of the flowers on the strap. "There. Now you're ready."

Tessa turned toward the mirrors and inhaled. She looked like a bride. A *beautiful* bride.

A pang of disappointment shot through her. Too bad the wedding was all for show.

She'd agreed to it, though, and in her heart, she knew helping Sebastian be free of Evangeline was going to be worth it.

For him.

She just didn't know if she'd get over walking down the aisle for the first time knowing she would be getting divorced a short while later. What if she and Sebastian didn't turn into anything? What if this was her one and only marriage? A sham that ended as quickly as it had begun? A flood of doubts filled her. She couldn't go back on her word. Sebastian needed her to do this, but was she just adding to the emotional baggage she was going to have to carry around for the rest of her life?

Refusing to go through with it could ruin Sebastian's life. Hell, it could cost him his life if Evangeline went to the council.

Jenna leaned around so Tessa could see her in the mirror. "You okay?"

279

Tessa forced a smile and nodded. "Just overwhelmed by the emotion of it all."

It would be too cruel to back out now with the wedding just a few hours away. And besides, she'd given her word.

Tessa lifted her chin. She was a valkyrie. A strong, capable woman. Whatever the price, she would pay it.

Sebastian was worth that much.

Sebastian had yet to receive the documents from his solicitor, even though the man had promised they'd be in his inbox in plenty of time. Hitting refresh made no difference. They weren't there. Sebastian closed his laptop and went upstairs to the bedroom to see how Greaves was coming along with his tux.

Duncan was lounging in the top-most perch of the cat tree, looking down on the room as though it were his kingdom.

Sebastian grinned at him. "Where's Greaves, little man?"

"In here," Greaves called out from the walk-in closet.

Sebastian leaned on the doorway. "Everything in order? Which one am I wearing?"

Greaves answered without looking. He hung the second tuxedo beside the first, then stood back.

"The shawl-collared Armani is the most classic, but the Tom Ford peaked-lapel is the newest and most modern. Your choice, really. They're both ready to wear, but I might want to give whichever one you choose a little steam."

Sebastian studied the two suits. "Which one do I look the best in?"

Greaves snickered, glancing over his shoulder. "I don't think you've ever asked me that before. Nor do I think I've ever noticed that you cared."

"Well, I do. It's my wedding. And if Tessa's going to see me as a groom, I want her to think that…I don't know, that I really could be *her* groom. Someday."

Greaves nodded. "I like her very much. She's done you a world of good. I approve your motives."

"Excellent. I was worried."

Greaves snorted. "Yes, I'm sure." He tapped his chin. "The Tom Ford is a little more youthful. And more James Bondish. Women usually go for that."

"And you would know this how?"

"I date."

Sebastian straightened. "You do?"

Greaves' irritation was plain. "Being your rook doesn't require me to be celibate."

"No, it doesn't but spare me the details. The Tom Ford it is."

"I'll get to work on it." Greaves stared at him for

a second longer. "Have you told your grandmother about all this?"

"No, and I don't plan to until it's the real deal."

"You're okay with the possibility that Evangeline could say something first?"

Sebastian snorted. "Evangeline wouldn't dare speak to Didi." The nickname was born out of Elenora's former title, the Dowager Duchess. It wasn't one she was overly fond of, so Sebastian and his brothers tended not to use it to her face. "If Evangeline values her life, she'll make sure Elenora doesn't even know she's in town."

"I doubt that's possible. Your grandmother knows everything that goes on in this town. Alice makes sure of that."

A very true statement. "Bloody hell. I suppose you're right. I'd better go see her." He checked his watch. He had time. And maybe his solicitor's email would arrive with the paperwork while he was out. "Tessa should be home soon. Let her know where I've gone, all right? And that I'll be home in plenty of time to get ready."

"I will."

Sebastian headed to Elenora's estate. The grand house sat on a vast piece of land near the vineyards owned by the one and only Nocturne Falls' winery, which meant that the land was rural and pretty and peaceful. He pulled into her drive, parked and let himself in, not waiting for her secretary, Alice

Bishop, to find him and escort him to wherever his grandmother was.

The witch wasn't one of his favorite people, despite her position as creator of the amulets that kept him and his family safe from the sun. More than once, Didi had used those amulets as leverage against them to bend their wills to hers. To say it was a thorn in his side to be nearly four hundred years old and still under the rule of his grandmother was an understatement. He loved the woman dearly, but it was a tiresome business.

Hugh had been working for years on a formula to sun-proof them, but had yet to achieve any real success. Until that changed, they were stuck with the amulets.

He strode through the great house, listening for sounds of life. He heard music and found his grandmother in her solarium, sitting at a wrought iron and marble table nestled beneath some palms and having tea. Vivaldi played softly on the hidden speakers.

"Sebastian," she exclaimed. "What a marvelous surprise. I'd begun to think you boys had forgotten I existed."

"Grandmamma, you know that's not true. We've just been busy."

"Oh? With what?" The question was as much of a challenge as anything.

He took a seat in one of the scroll-work chairs, buying himself some time to come up with an answer. "With this wedding chapel project of Julian's."

"I thought that was done."

"So did I but he keeps adding things to the budget. That makes work for me."

"Yes, crossing through all those lines must be very tiring." She nibbled on a tiny finger sandwich. "Have you left my poor Julie any money for anything?"

Sebastian barely refrained from rolling his eyes. As the youngest of the family, Julian had always been the baby and always would be to their grandmother. "There is plenty of money for this venture, I promise you."

"Good. Now, what rare treat brings you to me this afternoon?" She held up a finger. "I'll warn you. If you've come to scold me about the last Neiman Marcus bill, I won't hear it. A woman needs to stay up to date with the latest fashions and—"

"No, Grandmamma, that's not what I'm here about." But he'd take a closer look at that account next time he went over her bills.

"Then what is it, my darling?"

He took a breath, filling his lungs with the thick, loamy air of the solarium. It was more of a stalling technique than a necessity. "I have good news and

I have bad news. Which would you like to hear first?"

Her gaze narrowed ever so slightly. "The good."

"All right." He thought of Tessa. It was the easiest way to make himself smile genuinely. "I'm getting married."

She dropped her tea cup. It shattered on the floor but she paid it no mind. "You're getting married. Are you teasing me? Tell me this means Evangeline has given you the dissolution she should have centuries ago."

"Not exactly. But I really am getting married."

She gasped, the sound of pure joy. "When? To who? What's she like? Is she a vampire? Oh, Sebastian, this is the best news, my boy. I am *so* happy for you." Then, just like that, her wide eyes went down to slits. "What's the bad news? Is she pregnant? Because I don't consider that bad news. Not one bit. My word, I'll buy the woman an island if she gives me a grandchild. I'll declare a day in her honor. I'll—"

"No, Grandmamma. It's nothing like that." The idea of Tessa carrying their child was a thought that made his throat knot with emotion, but he swallowed it down. He was a vampire and she was a valkyrie. He had no idea what their chances of reproducing were. If they even stayed a couple.

"Then what is it, Sebastian? Stop tormenting me and tell me."

He sighed. There was no easy way to say this, no way to gentle the news. Best to rip the bandage off in one go. "Evangeline is in town."

A muscle in Elenora's jaw twitched. "I don't find this amusing, Sebastian. If this is some game you and your brothers have cooked up to poke at me, I will take all your amulets away for a week. Then we'll see if you think about bothering me with such nonsense again. I suppose you're not getting married, either."

He pinched the bridge of his nose before returning to the conversation. "I *am* getting married and Evangeline *is* in town. The two are, unfortunately, related."

"Please tell me this has something to do with dissolution papers being signed."

"It does."

Didi made a face. She wasn't altogether happy, but she was curious. "Start from the beginning."

Alice Bishop came plodding in. "Is everything all right? I thought I heard—oh, Sebastian. It's you."

"Alice." He wasn't in the mood for small talk and Alice Bishop wasn't high on his list of people he'd care to engage in that pointless endeavor anyway.

Elenora raised her hand. "Alice, bring me the Scotch."

"I should clean up that broken—"

"Scotch," she repeated. "Now."

"Right away." Alice trudged off, but not before she shot a questioning glance at Sebastian.

He ignored it. The witch's concerns weren't his priority. "Drinking already, Grandmamma?"

Elenora frowned. "I have a feeling whatever you're about to tell me will be made more palatable by some good whiskey."

"I doubt that. But I'll wait." He plucked up one of the finger sandwiches and downed it in one bite. It was delicious, even for something so mundane, but then Frauke was a perfectionist. All the more proof that he needed a cook of his own. Especially if he was going to be entertaining Tessa for meals on a regular basis.

Alice returned, put the crystal carafe on the table, then drifted off to the perimeter of the room. Elenora made no move to dismiss her and the woman would find out what was going on soon enough anyway, so he begin the explanation as Didi filled a new tea cup with Scotch.

"Evangeline came to town a few days ago looking to move in with me under the assumption that she and I would resume our marital life as if nothing had happened."

Elenora took her first sip of whiskey. It seemed to bring her back to center as she answered with a great deal more calm than her previous responses. "And you said?"

"I told her that couldn't happen. Specifically because...I was engaged." He grimaced, knowing his grandmother would only want more information. "She seemed flabbergasted that I might actually be involved with anyone else. She doubted it to such a degree that pride pushed me to lie. It was a foolish decision and one that's brought me to where I am now."

Didi frowned. "How so?"

"Forgive me if I skip the minor details, but as a result of my lie and an equally careless invitation to dinner, I needed someone to fill the role of my fiancée. That person came in the form of Deputy Blythe's sister, Tessa. She happened to be in town to interview for the new dean of library studies that we're hiring at Harmswood."

"And she agreed to do this for you?" Elenora looked skeptical. "How much did you offer to pay her?"

"Nothing. But we negotiated that the job would be hers in return."

Elenora nodded. "Smart woman to make that kind of deal."

"Actually, Deputy Blythe made that stipulation. Tessa was too shell-shocked by her sister volunteering her to say much on her own behalf. And I'll admit, I had my doubts about her ability to carry off the role of my fiancée, but she did beautifully."

Elenora settled back in her chair, keeping a firm grip on her tea cup. "I still don't see how this results in you getting married."

"Tessa and I both think that Evangeline truly wants me back. For what reason, I can't say. Maybe she's tired of life on her own. I don't know. Don't care. Because I have finally reached a place in my life where I'm over her."

"Remarkable. If that's true."

"It is. And I have Tessa to thank. Evangeline...ruined me in so many ways."

She reached out and patted his hand. "I know, my darling. You didn't deserve the rubbish she put you through. Why do you think I loathe the woman? For all the hurt and pain she caused you. If this Tessa has changed things for you, then I already like her."

"She has changed things. She's shown me that life can be so much more. That my sense of duty and responsibility don't have to be tied to my personal happiness. More than that, she's shown me how to be happy again. Something, I must confess, I haven't been in a long time."

Didi smiled at him in that way of all grandmothers, with unconditional love and caring. "You sound like you're in love with her. No wonder you're marrying her."

"We're marrying because Evangeline challenged us to, but I have definitely come to care for this woman. Evangeline said if we married tonight, in front of her, she'd sign the dissolution papers necessary to cut the ties between us. It means my freedom, Grandmamma."

"I wholly support this. Shocking, I know, but I do. I have no love for that awful woman and I don't know why you've continued to care for her as you have, but I am thrilled that this day has arrived. Put her behind you and move on. Marry this Tessa, whoever she is, and be happy, my darling."

"That's essentially the plan."

She stared at him. "I have to ask. Why not just tell Evangeline it's over? Why go through with the wedding? Do you need the papers signed that badly? You've gone this long. Why now?"

He rolled his shoulders, doing little to ease the tension that had settled there. "She threatened to go to the council."

Didi's eyes silvered and her fangs showed. "That ungrateful little tramp. How dare she? After all this family has done for her. Not to mention the history between our families! I ought to put a stake through her heart and be done with her."

"*Grandmamma.*" He glared at her. "Let's have some decorum, shall we?"

She thrust her hand out to point a perfectly manicured nail at him, causing the bracelet that held her amulet to slide free of her sleeve. "You ought to go to the council and report her. You have grounds for infidelity."

"Nothing I can prove, which is part of the problem. Whereas she's been led to believe that Tessa and I are cohabitating. She's seen it with her own eyes. And I'm her sire. You know how that changes things."

Elenora glanced toward the far wall, clearly upset and struggling to regain her composure. "I hate her."

"I know."

She sighed, took another sip of Scotch and seemed to calm again. "The wedding is tonight?"

"Yes, and no, you cannot attend."

"Sebastian." Her tone was pleading.

"If Evangeline sees you there, she will run. She knows you mean to do her mortal harm. Then I'll never have my papers signed. And it's not like this is a real wedding anyway. Tessa and I have already discussed it and as soon as it makes sense, we're going to divorce." Unless they didn't. Which could happen.

Elenora's artfully plucked brows knit together. "You're going to divorce the woman you're falling in love with? Why?"

"Because we've only just met each other. We need time to get to know each other, to see if we are truly meant to be a couple, without the weight of that marriage pressing down on us like a predestined future. She's going to be living in my guest house and we'll be seeing a lot of each other. But if it doesn't work out, she deserves to be able to walk away free and clear, not be legally bound to me by a marriage that's in name only."

He shook his head as he realized how much he didn't want to be married to Tessa under such contrived circumstances. "I had enough of that with Evangeline. You have to understand that."

He could tell Didi didn't like his reasoning. She put her cup down and gazed at him. "I guess I do. But if this goes wrong and Evangeline doesn't sign the papers, I can assure you that I will personally see to it she never has the ability to contact the council. I will not allow her to bring that kind of trouble to you or this family."

She leaned forward, displaying the sort of menace few ever got to see in her. It was a side he knew well, and was wise enough to fear. "I may be your grandmother, but I am also a powerful vampire with extremely powerful friends."

"You mean Alard Desmarais." The vampire who'd turned her and made Sebastian and his brothers' turnings possible. The man was ancient beyond days. Sebastian had a brief memory of the Frenchman, enough to know that with that sort of age came gifts none in his family had yet achieved.

"Yes."

"I didn't think you still knew how to contact him. Are you sure he's even still alive?"

"I do and he is."

"How old is he now?"

"Over eight hundred."

Sebastian shook his head at the idea of living another four hundred years. It seemed daunting and yet, he was halfway there. "Well, please don't go to any lengths just yet."

She nodded reluctantly. "I won't. But I'll be waiting to hear from you that everything's gone as planned."

He stood. "I promise to notify you as soon as it's done."

"And then you're bringing this Tessa here. I want to meet her."

"Why don't we give her a few—"

"You'll bring her here immediately. This is not open for discussion."

He clenched his teeth together before answering her. He had too much to worry about to argue with her any more this evening. "I'll do what I can."

She "hmphed" at him and waved her hand in dismissal.

He kissed her cheek and left, passing Alice without a second glance. The drive home blurred into muscle memory and thoughts of the night yet to come. He knew it was a very real possibility that Evangeline would refuse to sign the papers unless one more demand was met. Maybe an outrageous lump sum paid. Or a small nation purchased and her installed as queen. Nothing would surprise Sebastian at this point.

If she tried any of that, he might actually let Didi have her way.

He walked into the house and went straight to the bedroom to get into his tux. He pushed the door open and nearly ran into Tessa.

"Oh," she gasped. "You startled me." She was in her wedding gown.

"I'm sorry, I..." The ability to form words abandoned him, replaced by the sense that he should just be still and admire her. His heart ached with how beautiful she was. He stood there, gaping at her, praying this wasn't a dream he was about to wake up from, that this goddess of a woman wasn't suddenly going to disappear. If there was anything good about Evangeline showing up again, it was the gift of having Tessa in his life.

"You're not supposed to see the bride in her dress before the wedding, but I suppose that doesn't matter since, you know, this isn't that kind of wedding." She gave him a little half-smile.

He nodded.

She bit her lip. "Do you like it?"

He nodded again, and made himself speak. "You look stunning. Too good to be marrying me."

"I don't think that's true at all." Her smile

broadened and her cheeks went pink. "But that's sweet of you to say, especially since I haven't done my hair and makeup yet."

He smiled back. It struck him that whatever happened, he was going to fight to keep Tessa. Whatever that meant. Whatever it required of him. Because life without her around would be bleak. Just like it had been before she'd shown up. "Let me see the whole thing."

She did a little spin and as she got halfway around, he grabbed her shoulders and held her in place so that he could look at her back. "What the—" He whistled. "Unbelievable. I never would have imagined you'd have something like that."

Every detail of the sword marked on her skin was perfect from the hilt that started at the base of her neck to the blade that shot down her spine to disappear beneath the gown's white silk. Even the metal seemed to gleam under the light of the room, but that was surely just his eyes playing tricks on him.

She trembled under his touch. "What are you talking about?"

"This tattoo." He let her go to run a finger down her back, but as he made contact she whipped around and out of his reach.

She faced him, breathing hard and looking very much like she might bolt. "You can see that?"

"How could I not? It's life size, isn't it? I'll say,

for someone with your history, that's an interesting choice of artwork." And proof that they definitely needed more time to get to know each other.

"It wasn't a choice." She took a few steps back, eyes flashing with emotions he couldn't decipher. "And you shouldn't be able to see it."

There was no way, *no way*, Sebastian should be able to see the sword on her back. That was ancient Norse magic available only to valkyrie and berserker eyes. And yet, he clearly saw it. How else could he comment on it? He didn't know her sword's location. Unless he'd seen Jenna pull her sword. That was possible. Every valkyrie and berserker carried their weapon in the same place.

On their spine.

Whatever the reason he could see it, the fact rocked her to know that he'd laid eyes on this very personal part of her. It made her very afraid that he might never see her the same way again.

Sebastian looked completely confounded. "What do you mean it wasn't a choice? And why would you have a tattoo that no one can see?"

"Because I was born with it. All valkyries and berserkers are."

"So it's the mark of your people?"

"Essentially, yes." And not one she was proud of anymore.

"What does it mean that I can see it?"

She sat on the bed and tucked her hands under her thighs. "I don't know." Then remembering her long-ago lessons, she looked up. "You're technically undead, right?"

"Not technically. I am. The turning requires physical death of the body. It's why some don't survive it."

She pulled her hands free to rest her head in them. "That's it. It has to be. It's said valkyries and berserkers on the battlefields can be recognized by the dead they've been sent to collect." She lifted her head. "That would mean all vampires can see our weapons. I've never heard of that, but maybe Jenna knows. She didn't abandon her training like I did. I'll have to call her."

Tessa sucked in a breath. "Oh no."

"What?"

"If all vampires can see it, that means your family will be able to see it at the wedding. I can't do this." Maybe she could wear a shawl.

"Tessa, I promise you, they won't care. Wait— did you just call your tattoo a weapon?"

She sighed. She might as well tell him the whole truth. He *was* about to be her husband. And she'd already told him part of the story. "It's not a tattoo.

Well, it is. But it's more than that. It's genuinely a sword. My sword."

His gaze narrowed. "I don't see how that's possible, but then I'm a vampire and I shouldn't be possible. This is the magic of your kind, I suppose."

"It is." And maybe that was the end of it. Maybe his family really would understand. They were vampires, after all. She smoothed her dress out over her lap. "I should finish getting ready."

"Is that why you didn't want to show it to me? Because you didn't want me to know it was part of you?"

"Yes." His understanding made her feel a little better.

"So show it to me now."

She rubbed at the scar on her knuckles. It was the second time he'd asked. For a man who collected weaponry the way he did, he must be dying to see it. "I don't know." Except she did know. There was no way she wanted to hold that weapon again.

"Please."

"I...I haven't drawn my sword since *that* day." She glanced at the scar before meeting his eyes again. "I just *can't*."

He nodded but there was disappointment in his gaze. "I understand."

She wasn't sure he did. She got to her feet. "What that sword represents to me isn't something

I'm keen to revisit. I promised myself I'd never draw it again. Not after the last time. Not after what I almost did."

He smiled. It seemed a little indulgent and didn't quite reach his eyes. "I understand. I really do. If you haven't draw it since that day, you certainly shouldn't do it now. I'll leave you to get ready. I can change in the closet. Won't take me a second. I'll be in my office after that. Still waiting on the paperwork."

She smiled back, but it felt as if something had been lost between them. "If you really want me to take the sword out, I will." She reached back and her fingers grazed the hilt. She winced at the feel of the hilt beneath her hand and the buzz of anticipation that zipped through the weapon and into her like a small electrical charge.

"No. Please. Let's just forget about it, all right?"

She dropped her hand, happy it was over and yet sad that she felt like she'd created a rift between them. "All right. Where's Evangeline?"

"Getting ready, I suppose. I've asked Greaves to take her to the chapel as soon as she is. I'll drive us there."

"Okay, sounds good. I'll just finish up." She held her smile until she slipped into the bathroom where her makeup and veil were laid out.

Then the smile she'd been working at fell off her face and the twist of her stomach tightened. That stupid sword. She wished she'd never been born with it. Why couldn't she have been one of the generations that it skipped? It did happen. Very, very rarely. She just hadn't been so lucky.

But there was nothing to be done about it now. Not when she had this wedding to prepare for. She went to work on her makeup, following the advice of a YouTube video she'd watched earlier on bridal looks. It was pure vanity, she knew that. Sebastian would marry her with a bag over her head today if that's what it came to. Today wasn't about her, it was about him being free.

And about Evangeline's demands being met.

Seemed to Tessa that Evangeline got what she wanted quite a lot.

Anger made Tessa apply the eyeliner a little heavier than the video had suggested. She sighed in frustration and added a little more to the other eye to balance things out. Maybe she could call it a smoky eye. That was a thing, right?

She heard the bedroom door close and peeked out, realizing Sebastian must have gone down to his office.

Men really had it so easy. Put a suit on and they were done.

She finished her makeup, then went to work on her hair. When Corette had shown her how to twist a few strands back to clip the veil into while leaving a few wispy pieces around her face, Jenna had offered to come and help, but Tessa didn't want to bring her sister into this. When Tessa got married for real, she'd want Jenna with her every step of that way. But for this farce? It seemed wrong to involve her sister any more than Tessa already had. Like she would be using up a bunch of first time experiences on something that wasn't real.

Tessa finally figured out her hair, attached the veil and surveyed her work. Duncan probably could have done better.

She sighed. What did it matter? Again, today was not about her.

She stared at herself, getting angry. "Snap out of it. You're getting married. To an amazing man. Have a little pride. And stop being a quitter."

The pep talk fixed her mood a little. Enough that she pulled the veil free, laid it gently on the bathroom counter and picked up her brush. This day might not be about her, but she owed it to Sebastian and herself to be the most beautiful bride she could be.

If something was worth doing, it was worth doing well.

With that in mind, she went back to work on becoming that beautiful bride. Whatever that meant.

Sebastian had just unlocked his office door when Greaves stuck his head in. "Evangeline's in the car. Just wanted you to know I'm taking her to the chapel. She wanted to know why you haven't left the house yet."

"Because I'm still waiting on these documents to come through. Not that she needs to know there's an issue. Just tell her we're about five minutes behind you. Let the others know, too, will you?"

"Absolutely. See you there." Greaves left.

Sebastian turned on the office lights, went to his desk and fired up his laptop. The wall of antique weaponry flanking the fireplace gleamed softly in the overheads. He poured himself a whiskey while the computer came to life. There were some things his grandmother wasn't entirely wrong about. A drink could, on occasion, make things easier to bear.

And the fact that this marriage to Tessa was just about pleasing Evangeline was definitely one of those things.

He took his drink back to his desk and sat, opening his email. "Finally."

But the email from his solicitor had no attachments, just a note.

My apologies for not having the documents to you yet. We're having a terrible blizzard and the Internet is spotty. I'm sending this from my phone. As soon as I can get the office computer up and running, I'll have them emailed to you.

Damn it. He needed those dissolution papers. Without them for Evangeline to sign, this was all for naught. He picked up his whiskey and walked to the window. The sun was well set, leaving the sky burnished in purple and gold. As January evenings in Georgia went, it wasn't a bad one at all.

Even if he *was* still waiting on the most important documents of his life.

He sipped his whiskey and stared out, trying to think about something else. Tessa was the only thing that filled his head and the unsettled feeling that followed was completely his own doing. If Tessa didn't want to show him the sword, that was her right. One hundred percent. Was he disappointed? Yes, but her refusal to share that with him wasn't something that should make him feel poorly toward her.

He was being childish and he knew it.

He'd just thought...she'd want to let him in to the secret side of herself. She'd shared the story of her scar with him. But the sword was different, wasn't it? More than just a memory, it was a constant reminder of what had happened. A part of her past from which she would never be free. Of all people, he understood a burden of that magnitude.

Another sip of whisky brought further clarity. Truth was, she had no reason to feel differently about divulging something so personal with him. They'd known each other what? Three days?

No, he was being ridiculous. The woman was marrying him, for crying out loud. He owed her an apology. And he'd give it to her, along with a hearty kiss and a lengthy reminder about how beautiful she was and how grateful he felt for all she'd done for him.

To act otherwise would only bolster the general consensus that he was a grumpy, ill-tempered recluse.

The office door closed behind him. *Tessa.*

He turned, a smile at the ready. "I owe you an apology, my darling—"

Evangeline glared at him. "You're not supposed to be here."

"Neither are you." His smile thinned to nothing as he looked past her. "Where's Greaves?"

She strode forward. "Having some car trouble."

"Why aren't you at the church?"

Her glare morphed into a toothy grin. "I forgot something." She sashayed toward him, hips swaying in the little black dress she was wearing beneath what he hoped was a fake fur. Solid black was an interesting choice for a wedding.

Every alarm bell in his head rang. "What did you forget?"

Her fingers coasted down his lapel. "You look very handsome, Sebby. You always did wear clothes better than the average man. I'll give you that."

It would be the first thing she'd given him. But her attention wasn't something he was the slightest bit interested in. He stepped out of her reach and went to lean on the fireplace mantel. There was something comforting in being flanked by weapons while being confronted by this particular woman. "You didn't answer the question."

She came toward him again, her finger tapping her bottom lip. "What question was that?"

Oh, she could try a man's patience. "*What* did you forget?"

She stopped directly in front of him, her heels putting her just shy of eye-level. "So many things. Like how obtuse you are when it comes to the obvious."

He frowned at her. "What?"

She laughed. "Actually, I hadn't forgotten that at all. I've been counting on it."

"What in the hell are you talking about?"

She planted her hands on the mantel behind him and leaned in. She smelled of sandalwood and musk. "I'm talking about the real reason I'm here. The reason I got you to let me into your house, the reason I got you to let me stay here."

"I know why you're here. You want me back. Why that is, I have no idea. Life too hard alone, Evangeline?"

She snorted. "You are impossibly smart and yet, somehow one of the most clueless men I know."

In a flash of light and the hiss of metal, she grabbed one of the daggers from the wall behind him and pressed its point to his heart, the speed of her movements blurred by her vampire quickness. "I don't want you back, you boring fool. I want the secret to why you can daywalk. I've been trying to find it since I got here."

That explained so much. He'd found some books disturbed in the library, but had assumed Tessa had done that. As if a librarian wouldn't reshelve books when she was done with them. He really was a fool. Add to that the scratches on his office door lock and the copies of the newspaper stories that Tessa had found and Evangeline's scheme was clear.

She wasn't trying to get him back. She'd seen those pictures of him in the paper, pictures taken during the day, and realized he and probably his entire family were unharmed by the sun. Now she was trying to figure out how so she could do it too. "I'm not telling you a bloody thing."

"I already know it's some kind of magic. Your little librarian told me that much. So where is it? Give it to me and I'll leave you alone."

"I highly doubt that."

She pressed the dagger harder until the point pierced his shirt. "I will end you, Sebastian."

"You think threatening my life is going to make a difference? I've had no life to speak of thanks to the years I've wasted on you. And this is my reward? Threats from you? I've had enough."

"Oh please. The years you've wasted on me? As if you could have, what, spent them wining and dining women? Enjoying the world and all it has to offer? You're a sad creature, Sebastian. You're a vampire and yet you act like a church mouse, tucked away here in your cathedral, existing on crumbs."

The fact that she'd called him a mouse when he'd done the same thing to Tessa wasn't lost on him. He laughed, a loud, boisterous sound that bellowed through the room.

She jabbed the dagger in deeper. Pain radiated through him as blood trickled down his chest. "What's so funny?"

He stared at her, the woman he'd once adored and had determined that he would care for the rest of his life. If she slipped that dagger any farther, the latter might come true as his life would end right here. Although he'd stopped caring for her about five minutes into their meeting at the Black Rose three days ago.

Now she might actually kill him.

The time for secrets was gone. "You know your father offered to let me out of our marriage contract. On his deathbed, he told me there would be no hard feelings and that if I married you, you would make life miserable. He tried to warn me off, confessing that the creature you'd become was his fault. That he'd spoiled you into an uncontrollable brat. But I was too lovesick to accept that was true."

"I don't believe you." Her eyes blazed silver.

"Would you like me to show you the original documents in which he left me a generous sum to take care of you? They're rather fragile after all these years, but I'm sure you'll recognize your father's signature."

Her lip curled back, exposing her fangs. Angry tears lined her lower lids. Perhaps he'd finally hit a nerve with her. "You're lying."

"Why should I lie about such a thing? That money has been an albatross around my neck, just one more link in the thousand-pound chain that keeps me bound to you. Why do you think I never abandoned you after you left me? Or that I paid every bill you sent my way and refilled every bank account you drained? Because I still loved you?" He laughed bitterly, the truth lifting the cloud that hovered over his life for so long. "All of it was because I promised your father. And I'll promise you now that all of this is as true as the blade you're about to run through my heart."

"Lies," she whispered.

"You've told me I'm about to die. What more perfect time for confession is there?"

She swallowed hard and blinked away the tears, regaining her composure. "I don't care about the past, whatever it is. I want the power to walk in the sun."

"That's the last thing you should have. You're enough of a menace to this world at night."

She bared her fangs and growled at him. "Tell me the secret. This is your last chance."

He stared at her for a long moment, then slowly shook his head. He'd promised her father he would protect her, but the woman in front of him was a stranger. "I am loath to break a promise, but no."

"Then you leave me no choice." Her knuckles paled as her grip on the blade tightened.

The office door swung open. "Sebastian, I'm ready to—"

Tessa stopped dead in her tracks. Her face went from confusion to panic in a quarter second. "Get away from him."

Evangeline laughed. "Or what? You'll fine me for overdue books?" She leaned on the dagger, causing a sharp pain to pierce Sebastian's body as she looked up at him. "Maybe I'll torture your little librarian first. I bet that would loosen your tongue."

Fear filled Tessa eyes. "What do you want, Evangeline?"

"She wants the secret to my very special SPF." Sebastian shook his head. "But we're not telling her."

Evangeline's eyes flared bright. "The librarian knows more than she told me?" Her gaze turned calculating as she twisted toward Tessa. "And here I thought we were becoming friends."

Damn it. He'd slipped. "She doesn't know enough to help you."

"Too late, husband dear." Evangeline focused on Tessa. "Feel free to tell me if you'd like to save Sebastian's life. Otherwise, I'm going to turn him to ash right in front of you. Sorry to do that on your wedding day, but the choice is yours." Then Evangeline turned back to Sebastian. "Let's see if your *fiancée* really loves you, shall we?"

Tessa's panicked expression morphed into the war mask of a fierce warrior goddess. She went steely-eyed and her body tensed like a wild cat ready to pounce. The valkyrie in all her glory. "Don't. You. Dare."

Evangeline tossed her head back. "You don't scare me, librarian."

"Then you're a lot dumber than you look." The sweet hiss of metal sang out as Tessa did something Sebastian was sure he'd never witness.

The valkyrie drew her sword.

In a moment of brilliant clarity, Tessa understood that her vow to never again draw her sword had been made with the impetuousness of youth. Clearly there was a time and place and *this* was it.

The protection of the worthy.

Kettlingr hummed in her hand, happy to be unsheathed after so long. But the blade's joy did nothing to quell Tessa's building anger. Her ire at Evangeline's bold stupidity narrowed Tessa's focus down to the vampiress.

And the man she loved.

She leveled her sword at Evangeline, sighting down the metal length until Evangeline's heart was at the end. One quick thrust and it would all be over, even at this distance. "Put the dagger down, step away from Sebastian and I will let you live."

Evangeline glanced over at Tessa, and for the first time, a small crack appeared in her confidence.

She looked twice at the sword before speaking. "You'll let me live? Very cute. Put your little toy down and I won't run this blade through him."

Tessa laughed. The blade, sharp enough to divide a human hair into three parts, was a yard long and as wide as her fist. While its familiar weight felt like no more than a butter knife in her hand, it was no toy. "You're a lot dumber than you look."

Evangeline rolled her eyes. "I'm not the dumb one here. You have to actually know how to use a weapon like that for it to be effective."

The rage that tripped along Tessa's skin sank deeper to coil in her belly. It sent a wave of cold lucidity through her that cleared her head and laid out several paths of action before her. This was not the rage of her youth, the temper she'd fear for so long. This was something measured and powerful and worth giving room to.

Tessa examined her options and chose the path that ended peaceably. The others could be returned to later if need be. The peaceable path required a distraction. Tessa sent a little prayer to Freya that her lessons from battle camp had not been completely forgotten.

Letting memory take over, she started with what had once been a daily warm up.

She raised the sword two-handed and began to swing it in a figure-eight around her body, spinning it in one full circle around her hands on each side. It was a showy, elaborate movement that displayed the sword for the weapon that it was. *Kettlingr* purred through the air, a sound Tessa had forgotten. She laughed at the pleasure of hearing it again, reminded by the gentle thrumming vibrato of why she'd named her sword the way she had.

Kettlingr meant kitten, after all.

Evangeline was appropriately wide-eyed at the exhibition, while Sebastian beamed with what seemed to be a mix of pride and arousal, but not so much of either that he missed the opening Tessa was providing.

Evangeline was distracted.

He shot his arm up and around Evangeline's, twisting her arm and the dagger away from him and throwing her against the mantel. Blood spread down his crisp white tuxedo shirt.

Evangeline howled in anger and slid away from him, grabbing another weapon off the wall as she went. She brandished the short sword at both of them. "I will kill whoever comes at me first."

Tessa brought *Kettlingr* down to bear on Evangeline as she spoke to Sebastian. "Are you all right?"

"The shirt's in worse shape than I am. Bloody hell, you're a gorgeous sight to see."

"Now is not the time to flirt." She smiled, but kept her eyes on Evangeline despite wanting to kiss him and tell him how relieved she was that he wasn't hurt. "Better get Greaves to call an ambulance. Or a coroner. This could go either way."

"For you, maybe," Evangeline spat.

Sebastian shook his head. "I don't know where Greaves is."

"He's dead, or will be soon," Evangeline snarled. "Just like you'll be if I don't get that secret."

Sebastian cursed. "If you've hurt him—"

"Where is he, Evangeline?" Tessa liked the rook a lot. Her anger went up a notch but the blinding temper that she'd been so worried about for so long still had yet to rear its head. "If we can get to him in time to save his life, I'll go a little easier on you."

Evangeline lifted her weapon. "We've both got swords. I remember how this played out last time, so if you think I'm worried, I'm not." She made a coy face. "You should know I took it easy on you when we were fencing. I definitely could have won if I'd wanted to. My current lover has been teaching me."

Tessa stared her down, gaze steady and filled with the confidence of her training. "And you should know I let you hit me so Sebastian could see what you're truly capable of. Last chance to tell us where Greaves is."

Sebastian's phone rang. He fished it out of his tux pocket. "Ellingham." He went silent for a long moment. "I see. Thank you. I'll be there shortly. Actually, you should probably come here as soon as you're able."

He hung up and tucked his phone away, his gaze steely with anger. "Sheriff Merrow found Greaves in the Rolls on the side of the road on the way into town. He'd been hit on the head and the sheriff thinks possibly injected with some kind of paralytic. He's being transported to the hospital now."

Tessa sucked in a breath. "Is he going to be okay?"

"He'd better be." His hands balled into fists. "Either way, Evangeline's going to pay for this."

Tessa thrust her sword out a little straighter. "She's not going anywhere."

He nodded. "Keep it that way. I'm calling my brothers."

Evangeline's eyes were feral, fear expanding her pupils like the light in the room was betraying her. "Let me go. I'll forget about the daywalking. And I'll sign the paperwork. Whatever you want. I swear I won't go to the council."

Sebastian barked out a laugh. "Oh, you're going to the council. But this time the charges are going to be against you."

She snarled. "You can't do this to me. I'll tell them you're cheating on me with her."

He ignored her to speak into his phone. "Hugh.

Gather everyone and get to my house immediately. I'll explain when you get here."

Tessa recognized the crazed look in Evangeline's eyes. The woman sensed the end was near. She was getting desperate. Tessa took a few steps closer and slid sideways, eliminating a possible escape route. "Don't even think about running, Evangeline. I can and will hurt you if need be."

"You can't stop me. I'm a vampire. No one can stop me." Evangeline's laugh was shaky and wild. Then she charged forward, sword held out in front of her, flailing wildly with no perceptible skill in her efforts.

Without a twinge of the uncontrollable temper she'd feared for so long, Tessa reacted from the place within her that had never stopped being a valkyrie. Maybe she'd grown out of that rage. Or maybe it was because Evangeline wasn't an opponent to be feared, but rather pitied. She was mad with power and ambition and spoiled from a life of indulgence.

Or maybe it was because this time, Tessa was fighting for something—someone—that mattered.

Tessa flipped *Kettlingr* up and around, reversing her grip on the hilt so she could lead with the pommel instead of the blade. She danced out of the path of Evangeline's sword, coming around with *Kettlingr* high, and drove the pommel against Evangeline's temple.

The sword connected with a dull thud and Evangeline dropped to the ground like a rag doll, her borrowed weapon clattering to the hardwood beside her.

If Evangeline had had a pulse to check, Tessa would have put her fingers to the woman's throat. Instead, she dropped *Kettlingr* to her side and glanced at Sebastian. "She's not dead. I swear."

He nodded. "Well, actually, she is dead, being a vampire and all, but if you'd done enough damage to end her existence, she would have turned to ash."

"Good to know."

"I'm surprised you managed to lay her out, frankly. Not that you're not capable, because clearly you are, just that it can be done. Vampires tend to be pretty high on the tough scale."

"*Kettlingr* packs a wallop." She lifted her sword up a bit, admiring the blade. It really was a beautiful piece of craftsmanship.

"Apparently." He stared at Evangeline's prone form. "How long do you think that wallop will last?"

"At best she'll be out an hour or so."

"Good. Long enough for her to be taken into custody. The sheriff should be here soon."

"And your brothers are on their way?"

"Yes."

"Do you want to go to the hospital then? Check on Greaves? I can wait here and keep an eye on her." She didn't want to be separated from him, but her needs were unimportant at the moment, although she very much wanted to know that the rook was all right.

"We'll both go as soon as this is taken care of." He went to her, closing the gap between them. "You drew your sword for me. Thank you. I know that wasn't easy for you."

She managed a small smile. "Easier than I thought it would be, actually."

"It seemed to me that you contained your temper very well."

She shook her head slowly. "There wasn't much to contain. I was very angry, but it never took over. Instead it seemed to direct me. All these years, I've feared the return of those emotions. I thought that there was a part of me that was uncontrollable. Now, I don't know if that was ever true. Maybe everything I was afraid of was just…youth."

"Perhaps it was."

She stared down at *Kettlingr*. "I feel pretty foolish."

He caressed her cheek with the backs of his fingers, his touch light and sweet. "I spent my life watching over the woman who just tried to kill me, wishing for many of those years that I had been enough of whatever she needed to keep her at my side. If you're a fool, so am I. I guess we're perfect for each other."

She laughed. "Maybe." Then she lifted her sword. "This is *Kettlingr*."

He smiled. "It's as beautiful as its owner. May I hold it?"

"Only with my hands on it."

He nodded. "Whatever your conditions, I'm happy to oblige."

"They're not my conditions. They're part of the magical protection built into the sword. Watch. Hold out your hands and keep them flat."

He did as she asked, palms up.

With great care not to nick him, she balanced the blade on his hands, keeping hers on the hilt.

"Now watch when I let go." She took her hands away.

The sword shimmered and disappeared.

Sebastian frowned. "Where is it?"

"Where it belongs." Tessa realized she meant those words as she reached back and drew it free again.

He smiled. "So without your touch, it sheaths itself?"

"Not exactly." She walked to his desk and set the weapon down. It gleamed in the light almost as though it was pleased to be seen. "Pick it up."

With a curious expression, he joined her there,

hefting the blade with great admiration in his eyes. "Amaz—"

His hands were empty. He looked at her. "Let me guess. You have it again?"

"I do." She laughed. "The only person who can wield a valkyrie's sword is a valkyrie. The same goes for the swords of the berserkers."

He rubbed his chin in wonder. "I've never seen anything like it. Extraordinary. And very fitting that a woman of your caliber should own such an incredible weapon."

"Thank you."

"Thank *you*." He bowed his head. "I owe you a debt I will probably never be able to repay. You saved my life."

"You would have done the same for me."

"In a heartbeat. If my heart still beat, that is."

"Sebastian." The voice called out from the hall. Hugh, Tessa guessed.

"In the office," Sebastian responded.

Julian, Hugh and Delaney walked in a second later, the men in tuxedos and Delaney in a pretty dress of navy lace. Their wedding attire.

Julian walked over to where Evangeline lay sprawled on the floor. "How about that." He looked up at them. "Does this mean the wedding's off?"

Sebastian ignored Julian's question. Of all the good things that had come out of the day's events, not marrying Tessa wasn't one of them. Even though he knew it was for the best, he was curiously disappointed. "Evangeline was after my amulet."

Hugh's eyes held a warning expression. "Sebastian." He glanced at Tessa.

"She knows about the amulet," Sebastian said. "And if she hadn't, this incident would have led to it."

He grunted. "Fine, I suppose, but how did Evangeline know about it?"

"She didn't know about the amulet specifically. She just knew that I, that we, could daywalk. She was here to figure out how and gain the ability for herself."

Julian put his hands on his hips and stared down at Evangeline. "What happened to her?"

Sebastian grinned. "Tessa happened to her."

All three of them, Hugh, Julian, and Delaney, turned to look at the valkyrie.

Delaney's brows shot up. "Nicely done. I will never turn books into you late *ever*."

Tessa laughed and moved closer to Sebastian. He put his arm around her as she spoke. "She was going to kill Sebastian. I had to do something."

"That explains the blood on your shirt," Hugh said. "Start from the beginning."

Sebastian described how Evangeline had pinned him with one of his own weapons, threatening to kill him if he didn't reveal the secret to his daywalking. "And then Tessa came in at just the right moment and—"

He glanced at her. This wasn't his secret to reveal.

She smiled back at him with only the smallest bit of worry bracketing her eyes. "You can tell them."

"You're sure?"

She took a breath and nodded. "Yes. I'm done pretending I'm not who I really am."

His heart ached with affection for her. "All right then."

His cell phone rang. "Just a moment." He answered it. "Ellingham."

"Sheriff Merrow again. I'm on my way. Greaves is going to be fine. The doctors gave him something to wake him up. He's going to have an awful headache for a day or two, but that's it. The wound is already healing up."

Relief flooded Sebastian. "Thank you for letting me know."

"Also, he told me a woman named Evangeline did this to him. Said to talk to you about it."

"Come over and I'll fill you in. Any chance you have vampire-proof handcuffs?"

"I do. I'll bring them with me. Be there in ten."

Sebastian hung up. "That was Sheriff Merrow. Greaves is going to be fine."

Hugh frowned. "Greaves was hurt?"

Sebastian nodded. "Evangeline left to go to the chapel with him but I don't think she ever intended on arriving. She knocked him out, then came back here, probably with the intent to search the house for my secret. She'd already tried to pick the lock on my office door."

Julian walked to the bar and poured himself a drink. "I still want to know how the librarian knocked out a vampire."

"Yes, about that," Sebastian said. "Tessa came in, saw that Evangeline was about to run me through and—"

"What's going on in here? Is everything all right?" Elenora Ellingham walked in, her brow furrowed. Alice Bishop trailed her.

"How the bloody hell—never mind," Hugh sputtered. "Alice and her damned police scanner, am I right?"

Elenora lifted her brows as she surveyed the room. "We heard about Greaves. We were concerned. What's going on?"

Julian walked over to his grandmother and kissed her on the cheek. "Evangeline tried to kill Sebastian and Tessa knocked her out cold. We're not entirely sure how yet, but obviously it was very effective."

Elenora swung around to find Tessa. Her lips parted and her eyes filled with the brilliant gleam of unfettered joy. "You dear sweet child. You saved my Sebastian and you defeated that wretched excuse for a wife and vampire?"

Her hand went to her pearls momentarily as she swept forward and embraced Tessa. When she released the valkyrie, Elenora shook her head. "I'm not pleased my grandson didn't see fit to bring you to meet me, but I am overwhelmed with gratitude for all you've done today. I definitely give my blessing to this marriage."

Tessa blanched. "We're, uh, we're not getting married anymore. There's no reason now that…well…Sebastian?" She turned to find him, clearly looking for rescue.

He stepped up. "Grandmamma, we were getting married only so that Evangeline would sign the papers. I told you that."

"Yes, but this woman must love you if she saved your life like that." Elenora gave an imperious nod. "You should still marry her."

Delaney snorted.

Sebastian sighed. "We only met three days ago, Grandmamma. We need time to get to know each other. To make sure we're compatible."

Elenora huffed out a sigh. "Don't be an idiot. Of course you're compatible." She turned toward Alice. "See if—" She let out a bloodcurdling shriek as she pointed toward the hall. "What is that?"

They all looked in the direction she was pointing. A ball of brown and black fluff came scampering in.

Sebastian laughed. He scooped the little beast up and held him against his chest. "This is Duncan. Tessa's cat."

Elenora's lip curled. "Not you too." She sighed. "At least he's not the size of a horse like Delaney's creature."

"Aw, come on, Elenora." Delaney snickered like she was barely holding in a laugh. "You love your grandcat."

"Stop calling him that. I want *real* grandbabies. Not furred ones."

Julian made a small noise. "Now's probably not the right time to tell you I'm dating a werewolf then."

"Julian." Elenora glared at him.

He grinned, clearly teasing her.

Sheriff Merrow walked in. "The door was open." He took a long look around the room. "I'm pretty sure I missed something."

22

The next few hours passed in a whirlwind for Tessa. The sheriff carted Evangeline off to some special holding cell for vampires, which he said had never been used before.

Hugh, Delaney, and Julian all headed back to their homes to change out of their formal attire while Tessa and Sebastian did the same.

Then they all met up again at the hospital to visit Greaves, who was being held overnight for observation. The rook was rather cranky about that, but happy to see them and even happier to hear that Evangeline had been dealt with.

Finally, they regrouped at Sebastian's grandmother's house for a family meeting.

Tessa had never seen a house like Elenora's before. Well, sure, maybe on Downton Abbey, which gave her an instant love for the place, but in real life? Never. It was the sort of house that conjured up images of grand balls and hunting parties and life in the English countryside, which she imagined was what Elenora had been trying to re-create.

A bit of the past she still longed for, perhaps. It made Tessa sympathetic toward the woman, even if she was a bit bossy.

Despite it being the end of January, displays of fresh flowers were abundant inside, making the house smell like spring. It was a luxury Tessa had never experienced before, but she could see how easy it would be to get used to.

They were all gathered in a small sitting room— not so small it couldn't contain a baby grand piano—that was so pristine Tessa felt like it should have been roped off. The velvet chairs showed minimal signs of use, but then maybe this was a room reserved for family only. The way the old manor houses in England that allowed visitors kept wings of the house off limits. If there were grand balls thrown in this mansion, the guests of those events certainly didn't get to use this space.

The witch named Alice Bishop sat in a far corner doing needlepoint. The rest of them, Tessa and Sebastian, Hugh and Delaney, Julian and Elenora, were all seated in the center of the space in a grouping of sofas and chairs.

Elenora had everyone's attention. "There's only

one reasonable thing to do with Evangeline. We must turn her over to the council."

"I don't disagree," Sebastian said. "But she will bring charges against me. It's the only thing she has to counterbalance what she's done."

Elenora nodded. "I understand, but I doubt anything she has to say will carry much weight against what she did to you. You never raised a hand to her or threatened her in any way during the course of your marriage, did you?"

Indignation darkened Sebastian's eyes. "I know you're asking because you have to, but you must know I would never do such a thing."

"Of course I know that. I just needed to hear you say it." Elenora looked at Tessa. The woman radiated good intentions and gratitude, but that didn't settle Tessa's nerves. "Our dear, sweet Tessa. I hesitate to ask any more of you, but turning Evangeline over to the council means we'll all be required to give statements of the events that transpired. That will include you. Are you comfortable with that?"

"I am."

"So you're willing to participate, whatever it means?"

Tessa glanced at Sebastian before answering. "What could it mean beyond telling the truth?"

Elenora straightened and seemed to gather her thoughts before answering. "It will very likely mean a trial. That will require you to travel, possibly to Amsterdam or Madrid, and once there, you will have to testify in front of the council."

It was a daunting thought, baring her soul before an audience of ancient and judgmental vampires. But she would do whatever was necessary.

Sebastian took her hand. "You won't be alone. I'll be with you. Even at the trial."

"That would help immensely." She smiled at him and answered Elenora. "I will absolutely do it. In for a penny, in for a pound and all that."

Elenora put her hand to her chest and gave Tessa a short bow from her seat. "Thank you. I understand that this will not be easy, but as a family, we will be there to support you."

Delaney leaned forward. "You're so brave."

"Agreed," Julian added. "Who knew Sebastian was capable of finding such a remarkable woman? Now let's see if he can keep you."

Tessa lifted her chin. "Your brother is an equally remarkable man."

Then Sebastian spoke up. "What would you know about keeping a woman, Julian? For more than twenty-four hours, that is."

"Touché," Hugh said. "Until you can manage a lasting relationship, Julian, your opinion on Sebastian's love life carries very little weight."

Elenora cleared her throat. "That's enough,

boys. Let's focus on the task at hand, shall we? As I'm the most senior vampire here, I will contact the council about our issue. I don't know if they'll send someone for Evangeline or require us to transport her but either way we have work ahead of us."

Alice's small voice spoke from the back of the room. "Are you sure she was only after the secret for herself?"

"I can't believe I'm saying this, but Alice is right. Evangeline could have been working with someone," Sebastian said.

They all turned to look at him.

He held out a hand. "She was going to *great* lengths to find out what enabled me to daywalk. I know Evangeline better than any of you and for her to put that much effort into something, her motivation could have come from something more than her own desire to see the sun rise again. Losing that ability wasn't something she ever seemed to regret."

The thought cast a visual pall over the people in the room. Both Hugh and Julian muttered curses.

Tessa straightened, knowing immediately how to fix the problem. "Let me talk to her. I'll know whether she's lying or telling the truth, either way. So no matter what she says, we'll know if there's someone else involved." She glanced at the others in the room and answered the unspoken question.

"Valkyries can read a person's intent. It's our gift."

Elenora's eyebrows rose and she gave Sebastian a pleased look. "I may buy her an island after all." She shifted her gaze to Tessa. "We should do this immediately. This isn't something we can wait to find out."

Tessa stood. "Take me to her. Right now."

Sebastian hadn't been down to the Basement of Nocturne Falls in so long that Julian accompanied them. Only town employees with approved access could enter, which of course Sebastian was, but he rarely carried his keycard. This was more Julian's territory anyway, being the vast array of underground passageways that allowed much of the behind-the-scenes activities in town to take place.

And unlike Sebastian, Julian, always had his keycard on him.

He led them down the steps from one of several secret entrances tucked here and there around town. When they reached the bottom, Julian spread his arms wide. "Welcome to Nocturne Falls' best kept secret, Tessa."

"Wow." She glanced down both sides of the hall. "You could drive a truck through here."

"You can and we have." Julian smiled proudly

as he took off to the left. "This way to the detention center."

Tessa and Sebastian fell into step behind him. She looked at Sebastian. "What else goes on down here?"

"Through a room off one of these enormous tunnel the gargoyles who entertain the tourists at the fountain are hydraulically lifted into place." He looked over his shoulder. "I believe that's in the other direction. Also, many of the supernaturals who walk the streets posing for pictures and giving the town color use the passageways to come and go without fear of being followed by overeager tourists."

She nodded. "I think Disney uses tunnels like these."

"That's where we got the idea," Julian called back. "Although I don't think Disney has special holding cells built to accommodate supernaturals of any variety."

"No, probably not," she answered.

They turned a corner. Deputy Cruz was standing guard outside the locked door that led into the cells. Julian pulled out his keycard again.

Sebastian gave the man a nod. Cruz was a solid deputy and a panther shifter, but Sebastian didn't know much more than that about him. "All quiet?"

Cruz shook his head. "It was. Then she woke up." He grinned at Tessa. "I understand you were responsible for that. Nice work, valkyrie. Wait until your sister hears."

"I can only imagine."

"Here you go." Julian pushed the door open and held it for her.

Sebastian wished he and Julian could go in with Tessa, but she'd said the best result would come from one-on-one interaction so that no one else's emotions would interfere with sensing Evangeline's true motives.

"Who's there?" Evangeline called out.

They ignored the question. Sebastian squeezed Tessa's hand. "You won't have to get close to her to talk to her. When you're done, knock on the door and Julian will open it again."

She gave his hand a squeeze back. "I won't be long."

She slipped inside.

Tessa had expected a dark, dank cell. Why she'd pictured something that skewed medieval dungeon, she had no idea.

The room before her was bright white and more space ship than jail. Evangeline reclined on a wide molded bench on the other side of the thick glass that separated the free space from the confined. Small round holes perforated the wall at eye level.

More for sound than air, Tessa guessed, seeing as how vampires didn't need to breathe.

Evangeline scowled at her. "What do you want?"

Tessa walked to the halfway point between the door and the glass wall. "Just to ask you some questions."

Evangeline snorted. "Good luck with that."

Anger washed off her in waves. "It could make a difference with the council."

Evangeline gave Tessa the side eye. "What do you know about the council?"

"Enough." The woman's curiosity rose a notch. "Why did you want Sebastian's ability to walk in the sun?"

The question earned Tessa an eye roll. "I'm a vampire, you twit. We all want to walk in the sun again." Evangeline shifted, swinging her feet onto the floor. "Can you imagine what it would be like to give that up? When I saw Sebastian in the papers and realized he was out in the sun…" She shook her head. "I was his wife. He should have shared that ability with me."

"You knew losing the sun was the price to pay for being a vampire. But you also should have understood that Sebastian didn't owe you anything."

Evangeline barked out a laugh. "He's been giving me everything I wanted since we married.

Why should his daywalking ability be any different?"

"You could have asked him."

She huffed out a sigh. "Once I figured out all of the Ellinghams could daywalk I knew that option was out. You don't know what a tight grip Elenora keeps on that family. And she hates me. There was no way she'd agree to sharing that with me."

"So you assumed she was the one behind it?"

"Elenora controls everything that family does."

Tessa had yet to see evidence of that. She crossed her arms. "Did you miss the sun so badly you actually would have killed Sebastian for his secret?"

Evangeline glared at her, then turned away. "I'm not answering that."

But she already had. Indecision had whirled off her, finally solidifying into a positive. Tessa ground her teeth together to keep from lashing out as anger heated her belly. How dare this woman put her own happiness above the price of Sebastian's life? "One more question and I'll leave you alone." Unless she had been working with someone. Then Tessa would have to do her best to pull that information out as well.

Evangeline shifted toward the wall, putting her back to Tessa, and said nothing.

Tessa lifted her chin. "Were you trying to get his secret for yourself?"

Evangeline remained quiet, but her intentions were clear. She'd been after Sebastian's amulet because of her own desires.

"That's what I thought," Tessa said.

Evangeline shifted. "I didn't say anything."

Tessa walked toward the door. "You didn't have to."

Julian shut the door and leaned against it. "So what's your gut say? You think Evangeline is working with someone?"

Sebastian wanted to pace but made himself be still. "I don't know. Maybe. But who would have the patience to work with her? Although she claimed to have a lover who was teaching her self-defense or some such thing."

Which meant the possibility existed that she'd been doing this for reasons beyond her own desires. Evangeline could have promised another, more powerful vampire that she could provide him with the ability to daywalk in an attempt to curry favor or protection. Or money.

Or maybe she owed a more powerful vampire money and this was her way of repaying it.

If that was true, it would explain why she hadn't asked Sebastian for any cash in a long time. And her lifestyle required great sums of the stuff.

It was starting to make sense now. Someone else had to be bankrolling her. How else did she afford her life? He doubted she had the wherewithal to invest and plan like most vampires, learning to play the markets to increase their wealth to unimaginable heights.

No, Evangeline was the sort to rely on the kindness of strangers. Strangers she probably seduced and entertained until she grew tired of them. Or more likely, they grew tired of her. Perhaps she'd overstayed her welcome and had been forced to come up with something to repay the largess she'd been shown.

The secret of daywalking would be just the thing. Most vampires would give their right fang for that sort of knowledge. To be free of the one restriction of their kind would be monumental. Life changing. That kind of knowledge could shift the balance of power in the world if dropped into the wrong hands.

He'd about convinced himself that a horde of vampires were moments from descending upon them when Tessa's sturdy knock sounded on the door.

Julian whisked it open and she stepped out.

"Well?" Sebastian could barely contain himself.

She shook her head. "Just her. And it's exactly what we thought it was. She saw those pictures of you in the paper, realized what time of day it was when they were taken and wanted the ability for herself."

Relief washed the torment of thoughts from his head. Julian heaved out a relieved sigh as well. "All right then."

"She also figured out your entire family could daywalk and assumed your grandmother was controlling the whole thing."

Sebastian exchanged a look with Julian as Tessa continued. "She knew if that was true, asking you for the secret would get her nothing, but she thought you owed it to her. Mostly because you've given her everything she's asked for over the years."

Sebastian shook his head. "All because of that damned promise to her father."

Julian made a face. "What promise?"

"I'll explain later."

Sebastian leaned in and kissed Tessa. It was briefer than he'd have liked but being demonstrative in front of others was something he was going to have to work on. "Thank you for doing this. Did she say anything else?"

"Oh, all sorts of things, mostly about you." A mischievous glint winked in Tessa's eyes. It matched the playful tone of her voice. "But I don't use that kind of language."

Back on the street level, Tessa and Sebastian said goodbye to Julian. As he walked away from them, Sebastian turned to her. "Hungry? Because I'm starving all of a sudden."

She nodded. She was hungry. It had been a long, long day. "I could eat. But there's something else we should probably do first."

"What's that?"

A strange sadness came over her, but she knew that was nonsense. The game was well and truly over. She pulled the engagement ring off her finger and held it out to him. "Return this."

He put his hands in his pockets and looked at her. "I don't want it."

She frowned at him. "Maybe you don't, but I'm pretty sure that nice fae jeweler is expecting it back."

He gazed into her eyes and slowly shook his

341

head. "In case you haven't noticed, I am *mad* about you, Tessa Blythe."

She grinned back at him. "The feeling is mutual, Sebastian Ellingham."

"I am thrilled to hear you say that."

She laughed. "Did you think I'd changed my mind?"

"Meeting Elenora can have that effect on people."

Tessa shrugged. "She did say she was going to buy me an island."

He laughed and pulled his hands from his pockets. "So you'll take an island from her but not an engagement ring from me?"

She lifted the ring a little higher. "There's a pretty good chance I will. Someday. When it's right. But that time is not today and that ring is not this one. This one was about pretending. I would only want one that's about being genuine. We've both had too much pretend in our lives for a while, don't you think?"

He nodded and finally took the ring. "I agree with that. But..."

"What?"

"You've done so much for me. I feel as though I owe you something."

"You're still making me dean of library studies, right? And you already advanced me money for my new wardrobe. And hey, you're letting me live in your guest house. I think that's a tremendous start."

He sighed. "That's not what I'm talking about. What about a new engagement ring?"

She made a face. "Are you asking me to marry you again after what I just said?"

"Well, I didn't actually do it the first time."

She reached out and took his hand. "I'm really not ready for that proposal yet. But I'm not going anywhere either. I promise. Let's just take it day by day. Acknowledging my valkyrie side again is going to take some getting used to. And you're about to be free of duty and responsibly for the first time since Evangeline's father passed. How do you know you're not going to want to date other women and...you know, do what men do?"

He snorted. "You mean do what Julian does? I know myself well enough by now, Tessa. I am not that kind of man."

She smiled. "No, you're not, are you? I think that's part of why I like you so much."

His eyes took on the hint of a glow. "I might be that kind of man a little bit. Say, if we're talking about the two of us doing that thing you were referring to."

Her cheeks grew warm. "That's a very different conversation." And one she was surprisingly ready to have. Sebastian was an excellent kisser. It was an easy leap to imagine he'd be good at other things too. "But one we could…start."

A moment of silence passed between them until he finally spoke again. His voice was edged with something that sounded very much like desire. And maybe a little disappointment. "Day by day, then?"

She nodded. He might not be completely happy with delaying things, but it seemed like a solid plan to her. A chance for them to really get to know each other. And living in the guest house meant she wouldn't be tempted to sleep with him until they knew they were right for each other. Well, she wouldn't be any more tempted than she currently was.

Although, really, how could he be more perfect for her? She bit the inside of her cheek to keep from suggesting they do something very different than eating a meal.

He stuck his elbow out. "Dinner then?"

She looped her arm through his. "Absolutely. In fact, where's that diner, Mummy's? I could really go for a milkshake." Because sugar was a good substitute for just about anything. At least that's what she was telling herself.

"It's just up ahead." He sighed, a sad, melancholy sound. "This is not how I thought I'd be spending my wedding night."

She made a noise in her throat and stopped in

her tracks, staring at him. "Okay, this is not actually your wedding night since we didn't actually get married and did you think I was going to sleep with you just because we got married to satisfy Evangeline?"

He frowned. "No, not at all. I thought we'd be celebrating or...I don't know what I thought. I never thought I'd get married again, so I don't know what I thought I'd be doing, honestly. Not having a milkshake at a diner, that's for sure."

She stared at his beautiful face. She'd known him three days. Three long, weird, stressful, mostly wonderful days. Plenty of time for her to realize he was exactly the man she needed and wanted in her life.

The other thing she realized is there had been a time and a place for her to draw her sword, just like there was a time and place for plans and doing things by the book. This wasn't one of those times. A boost of valkyrie boldness charged through her. "Maybe we should get those milkshakes to go."

He tipped his head to the side. "Why's that?"

"Because I have a better suggestion about what we can do tonight." She leaned up and kissed him, long and slow and deep, then she rested against him until his arms wrapped around her and he pulled her closer.

The kiss was deliciously languid and easy. They were a perfect fit, the recluse and the bookworm.

The weapons collector and the sword wielder.

The vampire and the valkyrie.

When they finally broke apart, his eyes were as bright as Christmas lights and just as pretty. Anticipation created a haze around them, blocking out the rest of the world. "What's your better suggestion?"

From the look in his eyes and the roughness of his voice, she had a pretty good idea he knew perfectly well what she wanted to do but was too much of a gentleman to say so. Well, she was a valkyrie, a class of women who weren't afraid to ask for what they wanted.

She pressed her lips to his one more time, catching his bottom lip gently between her teeth and giving it a little tug before she let go. He let out a small, strangled noise that was something between desire and disbelief. It spurred her on. "Let's go home and play pretend one more time."

His words caught in his throat as he spoke. "D-did you have something specific in mind that you wanted to pretend?"

She nodded as she slid her hand down his chest. How she wasn't trembling from the buildup of nerves, she had no idea. Being bold wasn't something she was used to, but it was high time to practice. Which brought her back to her answer. "Our wedding night."

"Our"—he swallowed—"wedding night?"

"Um-hmm." She straightened his tie. "You know, just to see if we're any good at it."

As it turned out, they were as good at wedding night activities as they were at pretending to be married.

Which was very, *very* good.

.

Want to be up to date on all books & release dates by Kristen Painter? Sign-up for my newsletter on my website, www.kristenpainter.com. No spam, just news (sales, freebies, and releases.)

If you loved the book and want to help the series grow, tell a friend about the book and take time to leave a review!

Other Books by Kristen Painter

URBAN FANTASY

The House of Comarré series:
Forbidden Blood
Blood Rights
Flesh and Blood
Bad Blood
Out For Blood
Last Blood

Crescent City series:
House of the Rising Sun
City of Eternal Night
Garden of Dreams and Desires

PARANORMAL ROMANCE

Nocturne Falls series
The Vampire's Mail Order Bride
The Werewolf Meets His Match
The Gargoyle Gets His Girl
The Professor Woos The Witch
The Witch's Halloween Hero – short story
The Werewolf's Christmas Wish – short story
The Vampire's Fake Fiancée

Nothing is completed without an amazing team.

Many thanks to:

Cover design: Janet Holmes
Interior formatting: Author E.M.S
Editor: Joyce Lamb
Copyedits/proofs: Marlene Engel

About the Author

Kristen Painter likes to balance her obsessions with shoes and cats by making the lives of her characters miserable and surprising her readers with interesting twists. She currently writes paranormal romance and award-winning urban fantasy. The former college English teacher can often be found all over social media where she loves to interact with readers. Visit her web site to learn more.

www.kristenpainter.com

Made in the USA
Monee, IL
06 November 2019